Carnal Power

'Hurry up!'

Her imperious tone struck fear into him, fear that she would grow so impatient that she would change her mind and make him leave the bathroom before his task was over. The shame and frustration of such a prospect spurred him on to massage her midriff, feeling the heavy breasts tap against the backs of his hands as he worked, smooth as silk . . .

Now it was time to wash the pert full breasts themselves. He could see them straining for his touch and exulted in the sacred trust she had given them. Slowly he worked his way up the undersides with his fingertips, relishing the way they slid so smoothly over the wet skin. His fingers inched upwards, towards the tantalizing nipples . . .

Strictly Pleasure

Nadine Wilder

NEW ENGLISH LIBRARY
Hodder and Stoughton

Chapter One

Cordelia Blane opened the door of the deserted office with the air of a priestess entering an inner sanctum. It was eight-thirty. She liked to arrive half an hour before her boss, giving herself plenty of time to prepare for him. Cordelia loved the quiet atmosphere of the place in the early morning. It had a calming influence on her, allowing her to get into the right frame of mind for the day ahead.

The office suite consisted of her own small room with its computer workstation, the spacious and well-furnished area occupied by her boss, and the cloakroom, with its shower, WC and bidet. Cordelia appreciated having a proper bathroom. It was just one of the perks that working for Nigel Willoughby provided. She headed straight there, sliding open the door and examining the uniform that her boss had selected for her to wear that day. It hung on a rail just inside the door and she fingered the skin-soft material with relish, pinching and stroking it for a few seconds before kicking off her shoes and moving towards the shower. Turning it on, she allowed the water to reach the right temperature while she stripped off her clothes and hung them beside the garment on the rail.

With a shudder of anticipatory delight, Cordelia stepped beneath the stream and felt her body respond like a flower to the play of warm water on her flesh. She reached for the shower gel and began to massage it into her arms and then her breasts, which had already firmed up into slick mounds the size of footballs, each topped by an inch-long nipple. Her palms caressed the taut slopes, then moved down to the flat plane of her midriff. She was proud of her body. It was the source of her power over the two men in her life, and she made sure that she kept it in trim, tantalizing shape.

But she must not be too proud, Cordelia reminded herself, as the programme that she had painstakingly built up in her psyche began to kick in, stimulated by the ritual of the morning shower. As her fingers inched towards the base of her stomach she began to think about Nigel, her Master. An image of him came to mind at once, standing erect in front of his desk in his immaculate Hugo Boss suit, arms crossed and with one of *those* looks on his face. How expertly he could quell her spirit with a glance, or subdue her instantly with a subtle nuance in his tone of voice. He was truly her Boss, in more ways than one.

Cordelia began to recall that first interview, as she loved to do. Dissatisfied with the way her career was going, she had been seeking change, looking for something that she couldn't quite identify. But once she met Nigel Willoughby she knew immediately that he could give her what she needed. Not just a fascinating job with a good salary but something more, far more. Exactly what that was she had known only by instinct at that first meeting. The true nature of her need, and of his ability to divine and fulfil it perfectly, became clear gradually over the ensuing months.

How had they recognized that potential in each other, the silent rapport of heart to heart? Cordelia felt herself growing excited at the thought of the innocent she had once been. Her fingers crept lower, finding the damp cleft beneath her soggy pubic curls and the hard clitoral button that clamoured for her attention. She gave herself a few rubs with her forefinger, eliciting a sharp gasp as the sensual energy began to build, opening her up inside and out. Then she moved round to massage her buttocks, unwilling to take it further. If there was one thing above all that she had learnt in this job, it was how to pace herself.

Letting the shower sluice all the foam from her body, Cordelia stood motionless with her eyes closed and remembered, almost word for word, what Nigel had said to her that first time.

'My personal assistant must be a very special woman,' he'd told her, his dark eyes gleaming with what she now realized had been controlled excitement. 'I require absolute obedience in all things. I will not be crossed or disappointed in any way. If she should fail me then she must expect punishment.'

He had smiled then, continuing in a tone only slightly less severe. 'It's quite simple, you see. I'm a fair man, but I know exactly what I want. I believe in high standards and in keeping to the rules. My assistant must be able to accept that I know best: that I am not to be questioned, only obeyed.'

He'd paused, as if challenging her, assessing her response. She had nodded, lowering her eyes, and he had seemed satisfied because he'd continued with his lecture. 'There will be no false equality in this office. I am the Master and I need to be served – efficiently, impeccably. If I employ you, you will know exactly what to expect. The boundaries will be clear. It takes a very special sort of woman to appreciate my particular style in this modern, chaotic world where people chat matily to each other across the ranks and call each other by their first names. There will be none of that sort of thing here, do you understand me? Call me old-fashioned, but I believe in everyone knowing their place and sticking to it.'

'Yes, sir,' she'd answered with automatic deference, feeling rather shocked afterwards. She couldn't remember calling anyone 'sir' before.

Cordelia had taken on the job without knowing precisely what she was letting herself in for, but Nigel had insisted that the first month should be on a trial basis, both parties at liberty to terminate the contract immediately if they felt it wasn't working. He had offered her a very generous sum in compensation if that should occur, under no matter what circumstances, which seemed more than fair. Although Nigel Willoughby was more demanding than most employers, he was equally willing to offer greater rewards.

Cordelia stepped out from the shower and pulled a pristine white towel from the heated rail, wrapping it around her torso. The warmth was comforting, enveloping her like a security blanket. She tossed her cropped mane as vigorously as would a rampant stallion, so that droplets fell from her dark mop. There was a full-length mirror in the cloakroom and, once she had patted her body dry, she opened up the big looking-glass and surveyed herself.

As always the contrast between her rather masculine hairstyle and voluptuous female figure was striking, shocking even. It had taken her a long time to get used to her new image and even now she was sometimes caught unawares.

It had been Nigel's idea to have her hair cut short and at first she had baulked at it. 'I can visualize it exactly,' he'd told her, his voice holding just a faint hint of menace. 'It will be perfect for you, trust me.'

She hadn't, though, not at that early stage. All sorts of rebellious thoughts had run through her mind as she'd contemplated the ordeal of having her long, carefully nurtured hair cut off. It had taken her so long to grow it and she also had to consider the feelings of Ralph, her house-husband, who had always loved her shoulder-length tresses. Not that he would be a problem, of course, but her own self-image was at stake. Hair was surely the essence of femininity, the 'crowning glory' and all that. She couldn't help seeing its removal as some kind of punishment, as it had been for those Frenchwomen who had collaborated with the Nazis and,

4

after the liberation of their country, had had their heads publicly shaved.

'I shall hire an expert hairdresser to do it right here, in the office,' Nigel had told her. Already she knew that once he had made up his mind there was no stopping him. Not that she would want to, really. His wish was her command . . .

So it was done, one afternoon with the sun streaming around the blinds and Cordelia sitting on a single chair in the middle of the floor while Nigel sat behind his desk, watching. Her whole body was enveloped in a white nylon cape and beneath it, unknown to the hairdresser, she'd been tied to the chair by her boss. 'Just in case you are tempted to try to halt the process.'

Jason, the top stylist whom Nigel had paid a small fortune to hire, was theatrically gay. He made chirpy conversation at first until Nigel told him to 'please stop talking and get on with the job', which made him huff and pout, causing Cordelia great anxiety. She knew he was unused to being treated like that and feared that he might take it out on her hair.

It was bad enough having to watch her precious locks bite the dust. As the black, silky mound grew around her on the pink pages of the copy of the *Financial Times* that she had spread over the carpet, Cordelia felt panic set in and gritted her teeth to prevent herself from protesting. She half wished that Nigel had blindfolded her, but evidently he wanted her to see the evidence of her loss, to view it as a symbol of his autocratic power over her. She knew it was a test of her humility, of her submission to his will, but that didn't make it any easier to bear.

Jason stopped his relentless snipping and ran his fingers through her newly-shortened hair, making her spine tingle. He began to massage her scalp, but instead of relaxing her the tension was mounting beneath the plastic cape, putting her on heat. She could feel the sticky folds of her labia swelling with arousal, and the sweat trickling between her breasts as the nipples stiffened and the cleavage deepened. The nylon rope that Nigel had wound around her wrists and ankles chafed her skin when she moved her aching joints, making it agony both to wriggle and to sit still.

The fine-tuning of her hairstyle began but there was no mirror to enlighten her about Jason's progress. Cordelia could only guess at the radical transformation that was taking place and hope that she could trust her boss's judgement. He sat watching her with hawk-like concentration, his fingers steepled just below his firm chin, and she felt that he was not just looking at her but *reading* her, imagining the torment of suspense that she was going through, enjoying it vicariously. The very thought that he might be getting off on the procedure increased her arousal, making her ooze down below and wet her tight panties. She clenched her vaginal muscles and felt the hood of her clitoris lift, exposing the rigid nub that began to throb hotly. Did he know what effect all this was having on her? Of course! He always knew.

The waiting was unbearable. As the hairdresser primped and moussed and sprayed her hair into shape Cordelia dreaded the moment when she would have to face her transformed self. It seemed symbolic of her new rôle, like the branding or shackling of a slave, and she knew that after this there would be no going back. Her month's trial was over and this was Nigel's way of letting her know that she was worthy, that she had passed the test. Despite the physical and mental stress that she was under Cordelia felt her already tumid breasts swell another few centimetres, with pride.

'That's fine,' she heard her master say at last, as Jason stepped back with his comb poised. 'Here's an envelope containing the fee we agreed, plus a gratuity. Please leave us now.'

The hairdresser gave them both an odd look before he gathered up the tools of his trade and vanished. He knows something is going on between us, Cordelia thought, and the shame of half-letting someone else in on their secret made her flush. Nigel rose slowly from his chair – he never, ever, hurried – and came round the desk to face her. He surveyed her thoughtfully, no hint of his reaction to be read in his impassive features. Then he walked round behind her and untied the cape, letting it drift to the floor. He unfastened her bonds and told her to stand up.

'I want you naked,' he said. 'Then you shall see yourself as you really are.'

The thought sent a frisson of fear and exhilaration through her. She undressed carefully, folding each garment as he liked her to and placing it on the chair she had vacated. He watched her keenly, making sure she did nothing to displease him. By now she was used to doing everything under his scrutiny and it didn't faze her as much as it had at first, when it used to make her nervous and therefore clumsy, inviting retribution. She finished the operation without mishap and, when she was entirely nude, allowed her eyes to drift upwards to his face, seeking some response. Her head felt light and strange and she missed the familiar *swish* that her long hair had made. In his dark, fathomless pupils a light glimmered and she thought she detected the faintest suggestion of a smile at the corners of his wide, thin-lipped mouth.

He didn't chide her for raising her head, as he usually did, but simply led her by the hand into the cloakroom where the full-length mirror was. The image that had greeted Cordelia then was almost the same as now, except that her hair had been a fraction shorter, more severe, and she'd been unable to hide the look of shocked dismay that contorted her face. While she struggled to come to terms with her bold new appearance Nigel had stroked her bare buttocks soothingly, a gesture that said he was pleased both with her and with his own judgement.

'What do you think?' he had asked, teasingly, knowing full well that it made no difference now. The deed was done.

'It's . . . strange.'

'You'll get used to it. Come to like it, even. You are easily habituated, you like most things in the end.'

Cordelia had found it disconcerting at first when her boss described her nature to her, but now she accepted it as part of the game. Whether she was really like that or not was irrelevant. If he chose to see her in a certain way and treat her accordingly, that was up to him.

Nigel had made her turn this way and that in front of the mirror, forcing her to admire herself and, in time, she really had come to like her new image. There was a quirky disparity between the rather butch hairstyle, which could easily have belonged to an artistic-looking man, and the undoubted womanliness of her large breasts, slim waist and curvy hips, giving her an almost hermaphroditic appearance when she was without make-up.

Make-up! The little Chinese clock on the shelf in her office had tinged the three-quarter hour, making her scurry to the shelf beside the shower where Nigel had laid out the toiletries he wished her to use. Today he desired the scent of jasmine, rich and voluptuous. She poured some of the thick body-cream into her palm and began to apply it to her legs with long, sweeping strokes, making sure it was thoroughly absorbed. He liked her skin to be soft and scented at all times.

It would have been good to linger over the self-massage, to lose herself in the delicious perfume and the silken feel of her shaven skin, but there was no time. Finishing with a light dusting of jasmine talc over her pubic area, beneath her armpits and between her breasts, Cordelia went over to the rack and removed the costume she was to wear.

It was difficult at first to see how she was supposed to get into it. Fashioned in softest suede and of a dark purple hue, the top half of the garment consisted of a halter neck and straps that criss-crossed over her sternum but left the breasts bare. The bottom half was the same in reverse, leaving her navel exposed but providing strips at the top of her thighs for suspenders. At the back, two straps crossed from shoulder to waist, then a slim triangle pointed down between her buttocks, ending in a thong that was the only connection to the front, passing between her legs.

Cordelia got into quite a tangle trying to fit herself into what was little more than a harness, but in the end she managed it. The sight of herself with her large breasts hitched provocatively high and her sex only just concealed beneath the purple bands was a real turn-on, but not so much as the feel of the thong between her legs that cut right into her groove and pressed onto her already erect clitoris. As she walked the friction was delicious.

By five to nine she was sitting on the stool in front of the counter with the light on over the mirror, squinting as she applied her mascara. Nigel liked her make-up to be bold around the eyes and mouth, but her skin had to be pale as porcelain, 'like a china doll.' Thank goodness she didn't have to worry about her hair any more. In the days when she had cherished her long tresses it had taken her a minimum of ten minutes to get them brushed and styled in the half-up, half-down style that she had liked. For a wistful moment she remembered what that had been like, then shook her dark mop into shape and grinned at herself in the mirror, a wilful *gamine* again.

There was the faintest mechanical whine outside the office door. Cordelia knew it was the lift and that Nigel was inside it, which gave her approximately twenty seconds to prepare herself. She took a last cautionary look in the mirror: hair glossy and slicked down the way he liked it; eyes shadowed with a mixture of navy and purple, the lashes long and separated; mouth a tawny red, her full lips outlined in a darker shade. Then her gaze dropped to survey the skimpy arrangement of straps and pockets that passed for her uniform that day, the big pale breasts and matching buttocks nakedly exposed, jutting out from the velvety strips that framed them and looking cheekily obscene. On her feet were a pair of black patent shoes with three-inch heels that accentuated the plump curves of her calves and the trimness of her ankles in their light tan stockings.

Cordelia went through into her master's office and knelt on the floor, awaiting him. She was still as a statue, composing herself for the day ahead, repeating in her head the mantra that she silently relied upon to get herself into the right state of mind: 'Not my will but thine be done.'

The lift doors could be heard grating open and then his shoes were just audible as they slid across the pile of the carpet outside. Nigel paused and there was the jingle of keys, loud enough to send a tremor of fearful joy through her as she continued to kneel, awaiting his greeting, his bidding.

Often, just before they met for the first time in the day, Cordelia had an almost mystical experience. She was having it now, swaying on her knees as the wonderful sensations overtook her, swirling around in her head. There was a sense of completely knowing him, not in any of the normal ways but as if through some sixth sense, penetrating the heart of his mystery, perceiving in a flash the whole essence of the man called Nigel Willoughby. She believed him to be a man whose identity was extremely complex, far more than could be encompassed by any mere set of labels.

'Good morning, Cordelia.'

The words came out light and pleasant, a benediction, and her lungs exhaled in dizzy relief. Sometimes he was in a bad mood from the start and then she knew that she had to be extra careful.

Careful now to keep her eyes fixed on the carpet eighteen inches in front of her, Cordelia replied in a respectful tone, 'Good morning, sir.'

'Workstation, slave!'

'Yes, sir. At once, sir.'

Cordelia crawled over the beige carpet and went through the open door into her own office. She didn't always have to go to her computer straight away. Sometimes there were instructions to be listened to, other tasks to be done. On one occasion her boss had taken her on his knee and fondled her gently, making a fuss of her for no apparent reason before spanking her roundly on her bare behind and dismissing her for the day. She never did find out what that was all about. Hers not to reason why, et cetera.

'Wait, I'll get your tackle.'

She liked the way he said that word, 'tackle'. It was a man's word, redolent of the rugby club, the mass shove on the field followed by the mass grope afterwards, thirty-odd lusty lads with their tackle out. It made her hot to think of it, being gang-banged, a fantasy that she wouldn't like to experience in reality because of the damage it might do to her bits, but the *idea* of it was a real turn-on. As she crawled over to her desk the sticky folds of her vulva made a faint sucking noise and the sides of her breasts rubbed against her arms, making her even more aroused.

Waiting by her workstation like a patient horse, Cordelia felt her boss come up behind her with the soft leather bindings in his hand. He secured her feet first to the legs of the desk, winding the straps around both her calves and her ankles. Inside the leather was a layer of downy fur that both prevented chafing and allowed some freedom of movement, but although her restraints were minimal there was to be no kicking against the pricks. She hitched her behind up onto the swivel stool and allowed her elbows to be strapped tightly to her sides and secured to the back of the chair, with only her forearms left free for typing.

'That's better.' Nigel lifted her chin so she could see his dark eyes, and smiled down at her in an almost avuncular way. She wasn't fooled, though. Cordelia knew how swiftly that benign expression could change to one of forbidding menace, like a sudden change in the complexion of the sky.

Today she would give him no cause for complaint. But she told herself that same thing every day, and still she sometimes managed to cross him. He always told her why, but she couldn't always understand. What exactly was it about the look in her eye, the tone of her voice, that annoyed him so? He had his vocabulary: she was being 'sullen,' 'suspicious,' 'distrustful,' 'negligent'. He could categorize her crimes with forensic precision and yet she still ended up not knowing quite how she had failed, afraid that she would make the same mistake again simply because she could not recognize a fatal trait in herself.

'There's a good girl,' he crooned now, his hand heavy on the nape of her neck. She felt the touch of him like a breeze through her soul, gearing her up to expect more even though she knew it was unlikely, especially at this hour of the day. Her body seemed not to know that, going through the motions just in case. She could feel her cunt blossoming beyond her clenched thighs, opening up within while the soft exterior of her sex grew plump and moist too, readying itself. For a few seconds she thought of eight inches of solid meat inside her, ramming into her juices like a lubricated piston, and almost fainted with lust when she felt Nigel's fingers pinch her nipple casually, almost cruelly.

'You can pick your work up from where you left off yesterday,' he told her, matter-of-factly.

As Cordelia switched on her computer she heard him go back into his office, humming softly. She was glad he was in a good mood because her own spirits lifted too, in harmony with his. Her scheduler reminded her that there were standard letters to send out to clients today, and she set the wheels in motion, half of her listening out for the familiar noises of her boss's activity. Soon his voice could be heard on the phone, making the usual round of calls.

Nigel was a financial adviser, very successful at making money for others as well as for himself. He worked via the Internet and phone, always in control of the bewildering mass of information that poured into the office from the electronic jungle. He was the most brilliant man that Cordelia had even encountered, with a double first from Oxford and a laid-back manner that belied his restless, razor-sharp intelligence. A perfectionist, with the capacity for infinite attention to detail, he never smoked or drank more than one glass of wine with a meal – 'for his digestion's sake'. It was easy to admire such a man. Less easy to love him.

Cordelia wasn't in love with him, she knew that. Even so, he fascinated her and satisfied her needs in ways that her live-in lover, Ralph, could never aspire to.

For several hours Cordelia worked non-stop, her eyes focused on the screen in front of her. It wouldn't do to make a mistake. A decimal point in the wrong place could prove disastrous, so there was no margin for error. When she found herself growing tired she stopped, becoming aware of the ties that bound her to her place. There was something satisfying about being tethered to the spot, unable to get up even if she'd wanted to, but when her bladder began to call she felt the first pangs of anxiety, knowing she must wait to be excused.

Once Nigel had left it too long and she had wet herself. The memory of that day was seared into her soul, the terrible feeling of losing control accompanied by fear of the consequences. Sitting there in her soaking knickers she had hoped she might hide her shame from him but he had known at once, wrinkling his nose in distaste as soon as he came into her office.

'Have you had a little accident?' he'd asked her, with a sneer. 'I take a dim view of children who cannot control their bladders. They need to be punished.'

He had made her take off her urine-soaked knickers and wear them on her head for the rest of the day. Sitting on the damp office stool with her bottom bare had got her excited. The fabric covering the stool was rough and when she'd squirmed and pressed her thighs together her vulva had been very stimulated, the clitoris huge and horny. After a while she had found out how to manoeuvre herself around so that her libido increased, the thick labia growing slick with her juices as she stimulated her hard little button towards a climax. She eventually came despite, or perhaps even because of, her restricted state, the spasms racking through her with such force that she bit her lower lip hard to avoid crying out and being discovered.

Afterwards, tasting her own blood, she felt a deep sense of shame. She could hear Nigel on the phone, oblivious of the erotic cataclysm that had occurred in the room next door, and other emotions gripped her. She felt relieved that she had got away with it, and experienced a sneaky sense of victory. Up to then her boss had known everything she did during her working day (she suspected he even had a spy camera rigged up in the toilet) but now, for the first time, she had outwitted him, got her own back.

Her triumph had been short-lived. At the end of the day he had put her over his knee and spanked her bare bottom, an experience that she had found both arousing and humiliating, but which certainly had put her back in her place. She had gone home and masturbated wildly to ease the intense frustration she had felt.

Today, however, Nigel remembered in time and came to give her a break at half-past eleven. 'While you relieve yourself I shall check your work,' he said, his hand sliding in through one of the apertures in her outfit to find her breast, which he squeezed gently as he released her bonds. She wriggled on her seat and felt the tight thong stimulating her all the way from her clitoris to her anus, rubbing the sensitive perineum en route. Her desire had been growing slowly throughout the morning and Nigel knew it, but he was unlikely to give her the satisfaction she craved. His approach was always titillating, tantalizing, because he wanted her to remain in this state of eternal deprivation. It was all part of his game.

He patted her on the bottom as she got up stiffly, propelling her towards the bathroom. Once there, Cordelia pulled aside the restricting thong impatiently, then gasped out her relief as she peed, enjoying the sensual release of urine through her swollen vulva. She wanted to linger in the bathroom, to enjoy the heightened sensations that flooded through her when she touched her rearing nipples or the hard bud between her labia. But she dared not spend too much time in there or she knew that Nigel would come rapping on the door.

It was a mystery to her why she found him so exciting, even though she would not have picked him out in a crowd. Something about the way he spoke, looked at her, held himself, even, marked him out as a man with natural authority, someone to be feared and respected. Sometimes Cordelia thought he must be a substitute for the father she'd never known, although she wasn't much given to psychoanalysis.

She wiped her vulva with the petal-soft paper and refastened the thong between her legs. It seemed to cut even deeper into her this time, intensifying the friction on her clitoris, but still she maintained her self-control. If an orgasm took her by surprise that would be a bonus, but she would not stimulate herself. It was an unwritten rule of the office that she could never do such a thing unless she was given specific permission – and Nigel hardly ever permitted such indulgence. No, she would not betray his trust in her. Cordelia flushed the loo and, with her head held high, made her way back into the office, mentally prepared for whatever her boss might have in store for her.

Chapter Two

When Cordelia reappeared her boss had the picnic basket laid out on his desk. He sometimes liked to feed her at lunchtime the way you might feed a lapdog, getting her to sit up and beg for titbits. He indicated that she should kneel, then slipped behind her and tied her wrists behind her back, adjusting the straps of her costume so that her breasts were forced a fraction higher, his fingers lightly pulling at her nipples until they reached maximum proportions. Cordelia felt them burning and tingling long after his hands had left her body. The tight strap between her legs had slipped to one side and was tormenting her now with its hit-and-miss contact with her clitoris.

Nigel selected a forkful of potato salad and gave her the command. 'Beg for it!'

She raised herself up on her haunches, opening her mouth and putting her head back.

'Good girl!'

He slipped the food slowly between her lips and she relished the creamy smoothness of the mayonnaise against her tongue. Her lips brushed against his fingertips for a second in a transient kiss and the scent of his cologne was in her nostrils, filling her with sharp desire. If only he would let his guard slip for one moment and give her a glimpse of the powerful sexuality that she was convinced was lurking behind that cool, controlled exterior, she would be in heaven.

He wiped her mouth with an Irish linen napkin, then gave her a mouthful of ham, followed by half a cherry tomato and then some more potato salad. Pausing to open the white wine in its cooling sleeve, he held the glass to her mouth for her to take a sip of the fresh, herb-flavoured liquid that cleansed her palate after the oily dressing. The meal proceeded, in bite-sized chunks, with Cordelia waiting patiently to be fed and Nigel taking his time, until they proceeded to dessert.

'Strawberry mousse,' he announced. But instead of dipping a spoon in the pot he put a dollop on the end of his finger and spread it carefully over one of her erect nipples.

Cordelia, already in a state of erotic excitement, could hardly contain herself. The cool froth clung to the puckered folds of her nipple just asking to be licked off, and she imagined Nigel's tongue wiping all over her breast, savouring every globule of the sticky strawberry sweetness. It would be the first time he had used his mouth on her, signalling a new phase in their relationship. How she would relish such a development! Her nipples tingled urgently and between the humid folds of her labia she could feel her clitoris throbbing at the prospect.

But she was to be disappointed. Instead of doing the honours himself, her boss lifted up her heavy breast with his right hand while he placed the left on the back of her head, pushing the one down and the other up until the two converged.

'Lick it off!' he commanded her. 'Lick your own nipple.'

Cordelia found his order bizarre. She had never thought to perform such a deed, but now curiosity took hold and she opened her mouth, sliding her tongue out until it made contact with the tip of her mousse-laden nipple. The strong taste of strawberry encouraged her. She licked more thoroughly and felt the rubbery texture of the skin beneath. It felt strange, like giving herself a catlick, but was nonetheless stimulating. While she licked and sucked she felt Nigel placing more of the dessert on her other nipple.

'Now this one!' he said, hoisting up her right breast.

She continued, turning her second nipple into a shiny cone that was almost as strawberry pink as the mousse. Nigel watched her attentively. *What is he thinking?* she wondered. *What's he getting out of this?* He was more of an enigma to her than ever, but she had made up her mind that she would obey him in all things and this was just the latest in a long line of strange things that he'd made her do. He certainly had a fertile imagination, she would grant him that. The way he treated her was an education in itself. She had picked up so many tips, so many insights, even in the relatively short time she had been working for him that she felt privileged to be his office slave.

'Are you hot for me now?' he murmured in her ear. 'Do you wish I was the one doing that?' She knew better than to react. He went on, 'You're such a dirty little slut. Look at you, slavering over your own tits. If I ever catch you doing anything like this without my express permission I shall punish you severely. You know that, don't you?'

She remained silent, but he seized a bunch of her hair and yanked her head back, forcing her to look him in the eye. 'You're disgusting. You know that, don't you?' Without warning he thrust his forefinger in between her thighs and probed between her labia. 'See?' he held up his glistening digit. 'You're really getting off on it, aren't you, slut? Well, lick this!'

His finger was thrust into her mouth and, for an instant, she tasted her own musk. Then he untied her hands. 'Clear up!' came his curt command. 'I'm going out.'

Cordelia relaxed only slightly once he was gone. She suspected that he had video cameras rigged up all over the office – not just in the toilet – to spy on her, although she'd never detected any. It would be out of character for a meticulous control-freak like Nigel Willoughby to overlook such a precaution. So whenever he left her alone, even if it was only for a few seconds, she made sure that she did nothing behind her boss's back that she wouldn't do in front of him.

Carefully, she tidied up the remains of the picnic, putting the trash into the waste bin and the rest of the things back into the wicker basket, which she closed and fastened. She had no idea how long Nigel would be away from the office. Moving back into her section she saw there were instructions for the afternoon on her keyboard. She slid into place and began to type. After a couple of hours she heard the lift coming up to the third floor. She didn't waver but continued working, not even turning round when she heard the door open.

'You're dismissed!' she heard Nigel snap at her from the entrance to her office.

Startled, she turned around, unable to prevent herself from looking him in the face. As usual his expression was impassive, the dark brows level, the eyes inscrutable, the mouth a mean seam. A cold fear seized her and, in the same instant, she realized how dependent she was on him and how devastated she would be if she lost this job, that was so much more than just a job.

To her surprise, he smiled thinly at her. 'It's all right, I'm not giving you the sack. You're dismissed for the day, that is all. I'm expecting someone.'

Cordelia rose from her stool, filled both with relief and with understanding. There had always been just the two of them, locked in a world of their own making. She knew why he wouldn't want her to be there when he had a visitor.

He glanced at the gold Cartier watch on his wrist. 'Hurry up. You have five minutes to be out of the building.'

With obedient haste Cordelia swayed across the carpet in

her high heels towards the bathroom, the secret channel between her thighs squelching faintly as she walked. Although outwardly she was still the office slave, her costume and demeanour suggestive of extreme submissiveness, inside she was already distancing herself from the rôle.

Nigel was concerned that the two women might cross on the stairs or at the lift. But when Inez appeared she looked radiant as ever, with no hint of anything untoward marring the classical beauty of her face. His relief was accompanied by a feeling of renewed energy. The two women in his life were so utterly different that it was refreshing to go from one to the other, to make the chameleon change that allowed the contrasting aspects of his nature to flourish equally.

Inez glided towards him in a haze of *Paloma Picasso*, her dark eyes glittering wickedly at him. 'Darling! It was so sweet of you to invite me here. I can't wait for our little show to begin. Has the lovely Cordelia behaved herself today?'

He gave a sardonic smile, pulling out a leather padded chair for his mistress. She sat down with a regal air and crossed her long, elegant legs. Today she was wearing an outfit that Nigel hadn't seen before, a stylish two-piece in black grainy satin teamed with a cerise-and-black-striped blouse. The frill at the neck and the gold hoop earrings were the only sartorial hint of her Spanish gypsy blood but anyone could detect, from her olive complexion, dark brown eyes and jet-black hair, that she was of Mediterranean stock.

'You've had a picnic!' she exclaimed, noticing the basket in the corner. Her carmine lips framed themselves into a mock pout. 'And you saved none for me?'

'I've something much better for you, my dear!'

Nigel went to his minibar and produced a quarter-bottle of chilled champagne and a small bowl of beluga caviar. She gasped with delight as he popped the cork, saying, 'Here's to your first viewing of my office slave. I hope you like what you see.'

'I'm sure I shall. You know exactly what I like, sweetheart. And you have impeccable taste in women.' She preened, thrusting out her large breasts beneath the black jacket and throwing back her shapely head crowned by the tight, sleek bun.

'Inez, you are impossibly vain – but I forgive you!'

He was still feeling apprehensive as he poured the drink. Although he'd often told her all about Cordelia in minute detail – how she looked, how she behaved and responded to his treatment of her – there was no telling how Inez would react when she saw her for real.

Nigel handed her the fizzing glass and poured another for himself. He pushed the glass bowl in its saucer of ice towards her and she took a mouthful of the sturgeon roe on the silver spoon. 'Ah, delicious! Now make a feast for my eyes, darling. You've whetted my appetite enough already.'

He pulled down the blinds, making the faint hum of traffic seem even more distant and plunging the room into semi-darkness. Pressing a button on his desk activated a video screen that slid out from a concealed panel on the wall with only a faint mechanical murmur. Inez sat back in the swivel chair and let it swing gently from side to side as she licked the spoon clean of every tiny caviar egg, then took a mouthful of champagne to swill it down.

Nigel felt the nagging tension inside him ripen into apprehension as he tried to anticipate Inez's response to his video of Cordelia. He had spent six months training Cordelia to the point where he felt he could show her to Inez – but now doubts began to assail him. Suppose Cordelia wasn't Inez's type? What if all his meticulous training of Cordelia had been in vain because Inez simply didn't fancy her?

But as soon as he ran the video and Cordelia appeared dressed in her fetish costume he was rewarded by Inez rapidly clapping her hands together and gurgling with delight.

'Oh, she's charming, simply wonderful! If she's as sexy in the flesh as she is on film . . .'

'She's more so, of course,' he said, confident now. 'Just watch how she kneels before me, those big breasts of hers swinging down, and be sure to notice that lovely bottom. Don't you agree she's very well endowed, darling? And her face, such a picture. She's trying really hard to remain sedate, like a proper Little Miss Friday, but you can see how aroused she is -- as well as a little bit afraid.'

'But is she *obedient*?'

'See for yourself.'

Inez watched with rapt attention as Cordelia went through her paces, accepting the restraints without a murmur and staying at her post all morning, even though she must have been dying to go to the loo by around noon. Nigel was proud of what he'd achieved with her. After the fiasco of Anne-Marie he thought he might have lost the knack of training slaves, but Cordelia was shaping up beautifully.

And Inez would have to acknowledge that he had done a good job this time. Nigel knew she was impressed, and relief, like a river in full flood, surged through him. Of course, he'd come to believe in Cordelia after they'd made such a promising start and he'd expanded his own training methods to suit her particular nature. But he could never be a hundred per cent sure of Inez's reaction to anything. Maybe that was one good reason for loving her.

On screen, Cordelia was now being fed by her boss, her generous mouth opening in sensual anticipation and her breasts straining in the harness. When her nipples were daubed with pink mousse Inez exclaimed, 'Oh, you wicked creature! You knew I would love this, even though it's torture just to watch. Ah, see that tongue at work. Don't you wish it was your dick she was licking instead of herself, my darling? Oh, what tits, what torment!'

With a stifled moan Inez removed her jacket and Nigel recognized his cue. He gave her a nipping kiss on the nape of the neck where he knew it would inflame her most: her moans intensified. The jacket fell to the ground and he fumbled with the necktie of her blouse, soon releasing it. Without taking her eyes off the screen, Inez helped him undo the buttons until her pert breasts were fully exposed in their black-and-red platform bra.

'Lean on the desk,' Nigel whispered.

She rose as if in a dream and ambled over to the large, leather-topped desk from where she could continue to watch the erotic drama unfolding on the screen above. Nigel felt his balls grow hot and heavy as his cock reared in anticipation, nudging against the waistband of his pants. He pulled the black satiny skirt right up to waist height. It was lined, so there was no slip, only the black elastic of her suspenders and, as usual, her frilly panties were of the crotchless variety.

Inez parted her legs and leaned right over the desk with her sleek rump in the air, still looking up at the video with a glazed expression and uttering little moans of delight. Quickly, Nigel pulled down his fly and let his trousers fall to his knees. He released his erection which instantly sprang up to full cock, thick and hot and ready for it. Briefly he reached in front of Inez and groped at her full breasts, his hands passing across the deep chasm between and stroking the exaggerated swell before fastening on the large, red nipples. When he tweaked them they seemed to peak even more, growing as hard as the two brass buttons on her jacket, before his hands retreated and found the equally enticing globes of her derrière which he kneaded firmly, digging his fingertips right into the abundant flesh.

Then Nigel moved in close, his prick nudging its way between Inez's smooth, meaty thighs until it found the soft folds of her vulva, already open to him. He planted his legs firmly apart, aware that his knees might weaken as his arousal gathered force. She was wiggling her bum at him now, pressing it against his stomach as his glans sought her vulval entrance. He found the melting pool very welcoming and plunged straight in, knowing she was more than ready for him, feeling the first heady rush of unfettered lust as he slid his cock in easily right up to the root where her labia squeezed him subtly.

Over the dark head of his mistress Nigel could see the image of Cordelia sitting primly at her keyboard, her breasts jutting incongruously through the straps of her costume as she typed, and he knew that this was turning Inez on even more. She was all liquidized inside, the velvet walls of her vagina gripping him tightly in her excitement, and he put his hand down between her and the desk to feel the unmistakable sign of female tumescence, the erect and throbbing clitoris that was so excited it was thrusting right out from between her slack, engorged love-lips.

'Oh yes, please!' she murmured, her voice throaty and distant, as his fingers worked the hood of flesh that protected her love-nub. Beneath it he could feel the strong base of his penis thrusting in and out, which notched his libido up to danger level. He told himself he mustn't come before she did. Slowing down the rhythm of his penetration he concentrated on caressing her manually instead, feeling her small, protruding organ of pleasure becoming incredibly wet and slippery.

'Oh God!' he heard Inez moan. Now her eyes were closed, and whatever fantasy his video had induced was continuing to play on the internal screen of her imagination.

Nigel steadied himself and used his other hand to play with her breasts, passing lightly from one to the other in a teasing dance. Inez pushed her buttocks against him, almost tipping him backwards in her frenzy of desire, working her hips back and forth so eagerly that he was afraid she would injure herself on the desktop. He pulled her away a couple of inches and grasped her firmly around the waist to get a better purchase, then went in for the home run. Recklessly he gave his cock its head, shoving into her with abandon and making her squirm and squeal as her own climax grew imminent.

Somehow Nigel managed to hold back just long enough to let her pip him at the post, but the minute she began the high-pitched yelp that signalled her orgasm he felt himself gush into her, the release blissfully satisfying after all that pent-up energy. While her pussy convulsed around him he spent himself in a long, pulsating ejaculation that caused him to weaken and collapse onto her, pushing her face down against the leather top of his desk.

He lay for several seconds on that hot heap of abundant flesh, wallowing in her perfume, her sweat, her still-spasming sex. By the time he managed to stand up again the video had finished and was running blank with a noisy hum. He went around to the other side of the desk and hit the button to stop the film, then returned to attend to Inez, who was still lying in a state of limp exhaustion. Gently he wiped the black, wet strands of hair from her brow and helped her to the chair, which she flopped into like a rag doll, knees apart and showing the wet red fruit of her vulva between the frills of her crotchless panties.

Instinctively Nigel knelt beside her, kissing her fingertips. 'So you like my latest little prize, do you, sweetheart?'

She turned sultry eyes on him, not much more than slits beneath the sooty lashes. Her tawny breasts were heaving above the stiff shelves of her platform bra but the nipples were flaccid now, huge and spreading. Nigel suppressed an urge to flick them into life again.

'What do you think, darling?'

Her voice was deep-throated, still breathy. He found it very sexy indeed, especially with her Spanish accent. His penis began to stir again, but he knew that without the stimulus of the video Inez would not be interested. Her bisexual nature demanded that both aspects of her libido should be aroused before she could enjoy lovemaking to the full.

'I think it's time we thought about introducing her to you in the flesh, but we must tread carefully. We don't want to frighten her off prematurely.'

'I agree. It's been just you and her so far, hasn't it? Maybe you should introduce her to some others first. Get her used to the idea of playing her rôle before strangers.'

'I've been thinking along the same lines,' Nigel grinned, holding out his hand to her. 'Come on, up you get. When you've showered and changed we'll go out to eat. I've booked that new Andalucian restaurant in Muswell Hill but it will take us a while to get there.'

It was almost time. Ralph had somehow learned to sense when his mistress would come home, even though sometimes she stopped off to shop on the way back. Today she would be earlier than usual, for some reason. He'd heard that some dogs had the same instinct. Well, that was appropriate. He *was* her dog: sometimes her playful puppy and sometimes her wild animal but always looking up to her as leader of the pack.

The tinkling sounds of a Chopin waltz echoed through the house as Ralph put the finishing touches to the dining table. There were fresh flowers from the garden – delicately tinted irises, roses, sweet peas – in her favourite Lalique vase. From the kitchen issued subtle smells of cooking food: olive oil, lemon, thyme. He felt confident that she would be satisfied with his efforts. He did not hope for more: it was enough to know that he had done his best, as always.

Just before four he went upstairs to put on the uniform she had selected for him that morning. It was hanging in his wardrobe beneath a plastic cover. Filled with a pleasurable buzz of anticipation he took it out and shook it, to let the creases and folds settle. There would be time to shower and shave, to make his body sweet for her in case she wished to make use of it in some way. His prick stirred in his underpants, accompanied 'by the familiar twinge of longing. He hung the garment on the wardrobe door and made for the bathroom.

Ralph loved his mistress's bathroom, with its whirlpool tub set into the corner and the separate shower cubicle. Sometimes she liked to wallow in the bath while she watched him shower, her blue eyes roving greedily over his pecs and buns, making him feel naughtily self-conscious. He worked hard to get into good shape for her. Three times a week down at the gym and his own routine every morning at home had honed his lean body to something near perfection. At least she'd never complained, not in that department, anyway.

He stripped off his working overalls and turned on the flow of tepid water, stepping into the tiled area and shuddering with delight as the first spray douched him from the top down. He rubbed some *Xeryus Rouge* into his palm and smeared it all over his hairless chest and down his belly to the golden fleece above his cock, working it into a lather. That was her favourite men's fragrance these days. Once he had worn *Brut*. He smiled to think of how far he had come since those days. She had taught him so much, turning him from a raw twenty-year-old who knew nothing of the pleasures of the flesh into a skilled masseur and stud.

Yes, he reflected gleefully, he knew how to pleasure a

woman now, all right. Flashes of his past successes ran through his mind, images of his mistress coming with her lovely mouth open and a rose flush on her throat and chest, her exquisite breasts trembling. Then more images of her lying limp and perspiring after he had taken her to the limit and beyond. Thinking about how it felt to be permitted such liberties, how exquisite a reward after all the pain and humiliation, was making him unbearably horny.

Had there been more time Ralph might have played with himself there in the shower, but he knew if he delayed by even a few seconds he wouldn't be ready for her when she arrived and he couldn't risk that. He switched the shower to 'cold' and endured the icy stream until his cock hung quiescent again. It was a matter of pride to him to be always immaculate and relaxed when his mistress entered her house, with everything just so. He shaved lightly over his already smooth chest and chin, towelled himself vigorously, sprayed on more *Xeryus*, and worked some gel into his dark-blond hair, sculpting it into waves. Did he need more fake tan? Probably not. She liked him to be honey-gold, not mahogany.

For a moment he tried to recall a time when it had been not what *she* wanted but what *he* wanted. Those early days had been something of a strain, always focused on sex, sex, sex. He'd thought he was in hog heaven with a beautiful, randy woman loving it as much as he did, wanting him constantly. Yet he'd felt empty inside. He disliked being under pressure to keep up his initial performance ratio. And, he had to admit, his fancy had begun to stray. If he was honest, he had to acknowledge that the novelty of possessing a peach like her was wearing off. If they'd carried on for much longer like that they probably would have split.

Ralph knew her body intimately and he'd kidded himself that he knew her personality too. But did she have some surprises in store for him! She had approached him one night in her sexy underwear with a silk scarf between her hands. At first he'd thought she wanted to be tied up herself, and he was prepared to humour her, but when she asked permission to bind his wrists and secure him to the bedhead he was astounded. Yet he couldn't deny the rush of dark pleasure that had convulsed through him like a mini-climax at the thought. What more did she plan to do to him? A whole new arena was opened up in which they might play out subtle games of desire and frustration and satisfaction.

Their relationship had progressed from there into unknown – but exciting – territory. Before he knew the rules he had been afraid that she might somehow unman him, turn him into a wimp, but slowly he came to understand that, although she wanted him to be entirely under her control, she loved the dark male essence of him. She would command him but she wanted him no less masculine, no less sexual. In fact, he would become more so when his libido was harnessed to her will, a more perfect tool to service her rampant female appetite.

In the end it had been a relief to discover that no longer did he have to initiate the action, that he trusted her to take complete control of him. He had always loved doing things for her, cooking delicious meals, washing her hair and performing more intimate services. Being with her had brought out his latent talent for doing things for others. He loved being told what to do and putting the needs of others before his own. When she asked him to move in with her, to be her domestic slave, Ralph had felt deeply honoured.

Gradually she had subdued his will to hers, always in ways that delighted and surprised him, until he found he was spending most of his time in her service. His gratification was total: sexual, emotional, psychological. He gave up his day job and divided his time between share dealing via the Internet and his household duties. But the high point of his day was always the moment when she returned to the cosy world they had invented for themselves, a world where she reigned supreme and he devoted himself entirely to her pleasure.

Right now, however, the pleasure was all his as he surveyed the shiny black garment laid out on the bed. It was a stretch-fit vinyl, textured like silk and very constricting but with pores that allowed his own skin to breathe. The style resembled that of an old-fashioned bathing suit – but with most of the chest area sculpted out to show off his body – and cap sleeves that would emphasize his biceps. The briefs had flaps back and front, fastened with Velcro for ease and speed of access. He loved the idea of that!

Ralph rubbed talc into his body before easing the outfit on, relishing the feel of the thin second skin that encased his lower quarters and the faint, workmanlike smell of rubber that harmonized perfectly with the cedarwood notes of the *Xeryus*. He breathed in the complex aroma deeply, reflecting on how being with his mistress had enhanced all his senses, and adjusted the suit around his crotch. There was room for his cock to expand within the pouch that the flap created, but his balls were bound tightly against his body. He tried to imagine what she had planned for him that evening and his libido kicked into overdrive. His temperature was rising and the sweat was emerging in small beads on his chest and forehead.

This was only one of many outfits that she had procured for him, each affording him a unique satisfaction. He loved having parts of his body exposed with the rest of him tightly constricted. It made him feel safe and vulnerable at the same time, producing mixed feelings in him that were very arousing and which mirrored the way he felt about his mistress. Love and fear, relaxation and tension, familiarity and strangeness

– those were the twin poles between which his psyche made its ceaseless pendulum swing.

The long-case clock in the hall struck the quarter-hour, reminding him that he still had a few finishing touches to make before she came home. He wiped down the shower, threw the sodden towel into the bin and did his best to obliterate all other traces of his ablutions before making his way downstairs.

Chapter Three

Cordelia always enjoyed the forty-minute drive home. It gave her time to make The Switch. She could lay to rest any unresolved feelings she had about her day in the office and prepare for the new rôle she had to play at home. As she wound her way through the traffic south of the river she began to daydream about how she would resolve the frustrated feelings that Nigel's treatment had aroused in her.

It amused her to think of her boss's cocksure assumption that he was the only man in her life. She had told him she lived alone and had no boyfriend which, when she first took on the job, had been true. How stunned he would be if he ever found out the truth. Not that she had any intention of telling him. It was far more fun to nurse her little secret, to know that while he thought her world revolved around him she held another man in thrall.

The transition from Cordelia the slave to Cordelia the mistress occurred remarkably quickly these days. By the time she reached Clapham she was driving more aggressively, dodging the parked cars with practised ease as she skirted the common. At first it had not been so easy to make The Switch. She had sometimes been too assertive with Nigel, earning herself some painful chastisement without any compensating favours. Nowadays she knew the difference between genuine and token punishment, the purpose of the former being only to keep her in line while the latter served to titillate and pleasure her. She soon learned to avoid the careless lapses that made Nigel take out his cane or strap, but she sometimes performed minor misdemeanours on purpose. Only once in the past month had he submitted her to a real leathering, for supposedly being cheeky, and even that had afforded her a certain amount of gratification – even though she could hardly bear to sit down for the rest of the day.

At home she had forgotten herself only a few times, and even then she'd managed to turn it quickly so that she swiftly regained the upper hand. The worst occasion had been when Ralph had asked her in the morning which outfit she would be wearing that evening and she'd answered, unthinking, in her humble office voice, 'Whichever pleases you most, sir.'

The look on his face had been a study in disbelief. Cordelia had deftly covered her lapse by laughing shrilly and saying, 'Just teasing! I know that every item in my wardrobe delights you. It doesn't matter what I wear, I'm still your adored mistress, aren't I? So choose for me. I can't be bothered to do it today.'

Tonight, though, she would be choosing for herself. As she approached the quiet suburban road where her secret life took place, Cordelia mentally ran through her wardrobe. She was feeling feminine, romantic even. The pink silk corset trimmed with black lace would suit her mood perfectly, along with some *Shalimar* perfume and black fishnets with her patent leather spike-heeled boots. She wouldn't bother with panties, though. Her crotch was already so hot after Nigel's treatment of her that it needed an airing – not so say a tonguing! The only question was, should it be before or after dinner? She often had to decide which of her appetites she should satisfy first. However it was only – she glanced at the dainty watch on her wrist – five twenty-five. Ample time for a quickie between her shower and the evening meal.

Drawing up in front of the house, Cordelia felt a warm

glow of satisfaction fill her entire being. What a perfect life she led! Already the front door was opening to reveal her personal slave coming out in his black leather cape ready to garage the car for her. She switched off the engine with a faint smile and picked up her bag from the front seat. As she turned back round the door was being opened.

'Good evening, Ralph,' she said, getting out of the car.

He bowed his head in response. 'Good evening, madam.'

'I shall require your assistance upstairs in about . . . say, ten minutes.'

'Yes, madam. Very good, madam.'

Cordelia had long since stopped worrying about what the neighbours thought of her unconventional lifestyle. They only saw the outward show, a man in a black leather cape like some cult TV hero of the Seventies, but she knew that beneath the enveloping garment he would be clad in the sexy costume she had selected for their mutual delight. She could only imagine how paradoxically vulnerable and yet sensual he felt with that soft latex squeezing his balls oh-so-gently, yet firmly. She knew the effect of that same material on her breasts, the tight encasing of her nipples that sometimes made them itch unbearably and yet so deliciously. What other sweet torments could she devise for him that evening? Well, she would see.

With a last glance at his handsome blond head which he lowered as he entered the car, Cordelia walked up the path and into the small detached house that she called home. It served her purpose beautifully, being far enough away from the neighbours for them not to hear much on the rare occasions when she was obliged to raise her voice. The house and garden were not overlooked either, with a thick Leylandii hedge screening it on three sides. There was a neat rockery in front and a pretty suburban garden in the back with a pond and a patio, small lawn and flower beds. Ralph took care of it all. He was such a treasure.

But one who needed to be firmly disciplined, she reminded herself as she entered the cool, quiet house and embarked on a tour of inspection. In the kitchen she found a dirty spoon carelessly left on the worktop instead of on the china spoon-rest. In the dining room there was one wilting flower left among the otherwise pristine blooms, and she spied a few hairs on the carpet. In the lounge the top of a picture frame had dust on it and the curtain tie was twisted. All peccadilloes, to be sure, but she demanded perfection and every detail must be attended to. She had Nigel to thank for training her to have high standards.

Dismissing such inappropriate thoughts of her boss, she went upstairs and made her tour of the bedrooms and bathroom, finding them mostly in order. After removing her shoes she lay down on the queen-sized bed with its delicate lacy coverlet and thought about her desires. Sometimes the endless need to find ways in which Ralph might serve her was tiresome. But not tonight. She had returned from the office in a state of hot tumescence that required thorough satisfaction and the only question was, how did she want to achieve it?

Cordelia heard the car being driven into the garage, the whine of the automatic door, then the front door being closed, followed by Ralph's footsteps heading towards the kitchen. He was making some adjustments to the cooking, then he would come upstairs. She stretched languorously, reviewing the erotic programme she had arranged for herself. What luxury to have her slightest whim fulfilled at a moment's notice!

There was a respectful tap on the door.

'Come in!' Cordelia said. As soon as he appeared she felt a warm thrill of appreciation as she noticed how smooth and sculpted his chest looked, how handsome his tanned face was with its wide-set eyes in that ambiguous shade of greenish blue, his sexy mouth set in its habitual slight pout, his nose so classically long and straight and the whole picture framed by those gorgeous golden locks that she knew felt as glossy and sensual as a hank of embroidery silk.

Cordelia told him to prepare the bathroom for her shower, then come back to undress her. She knew he'd be hoping for more, longing to get his hands on her flesh as she sometimes allowed him to do, lathering her silky skin and feeling her nipples harden beneath his fingertips. But this time she would deny him – at first. She would make him stand and watch her as she washed herself. A little deprivation now would make him all the more eager to please her later.

When Ralph reappeared she stood up with her back to him. 'Unzip me!'

He obeyed her with reverential care, sliding the zipper down smoothly to the point below her waist where she could step out of the neat shirt-waister dress, leaving her in her underwear. He knew the routine, unfastening her bra at the back and pulling the straps down her arms from behind so that he ran no risk of touching her bosom. Cordelia let the garment fall to the floor and he picked it up, placing it on the bed with her dress ready to go in with the dirty linen.

Behind her back she felt Ralph kneel so he could unfasten her suspenders, unhitching her stockings and rolling them deftly down her legs, being very careful not to snag them. A hole or a ladder in her precious silk stockings merited a thrashing, as he well knew. Standing there in her lace-trimmed panties, Cordelia decided to call a halt to the proceedings.

'That will do. Find my pink basque, the one with the black lace, and lay it out ready. I shall require black fishnets and my black patent boots. Oh, and the rhinestone collar with the matching earrings. Get all that ready while I'm in the bathroom. Then you can come in and watch me take a shower.'

'Yes, madam. Thank you, madam.'

She knew the thrill he was experiencing at the omission of any mention of her panties. He knew better than to question her, of course. She smiled to think of her bush peeking out from between her suspenders, just below the frill of black lace. How tantalizing he would find it! But first she would provoke him by showering in front of him as, sometimes, she liked him to do for her.

The atmosphere in the bathroom was warm and steamy, the air already filled with the scent of her current favourite perfume. Cordelia stripped off her panties and stood beneath the coursing water that soon drenched her from head to foot. She dipped her finger in the shell-shaped bowl of turquoise gloop and began to lather her breasts, making them taut and globular, with the nipples rearing stiffly to attention. Then she called him in.

Ralph entered, the bulge that was leading up slantwise from his crotch more apparent now beneath the tight rubbery suit. Cordelia imagined it bursting free from its constraints, ready and eager to do her bidding, and a deep shudder of lust took her unawares and made her utter a small groan. She stifled it at once.

'Sit there on the stool and watch me!' she told him, sternly. 'Meditate upon my beautiful body and prepare to do me service.'

She knew that would excite him almost beyond measure. His eyes misted a little as he sat down on the cork-topped stool, his hand absently patting his crotch. Cordelia gave a secret smile of satisfaction and began to lather the shower gel into her public hair, letting her fingers delve into the mass of curls to where the slippery nub was already very evident at the top of her vulva. It was still pulsing strongly and crying out for stimulation but, hard as it was, she refrained from rubbing herself there. Ralph had been behaving impeccably since she had returned home and, despite his small oversights in the cleaning department, nonetheless he deserved his reward as well as some chastisement.

While she continued to soap herself with Ralph's eyes intent upon her, Cordelia devised a plan that would achieve both ends. She would make it hard for him to achieve her satisfaction. That way he would be frustrated but her own climax, when it finally came, would be all the more intense. An image of apple-bobbing came to mind and of Ralph blindfolded, with his hands tied behind his back. She would play Eve, tantalizing him with the sweet apple of her sex. The thought sent a wild shiver of sensual joy flooding through her. She stepped out of the shower and he was instantly alert, waiting to do her bidding.

'Turn off the shower, then prepare to massage me with the strawberry cream.'

He enfolded her in a large, warm towel that was as soft as swansdown and she made her way next door to the small antechamber that she'd turned into a massage parlour. There was a leather-padded table which she'd treated herself to out of her Christmas bonus. On it was another towel and nearby was an impressive range of oils and unguents. She'd chosen the strawberry-flavoured body-cream not just because it was edible but also because it would remind her of what had happened in the office that afternoon.

With a voluptuous sigh Cordelia laid her damp body prone on the towel and closed her eyes. This would be a wonderful preliminary to the pleasures ahead. Soon after their relationship had moved onto this more interesting footing she had paid for Ralph to go on a sensual-massage course and it had paid dividends. She heard him unscrew the jar and felt his warm breath on her back as he leant forward to do her bidding.

First he touched her lightly all over her back, bottom and thighs with the fruity cream. Then he began to rub it in, gently at first, but with increasing pressure as her skin absorbed the lubricant and grew sleek and smooth. Sighing, Cordelia sank further into the towel, feeling the soft leather give beneath her breasts and stomach. Relaxation came easily to her now that she trusted Ralph to do the job properly. His expert hands seemed to have a mind of their own, applying just the right touch to both soothe and arouse her at the same time.

She felt his palms circling on her behind and her thighs sagged apart, giving him access to the deep clefts, back and front, that were the most sensitive of her erogenous zones. His fingertips played lightly around her arse crack, making her moan gently with frustration as they made their teasing way along the steep inner sides of her buttocks. The strawberry perfume was growing musky, mixing with her essential body oils, and she knew that the smell must be turning him on a treat. He had proved very receptive to the mixture of animal and fruit odours. *Must be something to do with the pheromones*, she mused.

At last his fingers began to probe her, slowly opening her up to let him go deep into the greedy, shameful nether heart of her. Past the tight ring of her sphincter he went, easing his way, making every richly-nerved half-inch of her squirm with naughty pleasure. Then, with his other hand, he crept into the limbo between, tickling her softly on the perineum and preparing her for even more sensual delights. She groaned out her desire, unsure whether she was in submissive or dominant mode, 'Yes, both at once, front and back! Ah, that's better!'

His finger slid into her open cunt and began to move round and round in its entrance. Cordelia was caught between

wanting the whole of him inside her – his fist, if not his cock –
and wallowing in the external stimulation he was giving her,
the thorough kneading of both vulva and clitoris that she was
getting. And her breasts . . . they were tingling like mad now,
her nipples pressed so hard against the massage table that
they were hurting her.

'I want . . . to turn over!'

She spoke in tortured tones, half choking with frustration and pain. The crude need was strong in her now,
demanding instant gratification. Ralph withdrew his hands
from her and let her roll over onto her back with her knees
wide open, her pussy raw and exposed, her arse still open
and craving. Filled with all the pent-up lust of the day, she
spat out her final command: 'Bring me off, quick as you
can!'

He knew how to, as well. Cordelia knew her patient
months of training would pay off in situations such as this,
times when nothing but the most cataclysmic and mind-
blowing orgasm would satisfy her. Ralph went into action
like a whirlwind, impelled by his own lust as much as by hers,
licking and sucking at her itching nipples, thrusting his
fingers back inside both her orifices and plunging them in
and out without mercy. Then, just as she was building
towards a climax, he bent down and found her hot clitoris
with his cool, his blessedly cool, tongue.

Cordelia bucked and squealed like a wild mare as the
tremendous pressure of her coming rose to impossible heights
and then burst into vivid, pulsating life. She felt the fierce
contractions radiate from her pussy throughout her whole
body, filling her with powerfully voluptuous fire. Again and
again she peaked, her body arching in the extremity of its
bliss, until the delicious feelings began to fade and she fell
back against the cushioning bed with a deep and satisfied
sigh.

When she had composed herself she said coolly, 'That will do for now. I shall call you again when I need you to help me dress.'

Relieved to be alone, Cordelia went back into the bathroom and cleaned herself up, sponging cool, lavender-scented water over her hot breasts and even hotter pubis. Feeling more at ease now that she had sated her more urgent desires, she knew that Ralph's lust for her had only been all the more inflamed by seeing her in the throes of such a violent climax. Well, she would keep him on tenterhooks for a while longer. That might teach him to be more meticulous in the execution of his household duties.

It was time to do her make-up. Sitting at the large mirror, its strip light illuminating the pale contours of her face, Cordelia proceeded to apply a tinted moisturizer to her unblemished complexion, making it matt and even. A little shiny blusher on her cheekbones defined them beautifully, and she added a dab on the end of her nose, to shorten its appearance. She filled in the hollow above her lid with her favourite shade of purple, adding a lighter shade to the lid itself, then added some old-fashioned black cake mascara with a practised hand. To finish she outlined the upper bow and lower curve of her lips in a dark red lipstick, filling in with a more brilliant shade and topping it with a smear of gloss.

After surveying herself critically in the mirror she brushed her hair to shining sleekness and sprayed herself with perfume. Then she shook the dainty little handbell that would summon her slave at a moment's notice.

Ralph came into the bedroom just as she was surveying her clothes. She gave him a cursory glance, noticing how hooded his blue eyes looked and how smooth and golden his chest, like the finest kid leather. 'Help me put these on. Corset first.'

He held it out for her to step into, then adjusted it over her bosom, the backs of his knuckles dusting the tops of her breasts delicately as he fluffed up the lace, making her tingle with the first stirrings of arousal again. Then he began to pull the laces that constricted her waist and pushed up her bosom to enhance the cleavage, drawing them so tight that her breath came in harsh gasps. 'That's . . . enough . . . now!'

Somehow her ribcage adjusted to its prison and soon she was breathing more naturally again, although not so deeply as before. It was worth the torture, Cordelia decided, as she caught sight of herself in the long mirror on the wardrobe door. She had attained the perfect hourglass figure, her waist nipped in to two hands' breadths and her tits like Nell Gwynn's, enormous plump globes rearing over the frilly tops of the basque. At the nether end her fluffy muff was evident, a heart-shaped mat of dark, glossy curls.

'Now the stockings.'

Ralph brought the black fishnet stockings from the bed and lifted one of her feet with his hand. She loved the sensual way he rolled the stocking on, slowly unfurling it all the way up her leg, his fingers producing quivers of suppressed excitement when they reached the inside of her thigh. He was squatting at her side, carefully attaching the suspender to the welt, his fingers brushing against her pubic hair and tantalizing her again. The same procedure was repeated on the other leg. Then he brought her boots, easing them onto her feet with the same dedicated care and fastening the laces. Cordelia quelled an urge to pat his smooth, golden head as he crouched between her legs, his face on a level with her crotch. If he was finding it an impossible torment, as she suspected he was, he showed no sign of it.

I've trained him well, she thought, with satisfaction.

She was about to go downstairs when she remembered the

rhinestone choker. 'Fasten that round my neck,' she ordered him, pointing to where it lay on the dressing table.

It was a tight fit, constricting her windpipe, but once again the effect was so magnificent that she decided to endure it. The stones glinted flashily and, in the context of the rest of her costume, gave her the air of a Las Vegas showgirl. Cordelia didn't mind looking vulgar once in a while so long as the overall effect was sexy – and she'd certainly succeeded there.

'How do I look?' she asked Ralph. Then a thought occurred to her. 'Don't say anything. I'll find out for myself.'

She reached out and found the Velcro fastening in the front of his rubber suit. With a raucous tearing sound the flap opened up to reveal the full extent of his erection. His prick bobbed and danced cheekily in front of her eyes, making her smile. 'I see. Not much doubt about the effect of my outfit now, is there?'

'No, madam.'

For a few seconds she held the meaty length of his rammer in her hand, squeezing it gently. It was a good penis, smooth yet strong, and she loved handling it. But it was a pleasure she rationed, knowing that in so doing she increased its value. Now she saw Ralph's face register hope. It came to life in an instant, glowed and blossomed in the brief span when she was giving him what he wanted, then, as she let his tool go and refastened the flap, she saw his expression fall back into impassivity again.

'Put it away, Ralph, then come down and make me a Margarita – with lime.'

She left the room, stepping carefully because of her heels, and made her way downstairs where she entered the sitting room. Settling into her favourite armchair she allowed Ralph to put on a new CD of her choice. Then she closed her eyes and waited for her cocktail. The delightfully slow pace of her life at home was soothing, after the pressure of her working life where she had to be careful to play out her submissive rôle to perfection while being the perfect secretary. It wasn't easy, and she relished the fact that she could unwind completely the minute she arrived home, being as lazy as she pleased in the knowledge that everything would be done for her.

Ralph reappeared, holding aloft a silver tray on which a pretty glass stood, rimmed with salt and filled with the fragrant drink. Some of her sexy cocktail sticks were protruding jauntily from it, a pair of pink tits and a maraschino cherry on a stick bearing the motto 'Snatch my cherry now!' She took the slender stem of the glass between her fingers and raised it to her lips. 'Cheers! How long will dinner be?'

'Just ten minutes now, madam.'

'Good, I'm starving.'

He left her, the sight of his tightly-encased buttocks affording her much pleasure as she watched him go. Cordelia sighed as she sipped the fruity alcohol, replaying the scene she had planned in her mind. Would she judge it right? It was such a responsibility, having Ralph under her control. She didn't want to fail him, to be seen as weak, petulant or cruel. She wanted to be respected, above all.

The ache inside her pussy and the itch between her legs was returning with a vengeance. She would need some more satisfaction that evening, for sure, but now she had already sated her immediate lust it would be easier to hold back, to make him suffer before he had his share. A slow smile curved her lips as she thought of how she had tormented him in the past, making him wait, restraining and blindfolding him, chastising and teasing him until he was gagging for it. Tonight she must make it plain that she was displeased with him in certain areas. That way she would have an excuse to punish him before she let him have his reward.

The table looked beautiful, as always, when Cordelia went in and sat down at the place that had been laid for her. The silver cutlery and cut-glass goblets were spotless, as was the table linen, while the sweet peas offered the perfect fragrant touch and were a delight to the eye. She couldn't fault him in that department. And from the scents that were emanating from the kitchen she was sure that he had excelled himself there, too. Her bosom swelled proudly within its confines as she recognized how far he had progressed since he first came into her care, how diligently he had studied to improve his cookery and housekeeping. Perhaps it would be unfair to chastise him *too* harshly.

Ralph entered with the first course, a seductive mélange of fruits and sorbet on a bed of crisp salad leaves. She savoured every mouthful then, her palate cleared, went on to the salmon and delicate *sauce mousseline*. Only when she had finished the 'sticky-toffeed rice pudding', a recipe of his own invention, did she feel the time had come to mention both her pleasure and displeasure in the same breath.

'Ralph,' she began, in a conspiratorial manner, beckoning him to the table. She didn't address him by name very often. It was a sign that she was going to say something of importance. 'That was an utterly delicious meal. I don't know how you do it, night after night, amazing me every time with your prowess in the kitchen.'

He was about to murmur something self-deprecatory, something flattering to her perhaps, when Cordelia broke in, her tone only slightly more severe. 'What a pity your domestic skills are so inferior to your culinary ones.'

She saw him quail, recover, frown a little. He was wary now, unsure whether she really meant it. Well, it was up to her to prove she did. Throwing down her napkin she rose sternly from her chair and confronted him with the catalogue of his failings. As she ran through the list she saw him fall deeper and deeper into shameful despair. At the end she barked, 'On your knees, slave!'

'I . . . I'm sorry, mistress . . .' He stammered, as he knelt before her. 'I spent too long dealing today. I was short of time. I thought you would rather have a good meal . . .'

'Than a clean home, is that what you thought? Slovenly creature!' He cowered as she reached out and dealt him a clip on the ear. Like the first shot in a battle, the blow caused an adrenalin rush that increased Cordelia's libido. 'I have tried and tried to teach you high standards, and once again you have let me down!'

How he loved it when she was angry and towering over him! She saw the secretive, adoring look alternating with terror in his tanned, handsome face and knew that he would be hard down below, wanting and fearing her so keenly that it was torture to him. Aware that her breasts were heaving with emotion and her face was flushed, Cordelia continued with her tirade. 'Did you think I wouldn't notice your laxity? Or did you imagine that I would consider such details as unimportant, mere trifles?'

Ralph bowed his head. 'No, madam.'

She seized his chin, feeling the slight roughness of his incipient beard lurking below the surface, and tilted his head back, forcing his eyes to meet hers. 'Then why *did* you leave those specks of dust, that dead flower in the vase, the curtain tie twisted, those hairs on the carpet?'

'I . . . I was going to see to it all tomorrow, madam.'

Cordelia uttered a shrill laugh that had a visible effect on him. He shuddered. She continued icily, 'Tomorrow. And tomorrow, and tomorrow! *Mañana*, as they say in Spain. You think I am like some Spanish slut, some strumpet, who doesn't care how lazy or dirty her servants are?'

He shook his head. 'No, madam.'

She pushed his face back with the palm of her hand, in a

gesture of contempt. 'Then let me see you correct those oversights *now*. Right away. Jump to it!'

Ralph scrambled hastily to his feet and she slapped him on his rubberized behind, sending him into a frenzy of activity. First he whipped the dead blooms out of the vase, being careful not to disturb the rest of the arrangement, then he lifted the stray cat-hairs from the carpet with his bare fingers. Cordelia followed him into the next room, watching from her chair with her boots on the footstool as he dashed from straightening the curtain ties to dusting the picture frame. She always loved watching him working, but he was at his most fetching when he was motivated by the twin impulses of guilt and a desire to please. The abject haste with which he obeyed her was most gratifying.

When he had finished he came and prostrated himself at her feet in a ritual of self-abasement that had somehow evolved over the past months. 'You have corrected your mistakes and that is good,' she told him. 'But they should not have been made in the first place. I still have to find a way to punish you. Because your misdemeanours have been slight, on this occasion I shall not resort to physical chastisement.'

She saw the tension in his jaw relax and smiled, knowing that what she had in store for him might prove more taxing than a few strokes of the cane. Still smiling, she said, 'Go to the drawer and bring out the blindfold box.'

He obeyed her less eagerly than before, not quite so sure of himself now. Ralph disliked being blindfolded, she knew that and seldom used it, but on this occasion it was unavoidable. He brought the box to her and placed it in her lap for her to select. She rummaged through the masks and scarves and eye patches, searching for the one that would best serve her purpose. Eventually she pulled out a padded strip of black cloth with ties at both ends.

'This one, I think. Come here, let me put it on.'

Ralph bent his head like a proud hawk, submitting to the hood.

Chapter Four

Ralph knew that his mistress was preparing something for him, but he had no idea what. The blindfold was tight around his eyes and he had to rely on smell and hearing for clues. Scentwise, he was aware of the background smells of his cooking lingering in the other rooms. But in the foreground was the exotic aroma of his mistress's perfume mingled with the erotic perfume of her sex. It excited him greatly to know she was naked and open, her pussy delivering its sweet emanations directly to the air where he might sniff it.

Was she going to beat him for missing those silly domestic trifles? He did hope not. That would demean her in his eyes, since up to now she had only whipped him for what she called 'gross misdemeanours' and she'd already admitted that missing bits of hair and dead flowers were scarcely in that category. Kneeling there on the carpet, blind and with his hands tied behind his back, Ralph felt isolated and vulnerable. Just what was she up to? He strained to hear whatever he could of her movements.

She was putting on another CD. Within seconds the strains of her favourite Prince album were blaring out: hot, sexy rhythms that set his pulse racing and pumped up his cock. This track was real bump-'n'-grind stuff. He pictured her pelvis swaying and thrusting before him with the great plump cushions of her tits bouncing around on top, and his erection swelled painfully within the latex suit. How much more of this would he have to endure?

'Come closer, slave!' he heard her say, just below the volume of the music. 'Shuffle forward on your knees. You'll know when you've reached the right spot.'

Ralph obeyed, moving slowly over the carpet because he was in the dark. The musky scent of her was overpowering now and his exhilaration grew when he realized his face must be level with her crotch. His fingers itched horribly.

Suddenly her hairy muff was brushing his nose and he knew that he was right up against her moist, hot pussy. He nearly sneezed as the coarse hairs tickled his nostrils.

'Lick!' she commanded him.

He put out his tongue and the tip of it met a smooth button of flesh that was as succulent and scented as an overripe melon. With a groan he tried to probe further but the slippery nub evaded him and he tongued the empty air. Then he tasted her, briefly, before she moved beyond his reach again. When it happened a third time his suspicion grew that she was teasing him on purpose, dangling her vulva in front of him and then whisking it away. If that was so, she must be tantalizing herself as much as him.

But she'd already come once tonight, he reminded himself grimly: she could afford to play cat and mouse with him. Her fingers toyed momentarily with the skin of his exposed chest, brushing against his nipples in a way that she knew turned him on. The bitch! She was really testing his self-control tonight, bringing him close to the edge then leaving him dangling there. She'd played this game before, but perhaps never so earnestly as this.

The juicy fruit was pressed to his lips again, tempting him, but the minute he put out his tongue, hoping to delve into the sweet heart of her, the prize was whisked away. Ralph groaned aloud and heard her low chuckle of response. Deftly she opened up the flap that concealed his burgeoning erection and he took a sharp breath as her fingertips brushed his shaft from root to tip, making it stretch further. He felt her lips brush his hair as she whispered, 'You love this, don't you, me being such a prick-tease?'

Ralph pressed his lips tight shut and shook his head.

'Liar!' she snapped, cuffing him on the shoulder in what seemed like a fit of pique. 'It's obvious you like it. You can't hide your enjoyment from me. I know exactly what's going on.'

She sounded so sure of herself that he almost believed her. Yet the experience of her pussy being offered and then whisked away was tormenting him horribly. He might have an erection but it was a straining, hungry one and if she didn't give him some hope soon he would probably lose it. She had no patience with him when he lost it, but fortunately that didn't happen very often. He only had to think of screwing her, of entering again that private sensual heaven that he dreamed of practically all the time, and his cock would revive.

The scent of her pussy assailed his nostrils once more. With impeccable timing she let him have more of a nibble, and he found his lips suddenly pressed flat against the musky folds of her labia while his tongue landed on her clitoris and managed to get in a few strokes before she backed off. But Ralph could still taste her juices when he licked his lips and his cock jerked appreciatively – which persuaded her to give it another soft caress.

'More?' she murmured. Dumbly, he nodded. 'I thought so. You can never get enough of me, can you? But this time you must wait because you've been such a naughty boy.'

She made him wait too, long agonizing minutes when all he could hear was the sound of her sighs and moans and the faint, liquid noises of her pleasuring herself. It was torture not to be able to see and feel, only to hear and smell and imagine. She often played with herself in front of him, goading him with her luscious body, making him want her cruelly, but this time it was worse because he was burning for her in the dark, not knowing whether he would be allowed the least glimpse of her, let alone a touch.

But *she* was able to touch *him*. Quite unexpectedly he felt her mouth encircle his glans, sucking his cock slowly into her mouth, and he gave a shuddering groan that turned into an animal howl of disappointment when, after a few seconds, she let him go. He could feel how hot and taut his balls were, aching to deliver, and knew that she was probably enjoying his discomfort. He was too, in a way, he had to admit. The tension inside him was like a roller-coaster ride where you only travelled up, up, up, without the thrilling release of going over the top and starting the downward run.

'Shut up and lick me again!' she commanded him.

Eagerly he opened his mouth and tasted sweet, wet pussy once more. This time she let him have even more of her. With his lips pressed up against her vulva he managed to stick his tongue right inside the hot chasm, feeling his way through the folds until the tip of his tongue entered her. He sucked hard, his teeth grating against her hard clitoris, but she gave a yelp and pulled back, leaving him to mouth the empty air again.

'Oh God!' he moaned in his extreme frustration. 'Why are you tormenting me like this?'

Her voice came low, amused, perfectly controlled. 'Because you love it.'

He shook his head but soon felt the flat of her hand against his cheek. It was the kind of slap you might give a hysteric. 'Yes, you *do*. You know you do. You love being at my mercy, under my command. Everything I do pleases you, even when I am teasing you unmercifully. Tell me it's not true.'

He shook his head again, confused. She laughed. 'You won't tell me? That's because you can't lie to me. You know that there are no secrets between us because I can read you perfectly, and you trust me to know you that well. Crawl to me, slave. I want you to crawl and lick my feet just to show how utterly abject you are.'

Ralph began to crawl, his cock still obstinately hot and needy, a rod of iron that was punishing only himself. She was only a few feet away, on the sofa, but it seemed to take an eternity. When he got there she thrust one bare foot in his face. 'Lick it, all over!'

He started at the heel, licking up and around the ankle. She didn't taste bad. There was a faint smell of strawberries still, reminding him of the pleasure of his massage, and that gave him encouragement. She had dainty, well-shaped feet and they were very sensitive so she particularly liked him to caress and kiss them. Ralph licked all over her sole, feeling her squirm when she felt ticklish, and then bit into the thick skin of her heel, the way she liked it.

Her moans told him she was pleasuring herself while he did it, rubbing her breasts and her pussy, making herself come. When the convulsions racked through her body he fancied he could taste it, taste her orgasm as it emanated through the soles of her feet. It tasted mellow and electric-sharp at the same time, like overripe citrus fruit. He went on licking her as she writhed and moaned in bliss, imagining how she must be feeling, and his prick tingled in sympathy.

She was breathing heavily now, lying back sated, and Ralph knew she'd had enough of his ministrations so he sat back on his heels and awaited further orders. Nothing happened for several minutes and he was afraid she'd forgotten he was there. Then he felt her hands on his shoulders, and shortly afterwards his wrists were untied.

'There, now you can finish yourself off,' she told him casually, removing his blindfold. 'I'm off to bed.'

With a long sigh he watched her half-naked body move from the room. Once he would have been angry with her for leaving him in the lurch but over the months of training he had come to understand her better and, more importantly, himself. How well she knew that simple satisfaction was not what he craved. His sexuality was a great deal more complicated than that and between them they were exploring every byway, to their mutual delight. She was mistress of his heart and soul: he had delivered his body to her as a chattel, to despise or play with as she pleased.

Pulling back his foreskin, Ralph masturbated quickly just as he might scratch an itch, to relieve himself of the annoyance. His organ spurted into his hand accompanied by a brief climax that was about as significant as a sneeze. After rising from his knees he walked towards the bathroom where he would find tissues to wipe himself with.

Cordelia arrived at the office filled with a strange, buzzy excitement. She could think of no particular reason – was it something Nigel had said? Perhaps it was just a hangover from last night, when she'd put Ralph through his paces in a way that had been so very satisfying for both of them. Now she was ready for whatever her boss had in store for her.

The morning ritual always calmed her spirit. Today Nigel had selected a French maid's outfit for her, the apron and frilly knickers made from lace-trimmed cotton with the short black dress, with its sweetheart neckline, made of latex. She put it on after her shower, relishing the caress of the thin rubber as it clung to her breasts and stomach.

By the time Nigel arrived she was keyed up, sitting at her workstation and pretending to go through the previous day's accounts but in fact alert to every sound outside. When she heard her boss enter, her heart flipped and she crossed her legs tightly, feeling the swelling bud within her lacy panties grow more hot and tingling.

'Ah, you're at work already. Good girl!' Nigel smiled at her, putting his head round her door. 'You're looking very perky this morning, Cordelia.'

'Thank you, sir.'

'When you've finished what you're doing come into my office. I have some good news for you.'

It was uncharacteristic of him to be quite so cheerful this early, and Cordelia found her imagination racing ahead of her as she typed the last paragraph of a report, then prepared to send it to a client as a fax. She was feeling very warm in her leather costume, the sticky material clinging to her thighs and breasts. Beneath its constricting embrace she seemed to be expanding, her flesh soft and malleable.

When she went into the next room Nigel was on the phone. She waited patiently for him to finish, eyes downcast, but his first words to her caused her head to rise involuntarily.

'I think it's time we expanded your horizons a little,' he began, a secretive look in his dark brown eyes. 'Are you available this weekend?'

She was stunned. Nigel had never asked for her services outside the working week. What would Ralph think? While she deliberated he went on, 'Only I would like you to come to a conference with me. It's being held in a country club, near Oxford, and should be a pleasant occasion. I'm sure you'll enjoy it.'

'But . . . ?' Unspoken questions were crowding her mind.

He gave a soft laugh. 'Yes, you will be attending as my slave but you needn't worry. Everyone there will understand and be fully supportive. It will be a kind of celebration of our unique relationship, if you like.' He added, as if she needed some further inducement: 'There will be lots of pretty costumes for you to wear.'

'Well, I'm not sure.'

'I know. But to put you at your ease I've arranged a kind of trial run. I've invited a colleague here today, to put you through your paces. I know you've never served another man like you do me, but there are plenty more out there who would relish your talent. It seems selfish to keep you all to myself.'

Panic struck her as she realized that the cosy little world she had built up with Nigel was about to be invaded by an alien man. Yet the more she thought about it, the more excited she became. Her boss was right, it was a shame to waste the rôle-play they had perfected by keeping it all to themselves. So long as the other people appreciated it, were of the same inclination, it might be fun to put on a show for them. But the next minute she had cold feet again, the exhibitionist in her vying with her natural preference for privacy in these matters.

Nigel sensed her dilemma. 'We wouldn't take it any further than you wanted to go,' he assured her. 'There would be a safe word, an agreed code that would put an end to that particular activity immediately. No one wants you to be hurt or upset in any way. I would make sure there was no risk involved. Will you agree to meet my friend Morgan, at least?'

She nodded, slipping back easily into submissive mode. He came round the desk and caressed her lowered neck as one might pat a quiet horse. Cordelia felt her skin prickle at his touch, her spine becoming energized. His palm travelled down the smooth rubber from her shoulder towards her breast, feeling the taut curves until it reached her jutting nipple.

'Nice!' he murmured. 'I made a good choice with this outfit. Now we are going to have you silent for the rest of the day, I think. Morgan will appreciate that. Come!'

He led her over to the cupboard where he kept his array of paraphernalia: whips, restraints, gags and blindfolds as well as various costumes, each carefully packed in see-through plastic. Looking at them Cordelia was aware that he hadn't used more than a fraction of his collection on her. Were there other women who had enjoyed such things? She knew so little of his private life, his life outside the office.

Nigel selected a black rubber bung and strap. He held it up, frowning slightly, then said., 'Open your mouth.'

She obeyed and he pushed the bung between her teeth, pulling the straps around her cheeks until they could be buckled at the back of her head. 'Comfy?' he asked. She nodded. 'There's no need to bite down hard – that will only make your jaw ache. The thing is designed to stay put, so you can just relax.'

Relax, indeed! Cordelia couldn't remember when she'd felt this uptight. To meet a perfect stranger with this dildo in her mouth struck her as acutely embarrassing, even if he did know the ropes. Chained to her desk, she resumed her work in a state of extreme apprehension that had her wriggling in her seat for most of the morning, more from anguish than pleasure. Then, around noon, the stranger arrived.

As soon as she clapped eyes on Morgan, Cordelia knew she needn't have worried. He was a large, heavily-built guy with tattoos and piercing, who wore his smart grey business outfit like a suit of armour. But his face was open and friendly, with a large, sensual mouth and soft brown eyes that made their tour of inspection languidly, taking in every detail of her appearance with obvious approval.

'Nice gear!' he commented. 'Stand up, princess. Let's see what kind of arse you've got on you.'

She obeyed – there was just about enough give in her chains for her to get up from her seat – and he couldn't resist coming over to pat her on the behind. When Nigel chided him for taking liberties, he gave a full-bellied laugh.

'You invited me here to take advantage of her, didn't you?

Let's have a slave auction, shall we? I'd like that. I'd *really* like that!'

Nigel shrugged. 'I had something else in mind, but if you prefer . . .'

'We could ask the princess here, but she's hardly in a position to disagree so I think we'll take her consent as read, shall we?'

'Have it your own way.'

Nigel's expression had the hint of a pout about it and Cordelia found herself enjoying the dynamic that was developing between her two masters. The idea of a slave auction appealed to her, too. It sounded like fun!

Morgan looked as if he was enjoying himself too. 'All right, you shall be the slave master and I'm a potential customer. Now, extol the virtues of your wares to me. Bring her in, parade her in front of me, let the dog see the rabbit!'

He took up his seat in the leather armchair, his legs spread wide and a lazy smile on his somewhat boyish face. There was a huge bulge in his crotch that Cordelia couldn't resist staring at, and his smile only widened when he saw where her eyes were focused. Nigel unshackled her from the workstation took her by the hand and led her up and down, parading her in front of his guest and giving a running commentary.

'Now you have to agree that this is a very fine specimen of womanhood. Just look at her body, with its generous curves and perfectly sculptured limbs. Take off your dress, slave. Let the gentleman see what you have to offer.'

Trembling, Cordelia pulled the latex costume over her head and discarded it. Underneath she was wearing only the frilly white knickers, a white satin suspender belt, black stockings and high-heeled shoes. Her full breasts were nakedly exposed, the nipples temptingly pink and hard as they crested the pale cream mounds.

She bent to undo the suspenders and her heavy breasts

swung forward, but then Nigel said, 'No, wait! Turn around and let the gentleman see your magnificent behind. This is one of her greatest assets, I must say. A man would die for a *derrière* like that.'

Slowly Cordelia rotated on her three-inch heels, hearing Morgan's murmur of approval as her taut buttocks came into view beneath the thin cotton of her panties. Then he said, 'Get her to strip off completely now. I want to view her equipment at close quarters.'

'Do you hear, slave?' Nigel snapped in her ear. 'Off with the rest, but slowly, mind. Let him enjoy the gradual revealing of your beauties, and that way his desire for you will grow.'

She obeyed, first bending again to unsnap her left suspender and then roll down her dark stocking, inch by inch, until all of her white thigh was exposed. She turned around with her back to him, so he could see her bottom again, and continued to roll down the stocking until it hung in loose folds around her ankle. Then she started on the other one. When both her legs were bare she began to caress her behind, stroking her buttocks sensually as if in a dream.

The visitor gave a sharp intake of breath. 'Magnificent, back and front! The creature is tempting me, but there is a great deal more I need to know about her before I make my decision.'

'Yes, sir?'

Nigel was obviously relishing the play-acting, pretending to be obsequious to his guest. He walked up to Cordelia again and spun her round on her heel until she was facing the chair where Morgan sat. Then he lifted up one of her breasts from underneath, holding it in the palm of his hand. 'She's well upholstered, wouldn't you say, sir? And buttocks to match. She will provide you with good cushioning whichever way you decide to take her, I can promise you that.'

'Hm. Get those pants off her. I want to view her cunt.'

Nigel pulled the scrap of cotton and lace frills down, exposing her pubic mound to Morgan's eager gaze. The visitor leaned forward in his chair to get a good view. Then Nigel told her to lie down on the floor and spread her legs, saying, 'Let the gentleman see your pussy, slave. Open it up for him with your fingers. That's right.'

Lying on her back with her vulva fully visible, Cordelia suddenly felt horribly vulnerable. If it had been just Nigel she would not have been so nervous, but there was no way on knowing which way the script would go now there was another player. Even so, she pulled the swollen labia apart with her forefingers and felt the air bathe her fevered tissues with coolness.

She was aware of Morgan getting up from his chair and coming to kneel down on the floor in front of her, peering between her thighs. Looking down her body she could see his face frowning slightly in concentration as he took in every nook and cranny of her.

'Beautiful sight, isn't it?' Nigel said. 'Nice thick lips and a clitoris you can't miss. Very touch-sensitive. She comes like a steam train when she's aroused. Open wider, slave, and tilt your pelvis up so he can see right inside you.'

Cordelia struggled to find the right angle, delving in with her fingers to part the inner lips and give the two men a better view. Nigel stuck his forefinger just inside her vagina and wiggled it around. 'Hear that? She's good and wet almost all the time. An ever-ready battery, you might say. Just plug in and get stuck in!'

She had suddenly become very aroused, her whole body throbbing with excited tension as the two men discussed her like meat on the hoof at a farm show.

'Hm.' Morgan sat back on his heels, looking thoughtful. 'That's all very well, but appearances can be deceptive. How quickly can she bring herself off? That's always a good indicator of a woman's randiness.'

'Show him!' Nigel commanded, tersely.

At first Cordelia was very embarrassed at having to rub herself in front of a stranger. It was easy to do it when Ralph was watching. Somehow he didn't count. But she'd only done it once on command in front of Nigel, and then it had taken her longer than normal to come because of her shameful feelings. Now she was afraid the same thing might happen again. Nevertheless she set to with a will, pulling back her labia and easily locating the hard pleasure bud as it stood proud from its little niche, throbbing hotly and slippery with her juices.

It didn't take her long to get into it. Alternately pulling on her inch-long nipples and rubbing her slippery clitoris she felt the barometer of her libido rising rapidly. Secretly relishing the fact that the eyes of the two men were staring right at her pussy with concentrated lust, the show-off in her was driven to writhe and moan theatrically, putting on a real display for them. She heard Morgan give a soft groan and knew that she'd got him going a treat. The thought of his cock straining beneath those grey trousers, longing for the sweet release of orgasm as much as she was, brought her nearer and nearer to the brink until the sudden waves of ecstasy began rolling through her flesh, in spasm after delicious spasm.

'Oh, my God – ninety seconds flat!' she heard Nigel exclaim, and realized with a shock that he'd been timing her. Through bleary eyes she saw him turn to his guest and say, 'Will that satisfy you, sir?'

'It will more than satisfy me. From what I've seen I should say the creature is insatiable. But there is one more test I must put her to.'

'What's that?'

'I must discover if she gives good head. A slave who cannot

bring me off with her mouth is useless to me, quite useless. I must know if she has learned the art well.'

'On your knees!' Nigel commanded her, brusquely.

Cordelia rose, her thighs still shaking from the violence of her orgasm, and got onto her knees in front of Morgan. Eagerly he unzipped his trousers and brought out his cock. It was surprisingly long and rather slender, elegantly shaped and of a dusky colour with a rose-pink tip that winked up at her and oozed a single bead of white sap. She felt her mouth watering. Fellatio was something she prided herself on being good at, although she didn't often get the chance to practise.

'Right, princess, let's see if you can suck me off good and proper,' Morgan said in a low drawl that excited her.

She bent forward and took the tip of his penis between her lips without handling it. Her breasts swung down, full and round, as she began to lick all around the rim of his glans, encouraging him to lie back in the chair and relax into the sheer erotic pleasure of being serviced. Cordelia sucked the whole of the tip into her mouth and got to work on it with her tongue, still keeping her hands out of the way. She was very aware of Nigel standing behind her, watching her every move.

Anxious not to let him down, Cordelia began to take Morgan's long shaft into her mouth, inch by inch, relishing the cool feel of it against her tongue. When the tip reached the back of her throat she did not gag but it was more than she could do to accommodate the whole of it. She compromised by taking the inch or so that was left outside and fingering it deftly, making Morgan grunt like a pig in shit. She gently withdrew her lips halfway while she swung her tongue all around the shaft in a twisting fashion, and ended up going all over his glans with the tip. It tasted very salty and fresh, as if it was ready to spurt, so she decided to divert it.

Pulling herself up closer Cordelia took her mouth right away from the rampant penis and instead used it to caress her breasts. She let the shaft roll around the generous slopes and down the ravine between them, where she squeezed her tits tightly together, enclosing it. Morgan's eyes were open, watching her, his huge balls flopped over the seat of the chair. She grinned and bent her head down, flicking her tongue across the swollen eye of his glans until he moaned aloud and she tasted more of the hot spunk that was leaking out.

He was near to exploding now, she was sure of it, but there was no need to hurry. In this game delaying tactics were more effective than rushing to a speedy conclusion. However much a man felt he wanted to come she knew that to increase the tension made for a more satisfying climax, and she wanted Morgan to be very satisfied indeed! Her mouth travelled down the length of his erection and found the full sacs, hot and hairy beneath her lips. Slowly, she took first one, then the other into her mouth while she fingered his cock, being careful not to overstimulate him.

Cordelia sucked gently on the skin of Morgan's scrotum, enjoying the delicate sensations that the act gave her. She moved the skin of his shaft up and down while she did so, feeling the hard ridge beneath, and occasionally her thumb slipped over the viscid glans which seemed to become wetter each time. She noticed that his thighs were tense and rigid, sensed that he was on the extreme edge of endurance – and knew that it was time to let rip.

Quickly, she took as much of his cock as she could into her mouth and began to fellate it rapidly, keeping her teeth back behind her lips so that she could travel smoothly and swiftly up and down the shaft. Whenever she reached the top she tongued his glans, tasting the acrid fluid that was seeping from the slit, and soon she felt the first pulses working their way up his shaft accompanied by loud groans of ecstasy.

The fountain spurted into her mouth and she swallowed the lot, her fingers working the base of his shaft where she could feel the rhythmic pumping. When the last of his climax had worked its way through she fell forward, her hot breasts flattening against his thighs and her exhausted mouth slack and open. Morgan lay back in the chair, panting and groaning out the last gasps of his satisfaction. Then she felt Nigel's hand on her shoulder, pulling her away.

'So, does the slave meet your requirements?' she heard him ask, his tone amused.

Sitting back on her heels, Cordelia saw the man open his eyes. He stared straight at her, then his thick, sensual lips curved into a smile. 'By God, princess, you are one hell of a cocksucker!'

'Then you'll take her?' Nigel enquired, walking round to stand beside the chair.

There was silence while Morgan zipped up his fly, regained his composure and got slowly to his feet. He remained looking down at her as he said, 'I think I'll take a rain check, if that's okay.'

'Fine. Any time.' Nigel walked his guest to the door, talking to him in a low voice. He went out of the room and into the corridor with him, still chatting. Then Cordelia heard the whine of the lift and, in a few seconds, her boss returned with a smile.

'Well done! You passed the test with flying colours.'

She remained on the floor, bemused. 'What test?'

'Your first exposure to a stranger. And I think you enjoyed it, didn't you?' She nodded. He came up and helped her to her feet. 'Thank you for not letting me down. I told him how good you were, and now he knows for himself. I can't wait to show you off to more of my friends.'

'More?' She stared at him, wide-eyed. He obviously had an agenda that he hadn't told her about. A thrill of apprehension ran through her veins.

'Oh yes, I have plans for you. Big plans! At the conference this weekend. You did say you were free to come, didn't you?'

Cordelia knew that she could not refuse.

Chapter Five

Harley Grange was an old, brick-built manor house, tucked away between low hills by a stream. It looked most picturesque and Cordelia felt warmly excited as Nigel ferried her up the drive in his Mercedes. It was dusk, and the lights from the diamond-paned windows were gleaming on the gravel and flower beds, while coloured lanterns swung in the surrounding trees, giving the place a magical air.

'Nice venue,' she murmured.

'Yes, we always try to choose somewhere special for our conferences. Last year it was a health farm.'

He was cagey when she asked him about the other people. 'Oh, we're just a bunch of like-minded financiers who enjoy mixing business with pleasure.'

'Will Morgan be there?'

'Certainly. He's our entertainment manager for the weekend.'

Their conversation on the journey down had been minimal, strained. Cordelia had never accompanied him on a trip before and outside of her rôle she felt awkward with him, not sure how to behave. So it was a relief when he said, as they drew up outside the imposing porch, 'Now don't forget, from this moment on you're my slave. You must behave appropriately throughout the entire weekend. Understood?'

She did understand, perfectly. Getting out of the car first she opened his door for him and stood with head bowed and hands behind her back, symbolically tied, until he beckoned her to follow him with their suitcases. Slowed down by a large case in each hand, Cordelia arrived in the entrance hall to find him already chatting animatedly to two other men. She deposited the luggage and stood humbly by, still staring at the ground, as the trio approached.

'So this is your special treasure,' she heard one of the men say.

He came forward and put his hand beneath her chin, lifting her head up. His blue eyes searched hers for an instant with a hint of amusement, before they swept down over the neat lime-green business suit she was wearing, lingering on the swell of her bosom and the few inches of thigh that showed beneath her short skirt.

The other man clicked his fingers and a youth appeared. 'Take these cases up to suite seventeen, Giorgio.'

'Suite seventeen – I like it!' Nigel chortled.

'It's in the west wing. I hope you'll be comfortable,' the other man said, in a managerial tone. 'If there's anything you need, don't hesitate to ring the front desk.'

Nigel led the way to the foot of the grand staircase. Cordelia was aware of the sound of voices and general bustle elsewhere in the old house, rousing her curiosity, but she maintained her humble demeanour and felt the familiar sensations of fear and excitement mingling in her veins. She had no idea what was in store for her at Harley Grange, but she imagined it would be immensely gratifying in any number of ways.

The suite was small but delightful, with flowery wallpaper and matching bed linen, a fluffy pink carpet and an adjoining bathroom with whirlpool tub and shower. There were twin beds in one room and a double in the other. Unsure what Nigel would want of her, since she'd never actually slept with him, Cordelia was relieved when he told her to take one of the twin beds while he occupied the double next door. That, he told her wryly, would enable him to keep his options open. The double room had its own entrance and there was a communicating door between the two rooms.

While she showered, Nigel changed into a dress suit. Then he selected her clothes for the evening from the assortment he had brought. As soon as Cordelia's eye lighted on the outfit she knew it would be a great contrast to the neat suit she had arrived in. Fingering the glossy black-and-pink latex bikini, to be worn beneath a see-through pink plastic cape, she knew that she was destined to play an exciting part in the proceedings that evening. To complement the outfit she would be wearing elbow-length black vinyl gloves and self-supporting black lace stockings with the inevitable high heels.

'While you're dressing I shall be downstairs, sorting out a few details,' Nigel informed her, making for the door. 'You have half an hour, then I shall come for you.'

When she was alone, Cordelia found herself shuddering with suppressed excitement. Never before had she 'gone public' in her fetish fashion and she had no idea what lay in store for her downstairs. Would everyone be similarly dressed? Would the other men have brought their wives or girlfriends along? Nigel had given nothing away.

Cordelia smoothed scented body-cream onto her arms, legs, breasts and stomach, then sprayed herself with the same perfume. Nigel had chosen warm, spicy *Ysatis*. Everywhere her skin felt taut and tense, her pulses were fluttering wildly and a sensual heat was making her glow with perspiration. She flicked talc into the large cups of the bra and eased it on over her breasts, then tightened the straps to give them maximum uplift. After doing the same with the skintight latex pants, which were little more than two slim triangles joined with a few thongs, she looked at herself in the mirror.

The effect was striking. Her tits looked magnificent, encased in the smooth, liquorice-black material with her nipples poking stiffly through. However, there was a small problem with her bottom half. The bikini pants scarcely covered her pubic hair so she was obliged to get out her lady razor and smooth away the stray hairs until only a thin strip of curls covered her vulva. She wondered how it would feel to shave there completely, but she wasn't ready for that. Not yet, anyway.

Slowly Cordelia pulled on the lacy stockings, feeling the slight elasticity that helped them to stay firm around her calves and thighs. Her legs were lightly tanned, smooth and hairless, and beneath the peekaboo lace they looked magnificently shapely and would look even more so when she put on her high heels. First, though, she picked up the transparent cape and fastened it around her shoulders. It gave a softness to her appearance and enhanced the shine of the latex bikini, making her curves look all the more tantalizing.

She slipped into her shoes and gave a sigh of satisfaction as the picture became almost complete. Sitting down on the plush stool in front of the dressing table, she went into her meticulous make-up routine, her eyes growing huge and lustrous as she applied subtle shading and further lengthened her already long lashes. She chose a shade of pink lipstick that perfectly matched the flashes of pink on her bikini, then did up her blonde wig in the elaborate, yet sexy, style that she knew Nigel adored, with one or two curled strands falling gently around her face.

'Perfect!'

Her boss's voice from behind made her jump. He had come into the bedroom quietly so as not to disturb her and now his eyes were ravishing her, taking in every small detail and delighting in what they saw. In his black dinner jacket and crisp white shirt, with its discreet ruffles, he looked very handsome.

'Come here!' he commanded her.

Cordelia walked slowly over the thick carpet, confident that she was looking her best. Suddenly he took something out of his pocket and, before she realized what it was, her neck was encircled in a black leather choker with a chain attached.

'This is how we shall make our entrance,' he smiled. 'Come! They are waiting for us downstairs.'

He led her out into the corridor. Because of the collar and chain she couldn't bow her head so she held it high, putting on a blank, doll-like face. They walked slowly downstairs and into a large dining room to the right that was set with round tables. At the far end was a raised platform, probably intended for after-dinner speakers or cabaret performances. Although she was looking straight ahead, Cordelia was aware that the room was full, every table having its complement of four guests, and with a sinking feeling she also suspected that she was the only woman in the room. A flutter of applause had broken out when they entered and now this was rising to a crescendo, making her blush as all those male eyes swivelled in her direction.

Nigel made for what looked like the top table. There were three men already sitting there and Cordelia wondered where she would go. Her boss greeted his friends, then turned to her, barking a command: 'Sit!'

She made for the empty chair but he yanked the neck chain, making her yelp. Sternly he pointed to the floor. 'Sit!' he repeated.

Understanding now, Cordelia got down on the carpet while he tied the handle of the chain around the leg of the chair before sitting down. So she was to be his bitch for the evening! He confirmed it by stroking her hair and murmuring, 'Good girl!' before joining in the conversation around the table.

With startled eyes, Cordelia glanced around at the white tablecloths and black trousers, which were all she could see at that level. She strained to hear what the diners were talking about but it was all high finance and trading, which bored her. Many of them had upper-class accents and she concluded they were public-school Oxbridge types, like Nigel. That being so, they would be into corporal punishment, she had no doubt.

She began to wonder exactly why she was there, and a thrill of horror ran through her when she remembered what Nigel had said about Morgan, that he was their entertainment manager. Was she going to be the cabaret for the evening? Maybe what had happened in the office earlier in the week had just been a rehearsal, and she would have to go through that 'slave auction' routine before all these men! Overcome by a deep shame, Cordelia felt her eyes misting. What had been her dirty little secret, hers and Nigel's, was being aired in public. And she wasn't at all sure that she liked the idea.

Anger and resentment burned in her the more she thought about it. Had this been Nigel's intention all along? Had all those months of 'training' in the office had an ulterior motive behind them? She felt duped. For a moment she pondered what Ralph might think and feel if he saw her now, chained at the feet of her master, and she felt a giggle start to erupt. She coughed to hide it and almost choked.

A dish of water was placed before her with the instruction, 'Drink! Lap it up!'

She slipped quickly back into an obedient state of mind, dismissing both Ralph and her suspicious doubts from her consciousness as she bent forward and tried to lap up the water. It was hard to use only her tongue but she managed to get enough down her to stop her choking. There were murmurs of approval around the table before they continued their conversation. Waiters began to move between the tables and the delicious smell of the food was making Cordelia feel hungry. Nigel's table was served and then a plate was placed on the ground for her with small portions of food all cut up into bite-size chunks, as if for a child or an invalid. Nigel patted her head again, saying, 'There you are, lovely din-dins. *Good* girl!'

Trying to get the food into her mouth without spillage was a strain, and soon Cordelia had food stains on the plastic cape. Nigel noticed. He pulled on the chain and got her to stop mouthing the food around the plate.

'Look at you, you messy creature!' he said, loud enough to make heads turn in her direction. 'Making a real dog's dinner out of that, aren't you?'

The men all around laughed, which only drew more attention to her. Cordelia felt her cheeks grow red with embarrassment. Everywhere she looked there were grinning male faces, enjoying her discomfort while they took in the sight of her kneeling on all fours with her vinylclad bottom showing through the clear plastic.

Nigel took his dinner napkin and wiped with it to remove the food from what now seemed more like a baby's bib than a cape. He made a thorough job of it, brushing over her breasts repeatedly and making the nipples tingle with arousal inside their latex sling. The humiliation of it was making her feel resentful again, but at the same time there was a perverse satisfaction in having so many pairs of male eyes upon her, lusting after her and wishing they were the one to perform intimate services for her.

Nigel sat back in his chair, tossing the dirty napkin on the table. 'That's better! Now eat the rest of your food, and mind your table manners!'

Nervously Cordelia bent her head to the plate again. Soon the men lost interest in her and resumed their conversations once again, but try as she might much of the food still evaded her mouth, sliding around on the plate and spilling over the side. When she did manage to get a mouthful some of the sauce ran down her chin and onto the cape again.

Eventually Nigel noticed. He made more of a fuss this time, jerking her head up and exclaiming loudly, 'I don't believe it!' He turned to his fellow diners, seeking their support as he continued, 'Just look at this mess! You heard me telling this creature to be more careful, didn't you? Just look at the state of the carpet!'

Some of the men laughed, others asked him what he was going to do about it. Cordelia didn't like their tone of voice. They sounded knowing and sly, as if this was all part of the plan. Which, she realised with a shock, it definitely was. She was now the main focus of attention in that part of the room, and when she looked around it was to see a circle of grinning, lecherous faces that made her heart flutter as her imagination ran wild.

'What are you going to do?' a man's voice called, triggering off a volley of responses.

'Punish her!'

'Yes, give her a good hiding!'

'On her bare behind!'

Nigel nodded, slowly, and Cordelia felt the secret button between her legs begin to throb as she contemplated being chastised in front of all those men. She always responded erotically to being thrashed on the buttocks. Her boss told her to remove the plastic cape, his eyes glinting with suppressed enthusiasm for the sport ahead. She did as she was told, folding it up neatly and placing it on the carpet beside her plate. Now that her body was exposed in the black-and-pink latex bikini there were murmurs of approval all around. Men who were not near enough to see her properly had crowded round and some were standing on their chairs to get a glimpse of her.

Nigel got to his feet. 'Gentlemen, gentlemen!' he called, loudly. 'Please resume your seats. The punishment of my slave will take place on the platform, where you can all witness it.'

He tugged on the chain, pulling her forward slowly on all fours. As they made their slow progress between the tables towards the platform there were cries of approval on all sides and some of the bolder men gave her bottom a testing slap as she crawled past – which only served to increase her excitement.

When they got to the stage, Nigel removed the chain from her collar and helped her up. She knelt at his feet, eyes down, while he addressed the room. 'Friends, many of you have witnessed the sloppy behaviour of my slave this evening and I think we are all agreed that she deserves punishment.' There was a chorus of approval. 'Personally, I am averse to harsh treatment . . .' Cries of 'Shame!' and 'Rubbish!' ensued. Nigel waited for them to die down, then continued, 'So I shall call upon the services of one who is far more used to maintaining strict discipline. I give you, your friend and mine, Mr Morgan DuChêne!'

Cordelia couldn't help looking round as the man appeared, and she gave an involuntary cry when she saw him. He was the same Morgan she had met in the office. But now he looked very different, wearing all-black leather with lacing across his bare chest and his cock encased in a rubber pouch. From his belt hung an assortment of whips, dildoes and other paraphernalia that made her quail. Would he be using any of his armoury on her? She felt her insides turn to water at the prospect of having to endure stimulation of one kind or another in front of all those men.

The proceedings took on a formal tone as Morgan enquired, in a booming voice, 'What is the nature of the culprit's misdemeanour?'

Nigel answered, 'Breach of etiquette!'

Morgan's dark brows lifted. 'What form did this breach of etiquette take?'

'Disgusting table manners!'

There was silence in the room as Morgan stepped forward and addressed Cordelia directly. 'This is a very grave offence when others are dining,' he began. 'A sloppy eater puts others off their food. By your conduct you have insulted not only all those here present, but the hard-working chef and his assistants who prepared this magnificent repast for our delectation. This is not a minor matter. Your punishment should fit the crime.'

Cordelia sat on her heels with her head bowed, awaiting sentence. The whole place was tense, expectant. Although she knew that this was why she was here, to provide some 'entertainment' for the diners, her flesh trembled at the prospect of punishment. And what else was on the hidden agenda for the evening? She had a feeling that this was only for starters.

Nigel turned and addressed the audience. 'Any suggestions, gentlemen?'

A chorus of responses flooded towards the stage, making it impossible to single one out. Nigel placed his hand behind his ear and pointed to one diner, who was calling for 'six of the best.' Holding up his hand for silence, Nigel asked if they found this acceptable.

'Only if she takes her knickers down!' someone called.

His suggestion was greeted by laughter, shouts of 'Hear, hear!' and further vulgar suggestions that Nigel, mercifully, ignored.

'Very well,' he said at last. 'Bring on the whipping frame!'

Cordelia shrank as she heard the words. Frame? What frame? It sounded like something medieval, a variant on the village stocks. A buzz of excitement went around the room as a waiter wheeled in the wooden device and pushed it up the ramp onto the platform. Nigel's eyes were gleaming in that cruel way that both excited and terrified her, but Morgan was standing quite impassively as if he were only doing his job.

The frame was over six feet tall and equipped with bars and straps. It was immediately obvious to Cordelia that she was going to be secured to the thing in order to take her punishment, and an intense wave of orgasmic heat rushed through her at the thought of the ritualized public shaming she would have to endure. The men had been drinking all evening and were getting more noisy by the minute, obviously all looking forward to the sport.

'On your feet!' Nigel commanded her.

For an instant she looked straight into his eyes, hoping to see there some hint of complicity, some comforting sign that this was all part of the game they had been playing over and over since the beginning. But she received no such reassurance. He stared at her coldly, as if she truly had committed some gross transgression that merited a severe penalty. Anxiously, she stood with her arms crossed in front of her latex-clad breasts for protection while Morgan checked the apparatus, pulling on the straps and bars in a theatrical fashion that only increased Cordelia's unease.

Before she could register what was happening, Nigel took her by the hand and pulled her roughly towards the frame where Morgan was holding up one of the wrist-straps. She was pushed against the bars and first her right, then her left wrist were secured at shoulder height. Behind her she could hear the crowd of drunken men chanting, 'Off! Off! Off!' and she knew they were referring to her latex panties.

She heard Morgan say, 'I'll hold her,' but before the significance of his remark struck home Nigel had seized her nether garment and was tugging it down over her tense buttocks, then further down her thighs until the whole of her bottom was displayed to view. The audience broke out into spontaneous applause. While Morgan fastened the leather restraints around her ankles, Nigel addressed the crowd.

'Yes, friends, the creature is certainly well-endowed in the *derrière* department, as I'm sure you'll agree. Just how well-stacked she is elsewhere you might find out later. Let us proceed. Gentlemen, choose your weapon!'

Morgan finished strapping Cordelia to the frame. She felt horribly exposed and vulnerable, knowing there was a bright spotlight illuminating her round, pink behind. Soon that flesh would become even pinker. Out of the corner of her eye she could see her tormentor brandishing an assortment of whips and canes at the audience, trying to judge by the response which one they would prefer him to use on her.

She was trembling uncontrollably now, and her shame was that it was not all from fear but also from desire, the dark and inexplicable desire to wallow in the public humiliation that she was about to endure and to derive a secret pleasure from it. She could feel her labia growing wet and slack with lust, opening up as if to receive a full cock, and her clitoris itched and ached with suppressed longing. Knowing that the force of the blows on her buttocks would only increase her desire to insatiable levels, Cordelia couldn't help wondering what Nigel and Morgan had in mind for the rest of the evening. With no lack of willing volunteers among the dinner guests she could have her appetite satisfied many times over.

The thought made her quiver inside, notching up her arousal even more. There was a roar of approval from behind and she realized that the choice of implement had been made. She turned her head to one side and caught a glimpse of the long, supple cane that Morgan was brandishing. He tried it out on thin air, flexing and swishing it so that it made an alarming *whoosh*ing noise.

'Right!' she heard Nigel announce. 'I think we're ready.' He came close beside her and said, in a loud histrionic tone, 'Are you ready, slave, to receive your punishment?'

Cordelia nodded, bracing herself for the first stroke. It came suddenly, taking her completely unawares and bringing tears to her eyes as the stinging tip of the cane landed on the plumpest part of her left buttock. The sound of the men chanting, 'One!' didn't make it any easier.

She was more prepared next time. Trying to relax, she heard the cane make its singing descent onto the right half of her bottom and bit her lower lip, opening her eyes wide to stem the tears. Already her lower half felt inflamed, the hot friction exciting her almost as much as masturbation. Yet she was also torn in two, her inner turmoil centring on the knowledge that she was in danger of revealing her secret weakness to a room full of strange men, while her body shrank from the painful aftermath that she knew would follow the corporal punishment. Torn this way and that she found herself mentally counting the blows along with the men: 'Two, Three, Four . . .'

At last the sixth came, the sting mercifully less acute now she knew it to be the last. A sudden fear seized her that they would not play fair, that they would extend the sentence. But they were gentlemen, and once the applause had died down Nigel came up with a pot of soothing cream which he proceeded to rub into Cordelia's raw and inflamed behind. The massage did ease her pain but it also swung the pendulum of her sensuality firmly back towards pleasure, making her feel so randy that she squirmed against the barred confines of the frame and moaned aloud.

'You're enjoying this, aren't you? Shameful hussy!' Nigel whispered in her ear. 'Don't worry, there will be a better chance for you to get off later.'

While Morgan unshackled her limbs, Nigel clipped the

chain back onto her collar so that he could lead her from the stage on all fours, with her scarlet bottom in the air. Relieved when he allowed her to put her pants back on, Cordelia decided that the worst was probably over. *It's not me they're ogling*, she told herself, *just an entertaining doll, a piece of meat*. Even so, at some deeper level her boss's treatment of her still rankled like a betrayal.

The dinner proceeded almost as if nothing had happened, with Cordelia chained to Nigel's chair again. When dessert was served he fed her spoonfuls of the delicious chocolate-and-brandy mousse – her reward for being a 'good girl', she presumed. She sucked the spoon greedily, her senses craving stimulation from any quarter now, and was rewarded by a paternal pat on the head again.

At the end of the meal the tables were pushed back and chairs brought forward, facing the platform. With a sinking feeling, Cordelia realized that another show was being prepared for the men but she had no idea whether she would be involved. Surely she had done her bit for the evening? There must be someone else, a hired stripper for instance, who was going to put on an act for these drunken, randy beasts.

Because that was how they seemed, throwing lecherous looks in her direction if ever she dared raise her eyes, some even taking liberties and patting her on the bottom as they passed. When Nigel took up his seat in front of the stage he made her kneel in front of him so he could use her as a footstool and some joker asked if he could use her arse as an ashtray. Angrily, Nigel told him to 'fuck off', much to Cordelia's surprise.

'I won't have anyone treat my property as if she were theirs.' he explained to the man next to him. 'I haven't spent months training her just to let some ignoramus play stupid games with her. Let him get his own female. Let him find out how difficult it is to find someone with the right temperament, and then what hard work it is to spend months bending her to his will until she develops into the perfect slave.'

'I quite agree,' the man said, puffing out cigar smoke. 'And you have an absolute treasure there. I envy you, young man.'

There was a sharp rapping noise. Cordelia looked up to see Morgan standing behind a lectern on the stage, on which had been placed a top hat. He was bringing the room to attention with a baton, an action that caused her cheeks to flush, both top and bottom.

'Gentlemen, gentlemen!' he began in a drawling tone. 'As you know, we have sold a good number of raffle tickets tonight in aid of the Distressed Stockbrokers Association.' Loud laughter. 'So now we must invite the charming prize to come up and pick the lucky winner.'

He looked straight at Cordelia, making her spine tingle. She reran his words in her head, letting the implication sink in. Was *she* to be the prize? The thought that she might have to sleep with one of the men whose rapacious eyes had been feasting on her flesh all evening filled her with a confusing mixture of covert lust and dismay. Like those of a captive animal, her wary eyes passed through the crowd, noting the corpulence of this man, the powerful build of that man, the cruelly mocking expression on another man's face that told her he was exulting in her humiliation.

Nigel kicked her behind and she scrambled to her feet, almost toppling on her high heels. The chain was unhitched from her neck and Morgan beckoned her up onto the small stage again, smiling in a way that suggested he understood her apprehension and was amused by it. He held out his large hand and drew her over to the lectern on which the top hat stood. Picking up the hat by the brim he held it out towards her, saying, in his deep, ironic drawl. 'Pick a number, princess, any number!'

She did as she was told and gave the folded ticket to him. He read it out with a self-important air. 'The winning ticket is . . . green, thirty-two! Green, thirty-two, gentlemen!'

'I've got it!' An excited voice came from the back of the room.

Everyone's eyes, including Cordelia's, swung towards the winner. He was standing up, waving his ticket, and she saw that he was young and personable, quite tall and slim with an attractive, well-groomed look about him. Her heartbeat steadied itself, with relief.

'Congratulations!' Morgan grinned, after a waiter had verified the ticket. 'You have won a personal table dance from our lovely slave girl!'

Applause echoed round the room as Cordelia gaped with astonishment. *Dance?* They wanted her to dance, for heaven's sake? This was almost worse than the prospect of sleeping with a strange man.

Aware that both Morgan and Nigel were watching her, and fearing another beating for insubordination, Cordelia composed her features into the blank mask that signified her total submission to her master's will. All right then, she would dance, to the best of her capability. She would dance like Salome, like Monroe, like Madonna. She would use her body shamelessly to arouse him but never allow his hands to touch her, only his eyes. She would dance the eternal dance of the Prick-Teasing Whore.

But first, she simply had to go to the loo . . .

Chapter Six

Cordelia whispered her need to Nigel, praying that he would not make her wait for a pee as he often did in the office. She was relieved when he began shepherding her through the maze of tables, where the men ogled her with greedy eyes, until they went out into the hall, where the men's and women's cloakrooms were located.

Before he let her go, Nigel put his hand in his pocket and brought out something which he thrust into her palm. 'Stick these in your pussy,' he grinned. 'Then your dance will be more sexy!'

She opened her hand and stared down at the set of six small golden balls on a knotted string. Nigel grinned at her surprise. 'Japanese love-balls. Every time you roll your hips or rock your pelvis you'll get good vibrations! Now hurry up, or our prizewinner will be getting restless.'

Cordelia entered the plush cloakroom with the sex-toy in her hand, wondering what exactly it was supposed to do. She went into a cubicle and, after she had relieved herself, began to feed the string of balls into her wet and open quim. To her surprise they slipped in easily, all six of them, and once they were there she soon discovered their purpose. Every time she moved they gave her a delightful internal massage that set her pulses racing with erotic excitement. She experimented as Nigel had suggested, performing a sensual dance with her hips and pelvis that soon produced such exquisite feelings in her pussy that she wanted to carry on to orgasm.

But she thought of Nigel's words and realized that he wanted her to come while she was table dancing, to make her performance all the more erotic. Smiling to herself, she rearranged her wig to look more tousled and sexy, then went outside. Her boss came up at once and spoke softly in her ear. 'You're to strip as you're dancing – but slowly, make it last. The rule is look, don't touch. If anyone gets fresh with you they'll answer to me, so don't worry. Just relax and enjoy it. I'm sure you'll do fine.'

He led her back into the crowded room, where as many men as possible were surrounding the winner's table, all eager to watch the action. There was a good deal of pushing and shoving going on, but Morgan cleared a path for them and soon Cordelia was standing before the lucky man. He kissed her hand, then said, suavely, 'My name's Eric, and I'm looking forward very much to seeing you dance.'

'Okay, that's enough,' Nigel said, sharply. 'Don't touch her any more. Give the signal, Morgan, and let's get this show started.'

Morgan clicked his fingers at the waiter who was managing the sound system and soon the air was filled with a slow, raunchy beat. Taking her cue, Cordelia began to sway in front of the already mesmerized Eric and the other men moved back to give her more room. She stretched her arms languidly, still moving her hips and rotating her pelvis until she began to feel the balls moving inside her vagina. She gave a secret smile and began to caress herself, running her fingers lightly across the tops of her breasts and smoothing down her thighs, drawing attention to her assets.

There were small murmurs of appreciation all round as she bent down and arched her back, sticking her bum out, then wiggling it suggestively. She was beginning to enjoy the feeling of having all those men in the palm of her hand. Stripping for an audience had always been one of her fantasies and now the exhibitionist in her was coming to the fore, exulting in the opportunity to show off. Her movements became dirtier, more explicit. She patted her pubic mound and stroked her thighs again, put her fingers inside her bra and felt the nipples, hard and hot within the latex cups.

'Take it off!' someone shouted, and the cry went up, 'Off! Off! Off!'

She gave them an arch smile and pulled down one strap, teasingly, then the other. Her eyes were fixed on Eric, who was sitting back in his seat looking embarrassed. She could see the bulge of his crotch quite plainly beneath the dark trousers and knew that she was turning him on a treat. In true striptease style, she began to peel off the long black gloves, easing them off her fingers with her teeth and whirling them around her head before throwing them at the red-faced Eric. The first one landed on his head, making him look ridiculous and causing much hilarity among the crowd. The second landed in his lap, amid whoops and cheers.

She continued to dance for a while, approaching Eric's chair and thrusting with her pelvis so that her pubic mound was right in his face. Inside, the sneaky little balls were inching her nearer and nearer to the point where she would lose control entirely. There was a hot pulse throbbing continually in her clitoris and her pussy felt wringing wet. She wondered how much longer she could remain in control as her libido went into overdrive. She began to curse Nigel for making her job even more difficult. Did he know what a devastating effect those little love-balls would have on her ability to keep her balance? She suspected he did, the bastard!

It was time to push things along a bit. Putting her hands behind her back, Cordelia found the bra fastening and snicked it open, letting the garment hang loose over her large breasts. In no hurry to remove it, she continued to dance while the cups bounced free over her tits, barely concealing them. Eric's eyes were like saucers as he caught glimpses of the red peaks of her nipples and the rounded swell of her breasts. She enjoyed tantalizing him. It took her mind off the equally tantalizing action that was going on inside her.

At last she whipped the black bra away and exposed her breasts entirely. There was a round of applause from the bystanders and Eric goggled at her, readjusting his trousers. Cordelia tried to imagine his cock straining and swelling, wondered about its dimensions, but that train of thought only made it more difficult for her to concentrate on what she was doing so she pushed her palms down the back of her pants and began to stroke her buttocks. They were still rather sore from their beating, but they felt delightfully smooth after the cream Nigel had rubbed into them. She pulled the pants down to give the audience a mooning and, once again, spontaneous applause broke out.

The wonder balls were working her up into an erotic frenzy now, making her sigh and moan with genuine arousal. She was soon so intensely focused on the sensations taking place in her own body that she was almost oblivious to the bystanders and even to Eric. She pulled off the constricting pants altogether until she was naked save for the lacy stockings and high heels, then delved through the bushy delta until her fingers found the hair-trigger of her orgasm. Her clitoris was hugely swollen, and as she fingered it she continued to grind her pelvis, just inches from where Eric was sitting.

While she propelled herself towards a climax, Cordelia flexed her internal muscles so that they clenched onto the moving orbs inside her pussy. She heard Eric moan, 'Sit on my lap, please!' and automatically obeyed, straddling his trousered leg and clenching his thigh with hers. She was well aware of the thick ridge that was bulging beneath his fly, and she leaned forward to increase contact between his erection and her mons, thrusting her breasts right in his face and hearing his breath coming out in ragged bursts as he strained to control himself. She began to wriggle in his lap, oblivious now of everything but her coming climax. The friction provided by the rough material made her all the hotter and now she knew there could be no holding back.

When the first voluptuous waves rippled through her she flung her head back with a cry of triumph, her hands squeezing her breasts to enhance her pleasure. She could hear the laughter and applause echoing round about her but she was past caring. Even Eric's murmured words and moans fell on deaf ears as she entered the super-sensual world of orgasmic bliss where every fibre of her being was quivering with ecstasy.

After she'd recovered enough to notice what was going on around her, she realized that Eric was looking very flushed and exhausted, his eyes glassy. Blushing, she removed herself from his knee and did her best to regain her composure. The onlookers were grinning and murmuring, some openly winking and pursing their lips at her, so that she felt suddenly uncomfortable and looked around for Nigel.

But he was nowhere to be seen.

Overcome with shame Cordelia made a dash for it, picking up her scattered garments as she went, her high heels wobbling over the carpet. She left the room and took off the hampering shoes, holding them with her other things as she raced up the stairs towards Suite Seventeen. Her only desire now was to hide her embarrassment, to shower and rest before she had to face the crowd again. If Nigel wasn't there to protect her she wouldn't stay to become the prey of those lustful men, who had been eyeing her like ravenous beasts surrounding their timid prey.

Shuddering at the memory, she fumbled in her purse and found the key to her room. She slid the card down the slot and, to her relief, the door clicked open first time. Downstairs she could hear the buzz of conversation and the music still blaring out, but no one seemed to have followed her up the stairs, not even Morgan. She closed the bedroom door after her and threw her things into the corner. Then she took off the itchy wig and walked towards the bathroom.

Before she got there, however, she heard sounds coming from behind the communicating door to the next room, Nigel's room. She was about to knock on it when she realized the nature of the noises that she was hearing. It stopped her in her tracks. There were two voices next door, a man's and a woman's, and she was pretty sure that they were making love.

Cautiously, she approached the door between the two rooms and, even more cautiously, tried the handle. To her surprise it began to turn. Slowly, she turned it right round and pulled until the door was sufficiently ajar for her to squint through the opening. When she caught a glimpse of what was going on she gave a stifled gasp. There on the bed was a naked couple, the man clearly recognizable as Nigel. But he was lying on his back with a woman riding him, her shapely thighs and bottom moving powerfully up and down.

A flush ran through Cordelia's cheeks as she continued to watch, knowing that she shouldn't act the voyeur yet unable to help herself. Anger was flooding through her at the same time, anger that Nigel had deserted her in her hour of need just to go off and bonk some woman. Who the hell was she, anyway?

Through the chink in the door Cordelia took in the glossy dark hair that had come loose from its chignon and was falling in tendrils about the woman's olive-toned face. Her eyes were closed, the black lashes making lustrous crescents on her cheeks, and her red-lipsticked mouth was hanging open in one long gasp of bliss. Clearly she was in some private sensual world of her imagination. Nigel's face had a rapt expression, too, the pair of them appearing to be near to orgasm.

The woman's figure was impressive: large, pear-shaped breasts with long dark nipples that Nigel kept brushing with his fingers as he rogered her. She was agile too and evidently they had done this many times before since their copulation had a smooth rhythm and practised ease about it. Was she his girlfriend? Wife, even? Once again Cordelia realized how little she knew about the private life of her boss and an unmistakable pang of jealously took her by surprise.

Now they were both moaning in harmony, their breath issuing in short accelerating gasps that made Cordelia feel very excited. She squeezed down on the golden balls that were still rotating inside her, bringing exquisite sensations of pleasure. Soon she was watching the couple through half-closed lids, becoming more and more absorbed in her own sexuality. Her hands moved to her breasts, where she pinched the already turgid nipples and gasped as the in-creased pangs of desire ricocheted through her, making her feel weak at the knees.

But that loud gasp was her undoing. She could hear the woman mutter something in Spanish just before Cordelia gave herself up to paroxysms of pleasure that were sharp and intense, prickling like an electric charge through her nervous system. The slavering male audience that she had left down-stairs, plus the titillating effect of the love-balls, had resulted in such a fierce climax that she completely forgot where she was, forgot the need for discretion and just moaned her way through the peaks and troughs of her orgasm until she slumped, completely spent, against the door frame.

'So, we're being spied upon, are we?'

Nigel's dry tones brought Cordelia back to reality at the speed of light. She opened her eyes and saw him sitting on the bed in a maroon silk dressing gown with the woman kneeling behind his back, her hands on his shoulders, looking at Cordelia with a sardonic smile on her striking face. Something about the jet-black glitter in those almond eyes made Cordelia's blood freeze. Aware that she was wearing nothing but fishnet stockings and high-heeled shoes, she backed into her room, intending to find her bathrobe. But her boss was too quick for her. Bounding across the room in a few strides he seized her by the wrists and dragged her back towards the bed where the woman was still kneeling but with the bedspread concealing her nakedness, her smile widening by the second.

'I . . . I'm sorry,' Cordelia began. 'I heard a noise and . . .'

'What's going on downstairs?' Nigel snapped, still keeping tight hold of her wrist. 'How dare you leave before I gave you permission?'

'But you weren't there!'

Her tone was petulant. Too late she felt the back of Nigel's hand across her cheek. The woman on the bed commented. 'Such insolence!'

Nigel addressed her in a honeyed tone, without taking his eyes off Cordelia, 'You take a shower, my sweet. I can deal with this little minx.'

The woman got up off the bed, dragging the bedspread behind her, and came towards them, her movements slow and languid. Close to she was even more striking, her black eyes like tiny lumps of coal surrounded by sooty lashes and her red mouth full and pouting. She put a hand on Nigel's shoulder and cooed, in her sexy Spanish accent, 'Don't be mean, baby. I want to be in on the act, too.'

His eyes flashed sideways for an instant, then returned to scrutinize Cordelia with minute attention. 'You shall be, angel, all in good time. First I want to make sure this impudent hussy is placed in the correct position.'

Cordelia felt her pulses race. The woman gave her an

amused glance, staring quite blatantly at her breasts and then, with undisguised interest, at her half-shaven pussy. Despite her fear, Cordelia felt a thrill pass through her, and her vaginal muscles tightened on the slippery balls deep within. An orgasmic aftershock of startling intensity made her gasp aloud.

'Touch your toes!' Nigel rasped.

She did as she was told and heard him moving rapidly about the room until he came to stand beside her. The hissing rush of a shower in full spate came from the bathroom, adding tension to the scene. Suddenly Cordelia felt her wrists being bound to her ankles by a length of black nylon cord and she almost toppled over.

'Head down!' Nigel commanded. She stood there, trussed like a chicken and bent double, her butt high in the air and her breasts flopping heavily in front. The stretched tendons at the back of her knees were painful, but she vowed to maintain silence and endure her punishment the way she'd been taught. Her one fear was that she might let Nigel down in front of that formidable woman.

'Good!' She felt Nigel's hand on her, his palm warm and smooth as he caressed her backside. Then he left her to slip into the bathroom and join his mistress. Cordelia couldn't help wondering what they were getting up to. The only sounds were the low burble of conversation and the continually running shower. The golden balls were still tucked away inside her, giving their covert pleasure freely, but Cordelia was wary of letting herself have another orgasm in case she lost her balance.

It was excruciating to be made to stand in that uncomfortable position as the minutes ticked by. Eventually the shower stopped and the pair emerged. Although Cordelia kept her head low, her eyes flicked up to see the half-naked woman towelling her hair with another towel around her waist, the large breasts covered in goose pimples and the nipples firmly puckered.

'Inez, I think the red dress, darling,' she heard Nigel say. 'Do you want me to lace it up for you?'

'Yes, please.'

Their exaggeratedly polite conversation and saccharine tones were beginning to irritate Cordelia. She doubted whether they spoke to each other quite like that when they were alone. They seemed to be putting on a show for her. She heard the noise of hangers being moved in the wardrobe and caught a glimpse of the woman, 'Inez', stepping into a black corset trimmed with red lace. Then Nigel helped her fasten it, with much huffing and puffing.

'That's better,' he said. 'Now let's put on the dress, then you can do your make-up and hair so you really look the part.'

What part? Cordelia wondered. The strain on her knees and calves was immense now and she was beginning to feel giddy, although the couple seemed to have forgotten her. The blood was rushing to her head and the little balls were moving around inside her whenever her pussy twitched, teasing her unbearably. She wanted to do or say something to remind Nigel of her presence but she was afraid to step out of line.

Then, before her lowered gaze, she saw a pair of black patent boots coming towards her. They had very pointy toes and high heels, so she knew it was Inez. Cordelia couldn't resist the urge to look up.

The Spanish woman was looking magnificent in a vermilion latex minidress with black lacing across the bosom that squashed her breasts into great provocative mounds of flesh with a deep ravine between them. The dress had a swirly layered skirt reminiscent of a flamenco dancer's costume and at the waist was a small black-leather riding crop. On her head she wore a small black-lace mantilla. Inez gave a smug smile as her darkly glittering eyes met Cordelia's.

Nigel came hurrying up, as if he feared some kind of confrontation between the two women. 'Shall you administer the chastisement, sweetheart, or shall I?'

Inez turned to him with a smile that was glazed and distant. 'Need you ask?

Cordelia watched helplessly as the flounced skirt swished round her, three times, the pointed boots walking with a slow, deliberate tread. Soon Inez had the riding crop in her hand, caressing the leather loop at the end with suggestive, exaggerated gestures.

Suddenly she leaned forward and spoke into Cordelia's ear, her musk-scented bosom thrust almost into her face. 'How I hate a voyeur!' she murmured, her voice low and seductive despite the chilling tone of the message. 'It's so sneaky, spying on others. Six strokes should correct the problem, though, I think. After that you won't be so inclined to peep when others are taking their pleasures.'

Not again! Her bottom was still sore from the earlier punishment. Just how much more could she take? It angered her that Nigel had given this imperious woman the same power over her that he claimed for himself. Who the devil was she? It was clear that the Spanish woman was enjoying the situation immensely, and there was an erotic tension in the air too. Was she some kind of lesbian? If so, what, exactly, was her relationship to Nigel?

The first strike came swiftly and unexpectedly, a sharp thrash across both buttocks that had Cordelia crying in outraged pain. The indignity of it made her turn her head and scowl at the woman, who stared back with a mocking smile.

'Remember whose possession you are, slave!' she heard Nigel call from the wings, and she struggled to regain her self-control. 'If you will not take your punishment from Inez then I shall have to deal it out myself and you won't like that, you won't like that at all!'

Cordelia knew she wouldn't. On the few occasions when Nigel had resorted to vigorous physical discipline she had felt sore for hours afterwards.

The second blow was not so bad, since the flesh of her backside was already growing numb. The impact had its effect on her libido, however, which increased rapidly as the warming sensation spread through her cheeks, making her clench repeatedly at the pussy balls with her internal muscles. She knew she was growing excited again – and it was not just the beating. Inez herself excited her. There was something about the feline sensuality of the woman that was very exciting indeed, holding Cordelia in a spell of fascination. She was even coming to relish the complicity between Inez and Nigel, the dark conspiracy between them that was keeping her guessing about the sexual nature of their relationship.

'Such a peachy bottom!' she heard Inez murmur, and then a caressing hand passed briefly over that portion of her anatomy. 'But its naughty owner has transgressed and must take the consequences.'

Another sharp tap with the leather crop had Cordelia swaying on her heels. Suddenly a tuft of her short hair was being tweaked with such painful force that she yelped in pain. Her eyes shot upwards in fright and she found herself looking straight into the gleaming black eyes of her tormentress.

Inez smiled. 'You and I are going to have a lot of fun together, but first you must learn which of us is boss. This will teach you.'

Another swipe at her backside had Cordelia wincing in pain. She could feel the heat building up in her, a heat that was not just the result of the beating but was also lustful. It came as a shock to realize that the object of her desire was not Nigel but this strange, powerful woman. She imagined she knew how Inez must be feeling, experiencing the adrenalin rush of being in complete control and subjecting another being to her will.

For a moment she thought of Ralph. But it was only a fleeting thought swiftly replaced by a sudden overwhelming vision of being at the mercy of both Nigel and Inez, of having both a master *and* a mistress. The mere idea of it was so tantalizing that Cordelia felt her libido rise again, taking her to fever pitch and making her clutch at the love-balls with her quim. She continued working her muscles in a rhythmic stimulation that soon had her dangling on the brink of orgasm.

But then came the last of the blows from the leather and it wasn't quite enough to propel her into ecstasy. Still throbbing and aching inside, with hope and disappointment vying for possession of her heart, Cordelia felt hands on either side of her loosen the bonds that bound her wrists to her ankles. As she straightened up she saw both Nigel and Inez smiling complicitly, filling the space around all three of them with an ambiguous tension.

'That's good!' Nigel murmured, gently rubbing the smarting globes of her behind. 'Now you understand what is required of you. Complete obedience to your mistress at all times. I think you are ready in spirit to join us, but Inez will prepare your body first.' He threw his mistress a radiant smile. 'I leave her in your capable hands, my dear. You know what to do.'

'First, off with these!' Inez announced as Nigel left the room.

She pulled off the high-heeled shoes and tossed them over into the corner, then began to roll down the lacy stockings with their garters. Cordelia's pulse was flickering rapidly and her breath was coming in short bursts. The thought of placing her vulnerable body at the mercy of that formidable woman was both exciting and unnerving. Once Cordelia was completely naked Inez took her firmly by the hand and led her into the bathroom, where she turned on the shower.

'Stand there!' she told her, when she'd tested the temperature of the water with her hand.

Cordelia stood meekly below the fine spray, feeling her hair become sodden and wondering what on earth was in store for her. Inez put a loofah mitt on her right hand and lathered it with shower gel, then she began to rub it all over Cordelia's wet body. She was none too gentle and soon the rough glove had Cordelia's skin glowing and tingling with the friction. Not even her smarting buttocks escaped the treatment, and when Inez reached her breasts she was no less rough. Soon the pink nipples were standing out proud on their round, firm bases.

The expression in those black eyes seemed to change a fraction as Inez pulled off the mitt and began to run her bare hands over Cordelia's jutting breasts. While her palms smoothed over the curves her fingertips kept flicking rapidly over the throbbing nipples, increasing the torment.

'Now spread your legs!' Inez barked. Cordelia did as she was told and felt a soapy finger work its way around all the configurations of her vulva, filling the grooves with slick foam, working under the hood of her clitoris and even penetrating her by an inch or so. She gasped at the brusque, fleeting invasion of her sex.

'What is it, am I getting you hot, little girl?' Inez whispered, mockingly. 'Well, that's just how I want you, all hot and bothered. But if you think you're going to get any satisfaction, you're wrong. I'm working you up so you'll perform better down below.'

'P–perform?' Cordelia stammered, new trials now presenting themselves to her overheated imagination.

'Of course!' Inez pinched her nipples so hard it hurt, and Cordelia had to smother a yelp of surprised pain. 'You didn't think you were here for a holiday weekend, did you? You're here to work, like the rest of us. Now come on. We have to get you dressed.'

She slapped Cordelia on the bottom, then prodded her in the back so she would get out of the shower. When she was standing on the fluffy bath mat, Inez gave her a vigorous towelling until she was pink and roused, light-headed with the warm fizzing in her veins, then began to spray her from head to toe with a fine oil that had a lingering, seductive perfume. Inez's capable hands began to smooth the oil all over her in a business like fashion until her skin was gleaming like polished wood.

'That's better!' Inez took her hand and pulled, rather than led, her out of the bathroom and into the bedroom again, making her stand by the bed. She went to the wardrobe and selected a hanger that bore several garments. 'All right, let's get you into these!'

There was a corselette in baby-blue satin with marabou feathers just below the half-cups and tight lacing front and back. 'I'll never get into that!' Cordelia gasped, eyeing the wasp-waist.

Inez gave her a brief slap on the cheek that caused Cordelia more shock than pain. 'I'm the best judge of that!' the woman snapped. 'Guard your tongue, girl, or you'll have it guarded for you.'

Terrified, Cordelia lapsed into silence, reminding herself that the woman meant business. She had to admire her. Here was someone she could learn a lot from if only she did as she was told. It was easy to play the submissive with Nigel, but to submit to another woman was something new and strange to her. No wonder she was finding it hard.

Stepping into the corselette, Cordelia breathed in deeply and felt Inez pull the strings tight from behind. Already her respiration was severely restricted, but by the time the front laces were secured she could only make shallow movements of her lungs from the tops of her breasts and her ribcage felt crushed. It was quite tiring to breathe.

Inez turned her round so she could view herself in the full-length mirror on the wardrobe door. 'There, don't you look exquisite?' she purred.

Cordelia stared in amazement at her newly-acquired hourglass figure, with her breasts pushed right up almost under her chin and the pert nipples sticking up over the bank of white, fluffy feathers. Her shoulders looked very broad and her cropped hair made her head look small, but the contrast with her voluptuous figure was even more striking than usual. She turned around and looked over her shoulder at the round globes of her bottom beneath the high-cut corset. Her damp hair and bare feet were adding an incongruous informality to her appearance.

'Now these!' Inez said, holding out lacy pale blue stockings that exactly matched the outfit and a pair of white satin shoes with a pale blue rosette on each toe and very high heels.

'You're going to look fabulous!' she said. 'Stand still while I put these on you.'

Inez's deft fingers rolled the stockings up to where suspenders were dangling and she fastened them quickly, then helped Cordelia on with the shoes. Cordelia felt strange, restricted from head to toe and yet so exposed. When Inez asked her to sit on the stool in front of the dressing table she could hardly bend but had to flex her knees and lower herself down, keeping her torso rigid. At once Inez began to blow through her hair with a hand-held dryer. When it was dry she opened a drawer and pulled out a wig of long auburn ringlets.

'This is the one,' she smiled, stroking the soft curls then placing the wig over Cordelia's black natural mop. The contrast with the pale blue satin was very effective. Inez proceeded to dress the wig, lifting up the curls into fetching arrangements that both framed her face and gave her height. When she was satisfied with the style she sprayed it over lightly.

'Now, the finishing touches,' she said, picking up a vanity case from the floor. She opened it to reveal various compartments filled with make-up. Soon Cordelia had a face to match the outfit: long shiny lashes and deep blue shadows that gave a sultry look to her eyes, while her lips were a pouting, luscious pink. Then Inez drew a small packet from the case and opened it, scattering a cloud of tiny silver stars all over the wig and into her cleavage. The glitter stuck to her skin and hair, and when she stood up another handful went over her pubic area and clung to the mat of dark curls over her mons that was fully exposed to view.

'Wonderful!' Inez smiled, slightly ironically, continuing in a fake accent that came out more Mexican than American, 'You're gonna knock 'em dead, dahlin'!'

Cordelia wondered what she was going to be called upon to do downstairs, in front of all those men. She'd had a respite up here, away from the prying eyes, but now she knew she must face them again. A cold chill went through her. Despite the doll-like anonymity of her costume and wig she was still nervous, afraid of letting Nigel down.

And Inez too, she realized with surprise. Her attachment to the aloof beauty was growing, despite the strangeness of it all, and she wanted to live up to her expectations and serve her well. She already knew what punishment lay in store for her if she incurred her mistress's wrath, but what reward would she get if she pleased her? The thought of some lesbian dalliance with Inez thrilled her. Moving towards the door she alternately clenched her buttocks and pussy to heighten the exquisite effect of the little balls, and her desire grew to unbearable dimensions. Now she would do almost anything to get some relief.

Chapter Seven

Cordelia was surprised to find Nigel waiting for them at the bottom of the stairs, immaculate in his dress suit once more. When she saw what he was holding in his hand, however, her heart sank. It was a lace-trimmed blue satin mask, the same colour as her underwear – but there were no eye holes.

'You will be entirely in our hands for the rest of the evening,' Inez murmured as she noticed Cordelia's dismay. 'Don't worry, you can trust us.'

Could she? Cordelia felt her heartbeat quicken with anxiety as Nigel approached, the mask dangling from his fingers. She could see the naked desire in his eyes and knew that he was lusting after her more openly than ever before, but there was an irony in the situation. She had wanted him constantly ever since she first came to work for him, but his favours had been few and far between, keeping her in a state of frustration that had been hard to bear at times.

Now it looked as if her fantasy of being fucked by her boss might just come true except that it was likely to be in full view of a roomful of strange men, and possibly with another woman involved too. This was not how Cordelia had imagined such an event taking place and she found herself filled not only with disappointment but with resentment. Still, she was pledged to obey at all times and she had to trust Nigel and Inez to look after her interests as well as their own.

So as Nigel held up the mask in front of her eyes she forced herself to smile and submit willingly to the blindfolding.

Once deprived of her sight, everything seemed to change for Cordelia. She felt a stiff halter being put around her neck, forcing her to keep her head upright, and then her wrists were bound tightly behind her back, making her push her chest out. Knowing there was no use complaining, she tried to quell the lingering resentment that was still burning in her heart. But, although she switched into submissive mode and made no objection to having to crawl on all fours on the carpet, she couldn't pretend that she was entirely enjoying the situation.

There was a roar and loud applause as soon as she was led into the dining hall. Cordelia could smell the cigar smoke and hear the whispers and laughter as she crawled down the length of the hall with Nigel pulling her chain. Behind her strode Inez: every so often the toe of her boot would prod Cordelia in the rump, making her go faster.

Suddenly the trio halted, a gong was struck and the hubbub ceased. Cordelia was aching all over, longing for some relief from the constriction of the corset and her bonds. Her breath came in shallow gasps as she recovered from the physical effort of crawling the length of the dining hall, and her limbs were stiff and sore, not to mention her aching bottom.

Then came the announcement. Cordelia recognized Morgan's voice as soon as he began his speech. 'Gentlemen, I am sure you would wish to welcome our guest entertainers of the evening. A big hand, please, for the titillating threesome called . . . *Trio Los Paramores*!'

As the applause rang out again Cordelia's chain was tugged and Inez kick-started her rear end so that she was obliged to crawl forward, this time up some steps onto the platform. She wondered if the audience recognized her. In the auburn wig and mask, probably not. But what exactly would their 'act' entail? Evidently nothing that she needed to be briefed for, since she was as much in the dark as the men out there whose voices could now be heard whooping and cheering. What *was* happening?

There was a burst of sound and some raunchy rock music filled the room, hotting up the atmosphere. Suddenly Cordelia was yanked up onto her knees and, from the noises that issued in front of her, she guessed that she was facing the audience. They were laughing and cheering, so she guessed some kind of action was going on around her. She could feel Nigel and Inez moving about on stage, and then she felt herself being tethered to something by the neck. With her hands still tied behind her back she was now vulnerable, unable to escape whatever her master and mistress had in store for her.

The music quietened down and became slow and sultry. Cordelia recognized the tune: an old one – 'Pussycat, Pussycat'. Hands came onto her shoulders, soft yet firm, and she guessed they belonged to Inez. They worked around her shoulders, massaging the joints, soothing and calming her, readying her for whatever was to follow. The fingers inched down her cleavage where the skin was ultra-sensitive, lightly brushing the tops of her breasts. Cordelia felt a shudder travel swiftly down her spine and knew that her libido was on the up again. Her cunt gave an involuntary twitch and moved the balls that were still lodged inside, notching up her arousal still more.

Now the hands had found the laces at the front of her corset and were starting to untie them. As they loosened, Cordelia found she could breathe more easily, which was a relief. Her breasts were freed from the garment by eager hands and then she could feel someone groping her below, making her long for some real action. There were laughs from the audience and again Cordelia felt the frustration of not being able to see what was going on, knowing that she was the butt of their humour.

Something touched her lips, amid much applause and more laughter. It was only a fleeting contact but the musky smell was unmistakable. Next time it happened she put out her tongue and tried to taste it, relieved when she felt the slit in the glans. For one moment she had thought it might be part of Inez's anatomy and she wasn't sure she was ready for that yet. No sooner had she identified the male organ than it was thrust right into her mouth, filling it up and almost choking her as it pushed to the back of her throat.

Cordelia had only given Nigel head once before, but in her dreams she had relived it over and over. Now she felt the adrenalin rush through her as she began to suck at his thick, moving shaft and felt his balls bash against her neck. It would have been enough to satisfy her, fellating him while she worked her own little balls inside her pussy, making herself come. But the couple had something else in store for their willing blindfold victim.

Hands were stroking her thighs, pulling them apart slowly and gently until her sex was fully exposed to the entire audience. The watching men had grown subdued now, probably involved in their own intense fantasies of participation and, fully occupied with licking and sucking at the meaty organ, Cordelia hardly noticed the sly finger slipping between her labia and making her wet, so very wet. It was only when the exquisite sensations of cunnilingus made her toes curl that she realized what was happening: she was having her clitoris licked by another woman.

And an expert at that. With her attention now drawn away from Nigel's cock towards the busy work of Inez's lips and tongue, Cordelia felt herself ascending rapidly towards orgasm. Somehow the blindfold was giving her licence to enjoy it, shielding her from the full force of the realization that she was taking part in lesbian sex. The delicacy with which that small tongue was finding its way around her anatomy was something to be marvelled at. Cordelia sighed and moaned, her body twisting this way and that as the wellspring of ecstasy gushed inside her and fuelled her libido to boiling point.

Now the men were murmuring, some were cheering and applauding, as the big phallus drove in and out of her mouth, with her lips and tongue working automatically to pleasure it. At the same time she could feel herself moving helplessly towards a climax, wallowing in the feminine sensuality of the other woman's tonguing. Inez seemed to know exactly how and where to lick and kiss her, the soft lips seeming to be of the same texture as her own labia, the strong tongue protruding from the Spanish girl's mouth with the same defiant determination as Cordelia's clitoris was rearing rampantly from beneath its hood.

Long, sweet strokes were arousing her love-bud from root to tip, taking her nearer and nearer to the final explosion of bliss. Cordelia felt utterly abandoned now, despite the constriction of the collar that kept her head in a rigid position and determined that she could not escape the relentless battering her mouth was getting from Nigel's cock.

Suddenly she was being penetrated by something long, thick and smooth. Not a real penis, that was for sure: it must be a dildo. The men on the floor of the hall were going mad now, whooping and cheering, so she guessed that Inez must be putting on a good show. Somehow she was contriving to maintain contact between her mouth and Cordelia's pussy while she manipulated the dildo, twisting it around the dancing balls as she went. It was amazing that there was enough room for all that action inside Cordelia's cunt, but she could feel that her quim was so wet and slippery that there was no problem sliding the penis substitute in and out.

Cordelia came suddenly and violently, so much so that her lips pressed hard on Nigel's shaft and her pussy lips clutched so tightly at the dildo that Inez had difficulty moving it. The applause rang out, thunderous in her ears as she gave herself up to the swirling vortex of her orgasm, relishing every last shudder and spasm until she flopped down into Nigel's supporting arms, completely spent.

'Spend, darling, spend!' she heard Inez growl, close to her ear.

At first she thought the remark was addressed to her, and wondered how on earth she could be expected to give any more. But then Nigel began to thrust in and out of her mouth at an accelerating speed until she tasted the hot spunk shooting down her throat, almost choking her. Something else was going on between him and Inez, something she couldn't see, but she could hear the woman panting and then her lips fastened onto Cordelia's nipple and began suckling with fierce intensity.

The series of loud moans that followed left Cordelia in no doubt that Inez had reached a climax too, by whatever means. She didn't much care how it had been achieved. They had obviously put on a good spectacle as the cheers were still resounding around the hall. Nigel would be pleased with her, and that was all that mattered.

His strong arms lifted her up after a while and she was led back down off the platform. While he conducted her through the hall she could feel a hundred pairs of hands groping at her, some patting her damp pubic hair, others touching her breasts or thighs with lascivious intent. Now it seemed that the worst was over, Cordelia felt proud of herself. She'd enjoyed her first-ever session with another woman, and she hadn't let her boss down.

As soon as they were outside the hall Nigel pulled off the blindfold and united her hands. She saw him smiling at her, his dress suit now in disarray with the bow tie hanging loose over the discreetly frilled shirt. He smelt of sweat, sex and

Vétiver. It was a heady combination that instantly reignited her desire for him.

'So, my dear, we have come through with flying colours, haven't we?' he said in the deep, suave tones she adored. 'Now, what shall your reward be? Would you like me to fuck you, my little slave? Would that appeal to you, I wonder?'

Cordelia stared at him, her throat dry and her cunt twitching relentlessly, playing with the little balls as if they were worry beads and notching up her lust to fever pitch once more. 'Do you mean it?' she whispered, fearing it was just another of his games.

'Of course I mean it, silly girl! You'll have to give me a few minutes, of course, to recharge the old batteries, but I think we should be able to manage it. Come on, upstairs.'

Cordelia followed him eagerly, taking the steps two at a time now that her hands were free and there was no danger of her losing her balance. They went into his room and she was relieved to see him lock the door behind them. 'Now we won't be disturbed,' he said, removing his jacket and tie and throwing them onto a chair. She knew he meant they wouldn't be disturbed by Inez.

Unsure how to play it, Cordelia hung back, feeling rather silly in the loose corset. He sensed her mood and turned her round so that he could unlace the back, sliding the garment off her body until she stood there in nothing but her auburn wig, falling blue stockings and white satin shoes.

'Leave the wig on. I like it,' he told her, but his hands groped at the stockings, pulling them down roughly until they were wreathed around her ankles. Then he began unbuttoning his shirt. 'Now, sit on the edge of the bed.'

She did as she was told, still in her shoes and collapsed stockings. He took off his shirt, trousers and socks, then came to kneel before her in his underpants. Cordelia, unused to seeing him in a such a humble position, felt confused, but he seemed to want her passive so she just let him do what he wanted with her, taking the shoes off slowly and caressing the balls of her heels as he did so. Then he rolled the stockings over her feet very slowly, one by one.

'Lie down!' he murmured hoarsely, when her feet were bare.

By the time he'd stripped off his pants he had a hard-on and, seeing the great bulbous glans and the thick solidity of the shaft, Cordelia felt her insides twitch with anticipation. Nigel came to kneel over her, his great prong rearing up over her stomach.

'Touch it!' he grunted.

She did as she was told and the cock thudded against her hand, eager for action. Clasping it gently, she felt its silky warmth throb in her palm, making her want to feel it inside. Her vaginal muscles were squeezing at the balls, driving her on towards coming, but she didn't want to climax too soon. She wanted to be filled with hot, lively flesh, not the cold golden balls.

Nigel raised himself and Cordelia held her breath, hardly able to bear the suspense as he lowered his organ towards her open vulva. The glans began knocking gently at her vaginal door, opening up the tumid quim lips and making her gush with love-juice. When he finally began to nose into her she gave out a long, low moan of satisfaction that increased in volume as he pushed further in, and further, until she had accommodated the whole length of his formidable penis. She could feel it nestling among the little balls, her pussy full to the brim, and she was content.

Nigel began to move, slowly at first, which sent exquisite ripples of sensation through her, and then with gathering speed. Cordelia moved her hips in time with his and her arousal heightened as the root of his shaft connected with her bulging clitoris, making her pelvis buck and roll to increase the delicious friction. She could feel herself on the verge of an orgasm, her breath coming in rapid gasps and her whole body straining for release.

Then she felt his soft lips at one of her breasts, inching towards her nipple. When he reached it and began to suck, the floodgates were opened and the tide of sexual energy gushed out in one long flow, thrilling her with a series of spasms that seemed to spread right through her from head to toes.

Cordelia was lying in a post-orgasmic haze, revelling in the sense of utter satisfaction while her muscles continued to massage the still-erect cock lodged in her cunt, when there was a sudden noise as the communicating door to the next room burst open abruptly.

'Beast!' she heard a woman's voice say. 'You bloody bastard, Nigel Willoughby!'

It was Inez, of course. After her initial vague wondering about how the woman had got into her room, Cordelia was struggling to sit up, fully alert, as Nigel pulled out at speed and staggered off the bed.

'Inez, darling . . .'

'I want none of your "darlings"! You promised me that you wouldn't take her alone, that *I* could have her too! Bastard!'

'Please, don't upset yourself so, dear. I just felt randy and you were busy, that's all. I thought we could have a nice little threesome when you arrived. I was warming Cordelia up for it. Isn't that what you want, sweetheart?'

Cordelia felt sickened by the wheedling tone of his voice. This wasn't the Nigel she knew, strong and imperious, the boss who knew exactly how to bring her to heel. Why wasn't he dealing with Inez in the same way? And why was he talking about her, Cordelia, as if she had no mind or will of her own, but was just there to be the plaything of this pair?

She reminded herself that that was just what she *was* there for but, seeing these two squabbling over her, like dogs fighting over a bone, was putting her off. Somewhere along the line all the fun and titillation had gone out of it. Slowly she got up off the bed, just as Inez delivered a sharp slap to Nigel's cheek.

'I should thrash you for that!' he growled.

Ah, but would he? Cordelia thought not, somehow. She tiptoed round the couple, who were now far too engrossed in their own violent bickering to care about her, and found her way back into her room. What to do now? A great weariness had come over her, accompanied by a longing for home. What wouldn't she give for a long, hot soak in her own bathtub with Ralph on hand to soap her breasts!

The vague longing crystallized into action and she hurriedly dressed, collected her things together and crept towards the door. She could still hear Nigel and Inez going at it hammer and tongs next door, with the Spanish woman becoming more and more shrill and hysterical. Cordelia escaped down the corridor and into the lift, silently giving thanks for the cover that the quarrel provided for her escape. She phoned for a taxi to take her to the nearest station, then waited five anxious minutes for it to arrive before finally making a successful getaway.

Ralph had a strange feeling that his mistress might be returning that night and it didn't desert him, even when the midnight hour came and went. Instead of going to sleep he remained in his dressing gown watching television, his ears open for the first sound of a car drawing up. He had done his best to make the place spotless and knew he had nothing to reproach himself for, so his mood was one of pleasant anticipation.

Although he was soon dozing in his chair, the instant a car did brake outside the house he was awake and alert, up and peering through the curtains into the night. He saw the taxi at once, with Cordelia stepping out into the pool of light from the street lamp. How beautiful she looked! Her dark cap of hair was glossy and sleek, catching the yellow light, and her slim figure bent to pick up her case which had been dumped on the pavement by the inconsiderate driver. Ralph sighed. If only he had remained dressed he could have dashed out there and helped her with it – but it was too late to make amends. Now he must content himself with waiting behind the front door so he could take the burden off her the minute she came in.

Hovering there in the unlit hall, Ralph felt a sudden thrill of lust and his erection grew. He felt naughty, secretive, and just afraid enough to add spice to his situation. He never knew quite what kind of a mood Cordelia would be in when she came home from work, let alone when she returned from some unknown destination, like she was doing tonight.

She flung open the front door, flicked on the light and saw him. Her hand flew to her throat. 'God, Ralph, you gave me such a fright, standing there like a ghost!'

'Let me take your luggage, madam.'

'You're not the ruddy bellboy!' she snapped, dumping her case and striding into the sitting room from where she called, 'Leave the case and fix me a whisky and soda. I'm desperate!'

He hastened to do her bidding, his heart thudding loudly in his ears. It was so very quiet at that hour: surely next door they could hear her voice shouting commands at him? A faint flush rose up his cheeks as he remembered what weird looks they sometimes gave him when he was hanging out the washing or weeding the garden. But he hoped that the detached status of the house and the fact that most people were asleep at that hour would save him the embarrassment.

There was a clean glass in the cabinet – his mistress insisted on that at all times – and as Ralph sprayed the soda into the slug of whisky he began to feel more alert, more keyed up for whatever lay ahead. One thing he could say about Cordelia for sure, she always kept him on his toes. He handed her the glass with a slight bow and she gave him a frosted smile.

'And what have you been doing with yourself while I've been away? Nothing naughty, I hope. Not playing with yourself, or anything.'

Her clear eyes stared straight into his so that he found himself flushing guiltily even though he believed he had done nothing wrong. She reached over and parted the front of his dressing gown to view his erection, which had subsided a little by now. Her eyes narrowed.

'Not quite ready for me, are you? Don't you know you should be ready for me at all times?'

Ralph shuddered, not knowing whether she was going to punish him with a slap or get him going again with a caress. She did neither. Letting his robe fall closed she lay back in the armchair and shut her eyes sighing deeply and saying, 'Run me a bath now, then.'

He hurried up to the bathroom, listening out for any clue as to what Cordelia was doing downstairs. It was a habit with him, always trying to predict her movements, her needs, always wanting to be one jump ahead. Whatever had happened to her that evening she was in a strange, quixotic mood and he wanted to stay on the right side of her. He glanced swiftly around the bathroom, making sure everything was just so before he turned on the gold-plated mixer tap.

When the bath was full he went back down to see what bath oil she required.

'You choose!' she said, wearily. 'Something soothing, something to send me to sleep.'

He chose rose geranium, with a hint of sandalwood, and soon the room was filled with the perfumed steam. While he was testing the temperature of the water with his elbow, Cordelia appeared. Ralph jumped to his feet.

'Undress me!' she said.

He did so with the utmost care, making sure he didn't touch her body more than was strictly necessary, and when she finally stood naked before him he felt his cock rise abruptly to its former jaunty angle. Cordelia seemed to sense his arousal. Flinging open his gown she gave it a few tugs, then began to stroke it, as if it were a pet cat. Ralph swallowed, reddening, and she laughed, turning her back on him and stepping into the green water.

'I'm just going to lie here and you can wash me, all over,' she declared, leaning against the sloping back and closing her eyes.

Ralph couldn't believe his luck. His mistress didn't often let him touch her, let alone wash her. But then he began to have doubts. Would she be offended if he touched her intimately? What if he made an indelicate mistake and incurred her wrath? He stifled a yawn. It really was very late, but he must keep his wits about him if he was to do the job properly.

Picking up the fine-milled rose soap from the dish he wet his hands and got up a good lather, then lifted her arm and began to wash. When he got to her underarms he found she had some stubble there, just a little, and thought about shaving her. What a wonderful test that would be! Could she possibly trust him not to nick her skin? He could hardly bear to think about what his punishment would be if he did. Now he hoped she *wouldn't* ask him and, to his relief, she remained quiet until he had done both arms and the danger seemed past. He made more of the mousse-like foam and began to stroke it delicately over her face until she looked as if she were wearing a mask.

Cordelia gave a sigh of contentment which he found most

gratifying, and she lifted one leg out of the water as a signal that he was to wash that next. He paid special attention to her foot, delicately massaging the foam into her taut skin and being careful to go between each of her small, well-formed toes. She was proud of her feet, boasting that she'd never worn ill-fitting shoes and that therefore they had retained their perfect shape.

After he had done each foot Ralph worked his way up her shins and calves, making circular strokes around her knee and then washing her thighs as far as he could. He started to wonder how he could get to her body since it was half submerged, the magnificent breasts rising from the emerald waters like two pale islands, each topped by a coral tower. But then, divining his thought once more, Cordelia lifted her whole torso out of the water and lay poised in suspense, waiting for his ministering hands to do their work.

Ralph could hardly bear to look at her glistening, exquisite body that sparkled under the low bathroom light with warm, radiant life. He began by touching her navel, which seemed a safe place to begin, but his heart was in turmoil at the thought of going either above or below that central point. Those jutting breasts were so wickedly seductive! But then, so was that saucy little mound, the pouting slit just visible beneath the neat fringe of hair.

'Hurry up!'

Her imperious tone stuck fear into him, fear that she would grow so impatient that she would change her mind and make him leave the bathroom before his task was over. The shame and frustration of such a prospect spurred him on to massage her midriff, feeling the heavy breasts tap against the backs of his hands as he worked, smooth as silk. Cordelia gave a sharp intake of breath and he knew she was enjoying the experience. It was not often that she allowed herself this degree of sensual indulgence.

Now it was time to wash the pert, full breasts themselves. He could see them straining for his touch and exulted in the sacred trust she had given him. Slowly he worked his way up the undersides with his fingertips, relishing the way they slid so smoothly over the wet skin, leaving a trail of froth that melted into a slick film. His fingers inched upward, towards the tantalizing nipples that crowned the breasts and which, he knew, would provide his mistress with the most voluptuous pleasure once he got going.

His thumbs and forefingers found their twin goals and began to softly pinch and pull, eliciting the most yearning and appreciative moans. Ralph felt his cock twitch, knocking against the side of the bath quite painfully. He made broader sweeps over her breasts with the flat of his palm and then returned to her nipples, finding them even harder and more tumid than before.

What a beautiful bosom his mistress had! He'd like to place his head there and have her stroke his hair. He'd like to place his cock there and – Oh God! – have her stroke his shaft! The very idea of it made him throb down below and turned him light-headed. What a disgustingly presumptuous worm he was, to imagine such bliss! Yet he couldn't resist stroking those large rotund breasts over and over. It had a mesmerizing effect on him, and on her too, he could tell. They heaved and fell in a sweet rhythm, in time with her breath that sighed from her luscious lips.

Ralph was lost, quite lost, in his reverie when Cordelia suddenly opened her eyes.

'I can't stand this any longer!' she snapped. 'Help me out of the bath, slave, and then I want you to suck me and lick me until I'm almost there – I'll tell you when.'

All Ralph's pulses were quivering with excitement. It was late, so late, and they were being so very naughty alone in the house together in the dark, secret middle of the night. Feeling as if they were acting out some nursery story he fetched the big white fluffy towel and held it up for her, his eyes feasting on the vertical strip of hair at the bottom of her beautiful belly, the place where he had just been invited to take the most incredible liberty. His cock was so hot and rigid he was afraid it would spurt at any second and spoil things.

She lay down on the big bath mat and put up her knees, giving him a glimpse of the pink, soft folds of her pussy. Ralph didn't dare look too closely, afraid of being overcome with an obscene burst of lust. Helplessly he watched as she placed her hands on each side of her crotch and used her fingers to spread her labia wide, giving him an invitation no man could possibly refuse. He got down on his hands and knees, stuck his bum in the air and began to lap at her like a dog.

'Oh yes, faster, harder, more, more!' she murmured, a crazed litany that was driving him on, on. He tasted the soapiness of her vulva, poked right into her with his tongue-tip and felt the sweeter, fresher juices lave his tongue while she twisted her hips and thrust her mons in his face so that he could hardly breathe. He found the jutting clitoris and licked it tentatively, the exquisitely sensitive source of her pleasure, feeling the electric buzz that ensued as if it were his own. And all the time he was performing his hips were swinging his huge erection back and forth in the air, in readiness for the action that he hoped would follow.

The musky aroma of Cordelia's cunt was like a drug to him, making him faint and tired. After all, it was the middle of the night, but what did he care? He was her servant, and if she woke him in the middle of the most wonderful wet dream he would still be up and running, eager to serve her in whatever way she wished. Sneakily he touched his cock, felt the viscous glans and the hard shaft, reassured himself that all was in readiness for her when the time came.

But she was lying right back on the floor now, her breasts growing flaccid as her breath steadied and her eyes closed. Ralph slowed down to match her listlessness and felt a warm languor creep over him, his cock wilting just a little. *This will never do*, he thought, but there had been a change of mood that he was helpless to resist. Something was creeping over them both, a deep fatigue that was conquering even the will to pleasure. He continued to lap at her pussy, more like a cat now, and there were still little fluttering sighs from time to time. But he no longer imagined that he could bring her to a climax. The idea of all that excitement was so fatiguing, so very tiring. And, after all, it *was* the middle of the night . . .

Chapter Eight

'I'm going to give a dinner party.'

Ralph received his mistress's words with a mixture of pleasure and trepidation. The pleasure came from the prospect of devising a menu and cooking elaborate dishes. The trepidation came from memories of previous occasions, when he'd been handed round after the meal like a sweetmeat with the coffee.

Had Cordelia dreamt up some fiendish plan as punishment for him falling asleep on the job last night? He wouldn't put it past her. She knew so well how to humiliate him, in public and in private. Knew, too, how a despicable part of him lapped it all up, even though he hated himself for it.

'It will be for six people, including myself,' she went on, coolly. 'Devise a menu and let me see it. Nothing you've ever done before, of course, just in case I decide to invite someone who has been to one of my previous dinners. Remember, you have a high standard to maintain.'

'Yes, madam.'

'A theme would be nice,' she went on, musing. 'Perhaps something we could dress up for. Let me see . . . I know, let's have a Middle Eastern evening! Shades of the harem, and *you* can be our chief eunuch!'

She let out a stream of tinkling laughter that grated on his nerves but excited him at the same time. Already he was thinking ahead: succulent kebabs, perhaps, or couscous. And some of those delicious little cakes flavoured with orange and rose water. Stuffed dates, and Turkish coffee, of course, boiled thrice in the correct manner . . .

'I'll leave it to you, then, to come up with some bright ideas.'

Ralph had two weeks. The dinner party obsessed him so much that he started to neglect his other duties and Cordelia grew displeased with him. Coming home one evening to find the kitchen table awash with cookbooks and the evening meal scarcely begun, she let loose the full force of her wrath.

'Lazy layabout!' she screamed, throwing one of his recipe folders at him. 'Get all this cleared and put the dinner on, then strip naked and come into the sitting room for your punishment.'

He knew he had done wrong, becoming so engrossed in his plans for the future that he had forgotten his present duties. Hastily he put the oven on for the dish he had prepared and lit the gas burners under the pans for the vegetables. Then, his heartbeat increasing at every pulse, he began to get out of the rubber pants and vest he was wearing, stripping the clinging fabric off like a beetle shedding its carapace until the soft, vulnerable flesh of his body was exposed. Falling onto his hands and knees he crawled into the front room, ready to do penance.

Cordelia was standing there, looking magnificent in a leather outfit with lots of straps and buckles, her breasts covered by moulded metal plates complete with nipples. She stood with her legs apart, holding a short whip behind her back, the close-fitting high black boots making her legs seem incredibly long, and she wore a voluminous blonde wig that threw her huge bright eyes and glossy red mouth into startling relief.

'I'm so angry with you that I'm inclined to give you a dozen lashes,' she announced, flexing the whip before his eyes. He cringed, but then her tone lightened a little. 'Unless, that is, you can suggest some more appropriate penalty for your misdeeds. I want you to grovel to me, worm! Plead with me to lighten your sentence, or your buttocks will know the taste of this!'

Ralph's mind, which had been so fertile all day as he planned his menu, went blank. He tried to think of something he could do to make amends and avoid the stinging pain of a lashing, but nothing came. Then inspiration struck. 'I would . . . I would lick your leathers clean, mistress.'

'Lick my leathers!' she laughed, mockingly. 'Can't you see that my outfit is already impeccably clean, you imbecile? You'll have to do better than that!'

He looked desperately around the room for some clue to help him out of his predicament. His cock dangled uselessly, reminding him that it was no use offering her sexual favours. Besides, she would scorn that as an offer since she was entitled to it at any time. No, he would have to think of something ingenious to evade the torture of a whipping. The seconds were ticking by and he was growing more and more desperate, when he had an outrageous idea.

'I would drive you anywhere you wish to go, madam.' He gestured towards his nude body. 'Just like this.'

Ralph knew it would appeal to her perverse humour, and it did. Her face broke into a deliciously wicked smile. 'You mean, totally naked?' He nodded, eyes downcast. 'A butt-naked chauffeur, how delightful! You know, I think that might just do. But where shall we go?'

He waited, abased before her, his pulse racing with apprehension. What had he got himself into? A possible indecency charge, that was for sure. He prayed that she wouldn't choose to be taken anywhere too far away, or too public. The seconds ticked by, and then she announced with a flash of enthusiasm, 'I know! You can take me to work tomorrow!'

His heart plummeted. The idea of driving her to the office stark naked in the rush hour filled him with utter horror, yet he knew that he must keep his side of the bargain. He could tell how much she was relishing the idea of it already. If he reneged on the offer and opted for the physical punishment she would be angry and whip him more severely. His flesh shrank from the prospect.

'That's decided, then. Just this once, you will drive me to work. Talking of work, get back to the kitchen. I'm hungry.'

Ralph obeyed, full of dread at the thought of what he had landed himself in. But there might be compensations, too. He had no idea what Cordelia did, he'd never been to her office, he had no idea where it was, even. She had always kept her working and private lives strictly separate. Now a curiosity that he'd suppressed in himself long ago suddenly surfaced, so that the prospect of driving her into work became enthralling, even despite the unfortunate circumstances under which he must act as her chauffeur.

He was on tenterhooks for the rest of the evening, wondering how he could possibly face the ordeal. Cordelia left him alone after the meal, wanting to watch a video, and once he'd cleared away in the kitchen, tidied up the dining room and made sure madam's bedroom was in perfect order, it was time to see if she wanted a nightcap.

'I'll have a Brandy Alexander,' she told him, still absorbed in the lesbian video she was watching. Ralph couldn't help wondering why this sudden interest in girl-on-girl sex, but he reminded himself it was none of his business and hurried off to do her bidding.

Ralph spent a restless night and, when he did sleep, he experienced nightmares about being in the middle of crowded rush-hour traffic – a bad dream that, for once, was not just a fantasy. Tomorrow it would become reality, and he was far from prepared for it when he finally rose at the crack of dawn to wash and shave. He only put on his dressing gown. After taking his mistress's breakfast in to her on a tray as usual, he spent quite a while being discreetly sick in the loo at the thought of what he had to face that morning.

Cordelia was up and ready by eight, dressed in a trim navy suit with a fuschia silk blouse and looking as if this was just a normal day. Which, for her, it probably was.

'Ready?' she inquired, seeing him hovering in the hall. 'If you like I'll pop out and start the engine to get the heater warmed up. No need to freeze your bullocks off, after all, is there?'

'That's very kind of you,' he muttered.

'Yes, isn't it?'

She smiled sweetly at him and let herself out. Shivering already in the draught from the open front door, he watched her go down the path and wondered how on earth he was going to pluck up the courage to walk down that same path completely starkers. Perhaps she would let him keep his dressing gown on at least, just until he got into the car.

But his hopes sank when, after revving up for a few seconds, she saw him at the door of the house and beckoned to him. He started out in his dressing gown but she shook her head and wagged her finger at him, so he was obliged to discard the garment in the hall and venture forth in the altogether. Shivering, he closed the door behind him and looked warily up and down the street. Fortunately there seemed to be few people about. One car was driving down the road and there was a newspaper boy delivering a few doors down, but with luck he would make it to the car unnoticed.

Trying to look nonchalant, just in case any neighbours were watching from their windows, Ralph sauntered coolly down the path. He had no idea if anyone had seen him or not, but there was no point in worrying about it. As he got into the driving seat that Cordelia had vacated for him she murmured her congratulations from the back while she plonked a chauffeur's peaked cap on his head. 'Well done, thou good and faithful servant. Now drive on!'

Although the side roads were fairly quiet at that time in the morning the main roads were starting to clog with traffic and Ralph realized that, sooner or later, someone was bound to notice his state of undress. He was dreading stopping at traffic lights. It was easy to look straight ahead while he was driving and ignore any startled glances, but once another vehicle pulled up alongside and they were stuck there waiting for the lights to change he would be especially vulnerable.

Hunched well down in his seat, Ralph steered the vehicle out into the stream of traffic and braced himself for catcalls, whistles or ribald remarks. But none came. He began to relax, even enjoying the sensation of freedom and daring as the car warmed up and his cock began to respond to the subtle perfume of his mistress, excited by the novelty of the situation despite his fear of discovery. Cordelia was sitting back in her seat, comfortably relaxed and obviously enjoying being driven to work instead of having to do it herself.

Normally, of course, Ralph would be required to perform his domestic duties while she was at work, but today was special. There was a charged atmosphere in the car, an unspoken conspiracy against modesty and decency that could be challenged at any moment. Every second that Ralph got away with it he felt exhilarated, as if he was challenging society at some fundamental level.

Was this how criminals felt, he wondered, when they pulled off a really big con trick?

Up ahead, the lights were red. This was the first real test and Ralph felt his body gearing up for it with a rush of adrenalin that set his pulse racing and his heart skipping beats. A light sweat broke out on his forehead and the back of his neck as he applied the brakes and drew up at the back of the queue. At the moment it was single-line traffic, but he could feel the pressure building up and knew that another car might pull up alongside him before the lights changed. It was, literally, a race against time.

Then it happened: a white Vauxhall slowly cruised up alongside his and a female face looked casually in his direction. At first her expression was vague, then she did a double take and her jaw dropped. She turned to the male driver beside her and pointed in Ralph's direction, but at that moment the lights changed and he put his foot down. To his relief they left the white car standing and it wasn't long before the road cleared again.

'I think you gave them something to think about!' Cordelia chuckled, and he realized that she had watched the whole scenario unfold.

After that first encounter Ralph began to feel it wasn't so terrible after all. What if someone *did* see him: so what? He felt safe inside the car, reckless even. When the next set of lights loomed he approached them with a devil-may-care attitude that was abruptly shattered when the white car came up on the other side of him and the driver rolled down his window, clearly intending to give him an earful.

'You're disgusting!' the man shouted, rapping hard on the side window. Cordelia giggled, which didn't help Ralph's state of mind one bit. He quickly took off the chauffeur's cap and popped it over his burgeoning erection which was, in any case, starting to wilt again.

'I've taken your number!' the man, a City type with apoplectic cheeks, yelled. Verging on hysteria he added, 'You've completely traumatized my wife! You've completely ruined our day. No one expects to see that kind of thing this time in the morning.'

'When does he expect to see it, then?' Cordelia remarked, dryly. She was clearly enjoying every minute of it but Ralph was shit-scared. What if he had his licence taken away? A court appearance would be so horribly embarrassing. Could they fine him, even send him to prison?

He let the Vauxhall pull away first, praying that there would be no more trouble. Their route soon took him off the main road and down a side street, where he began to feel relieved. His progress turned a few heads, but he wasn't held up anywhere and so there was no danger of anyone getting a look at his credentials again. But the last lap of the journey worried him, since they would be joining the mainstream traffic once more.

'Chin up, Salter, only another ten minutes to go,' Cordelia said.

Ralph felt strange. She hardly ever called him by his surname and, coming from her lips, it sounded almost alien to his ears. They turned into the main road and joined the slow-moving traffic. This was going to be the trickiest bit of all. When a young girl, a rough type, drew up alongside on a bike and suddenly stared right in at him Ralph felt himself blush all over. The girl tottered and almost lost her balance, putting her hand on the car to steady herself. While Cordelia smothered a laugh Ralph looked steadfastly ahead, praying that the traffic would pick up speed, but they continued at a snail's pace towards a roundabout. Once they were past that, Ralph told himself, they'd be okay.

Cordelia told him her office block was almost within sight, but the worst wasn't over yet. The girl looked over her shoulder and shouted something, Ralph's first clue that she wasn't alone. There was a young man following on another bike – her boyfriend, probably – and now the pair of them were staring in through the side window, pointing and giggling. Pedestrians were taking an interest too, craning to see if some celebrity was in the car and frowning bemusedly when they caught sight of Ralph's naked chest and shoulders.

'What's up, you oversleep this morning?' the young man shouted, loud enough for several heads to turn in their direction.

'Just ignore him,' came Cordelia's advice from the back seat.

Easy for her to say, Ralph thought sourly. He tried to keep his eyes in front but it was difficult now the pair were hammering on the window and swearing at him, causing a disturbance. He lifted one finger to them and their verbal assault intensified.

'Pervert!' they called.

'Bloody exhibitionist!'

'Flasher!'

As the queue started to ease along the bikers kept up with them so there could be no escape. He could tell that Cordelia was thoroughly enjoying herself, especially when they turned their attention to her.

'Are you his girlfriend?' the youth challenged her. 'Why don't you buy him some clothes?'

'Do you like to fuck him?' the girl leered. 'Is he your husband, or your chauffeur?'

Cordelia rolled the window down an inch, announced coolly, 'He's my personal slave!' and rolled the window up again.

Ralph wanted to sink through the floor of the car, he was so embarrassed. The pace of the traffic was picking up a little so he swerved in front of the cyclists and joined the other queue, effectively blocking them off. When his turn came at the roundabout he was off like a greyhound from a trap and soon the home stretch was in sight. Even so, he got some strange looks from other motorists who had heard all the commotion behind and wondered what it was all about.

When they caught a glimpse of his naked torso most of them gaped or turned to their companions with incredulous exclamations and pointing fingers. Ralph could see himself leaving a trail of shocked disbelief in his rear-view mirror, but now that he was almost at their destination he could afford to smile.

'Turn right,' Cordelia ordered. 'There's usually a parking spot down here.'

As he did so, Ralph was starting to think about the homeward journey. That was going to be more tricky, without a passenger to give him even a hint of respectability or to stick up for him if things got out of hand. Then he remembered that there was a tartan travelling rug on the back seat. He might end up looking like an eccentric Scottish laird with the thing wound around his torso but at least he would be spared the ignominy he'd had to put up with on the outward journey.

Ralph found a space between two parked cars and drew up. Cordelia reached forward and tousled his hair affectionately. 'You did well,' she said.

He heard her open the car's back door and step out onto the pavement. As soon as she'd gone he would reach over to the back seat and find that rug, he decided. He looked up with a grin as she came to the driver's door but his grin froze to a rictus as he saw what she was carrying over one arm. It was the red-and-navy tartan.

'Just in case you tried to hide under it on the way home,' she smiled sweetly. 'Goodbye, Ralph. See you back at the house around six.'

There was a slight problem with the guest list for Cordelia's dinner party. Her friend Karen's partner was unable to come, which left them short of a man. So when Karen suggested that she should bring along a French acquaintance of hers called Lucien, Cordelia reluctantly agreed.

Reluctantly because she was afraid the presence of a relative stranger might upset the delicate balance of personalities that she had carefully orchestrated. She wanted her guests to be liberal in outlook, especially concerning sexual mores, but also still shockable. None of them knew the precise nature of Ralph's relationship to her, and she wanted to introduce them gradually to the idea that he was her slave. This Lucien was a potential loose cannon.

As the date drew near, however, Cordelia started looking forward to the evening. She was in a strange impasse at work with Nigel being very distant with her, continuing to treat her as the office slave but making her life all drudgery and no fun, giving the impression that he was looking over his shoulder all the time. She suspected that he'd received a drubbing from the formidable Inez, and was trying to keep in line. She was now even more convinced that he must have spy cameras set up in the office and that Inez must have access to the videos. Why else would her boss behave in such a paranoid manner?

So the prospect of a pleasant evening among friends was all the more welcome. She knew that Ralph had planned a splendid menu and would do her proud. Then there was the 'harem' theme, which the two female guests had promised to dress up for, although they couldn't vouch for the men. Cordelia had found herself a pair of gauzy pink-and-gold harem pants that she planned to wear with a turquoise bolero, low-necked and sewn with pearls. A band of gold braid secured it beneath the bust, making her sizeable breasts look even more impressive.

Ralph's behaviour had been impeccable ever since he'd played the naked chauffeur, and Cordelia had begun to plan other public humiliations to be kept up her sleeve in case they were needed. She would go easy on him at the dinner party, however, dominating him so subtly at first that the guests wouldn't twig what was going on, and becoming increasingly blatant over the course of the evening. Those who were clued in to such matters might make remarks, of course, which would be her cue to bring things into the open if the general climate seemed right. But she would enjoy testing the water first.

On the Saturday afternoon, Cordelia had a long, scented soak in the bath while Ralph made the preliminary preparations for the meal. Then she made him give her a manicure and pedicure, painting her fingernails – and toenails a pretty sugar-pink to match her outfit. Feeling cosseted, she got into her sexy costume and put on a black, Cleopatra-style wig, then made herself up with turquoise eyelids, plenty of kohl and long, thick lashes, using a lipstick that was a perfect match to her nails. Pleased with the finished effect, she added some dangly gold earrings and plenty of rings and bangles to give an opulent effect, then went downstairs to await her guests.

'Mix me a cocktail while I'm waiting,' she said to Ralph, who was dressed in baggy black silk pants and a gorgeous loose white velveteen shirt, with a pair of embroidered curled-toe slippers. Cordelia had found them on a market stall, along with her bolero, and was very pleased with the exotic touch they gave to his costume. He had put some gel on his dark-blond hair and sculpted it into waves, and the fake tan brought out the brilliance of his eyes. He looked as tasty as the dishes he was preparing!

Around eight the first couple arrived, Jayne and Simon. Cordelia had met them when she had been holidaying alone the previous summer, and they'd kept in touch. She had spent a pleasant weekend at their country cottage just outside Oxford and now it was time to return their hospitality. They wouldn't be staying the night, however, as they were visiting relatives in London.

They embraced warmly, and Cordelia stood back to view their appearance. Simon had made a token gesture by wearing a black velvet caftan-style shirt over black jeans – not exactly *Arabian Nights*, but it would do. Jayne, however, was looking stunning in a belly dancer's outfit that she had purchased on a trip to Egypt. The close-fitting red-and-gold top outlined her small shapely breasts and the low-slung matching pants showed off her slim waist and the jewel in her navel.

'Like it?' she grinned, pointing to the glittering stone. 'I had my belly button pierced for my birthday and Simon bought me the diamond to show it off.'

'Is that the only thing you had pierced?' Cordelia asked, her eyes dropping suggestively to where the flimsy pants showed the shape of her pubic delta.

Jayne flushed and giggled. *A promising sign*, Cordelia thought, feeling a rush of erotic excitement. Her experiences with Nigel and his friends, although they had been soured by Inez's jealously, had left her hungry for more of the same. The thought that this outwardly respectable dinner party might possibly turn into something approaching an orgy was exciting her already.

She turned to Simon, who had also caught her drift. 'How many diamonds can one woman wear?' he asked. 'If you start giving her ideas . . .'

'I'm sure she doesn't need *me* to give her ideas,' Cordelia smiled. 'Come on through. I'll get Ralph to make you a drink.'

'Ralph?' Jayne's eyebrows shot up. 'You never mentioned you were living with anyone.'

'Oh, he's just the hired help,' she said, airily. 'I clap my hands and he comes running – look!'

He appeared from the kitchen at once and took their orders with cool efficiency. 'I'm impressed,' Jayne said. 'What else can he do?'

'Oh, absolutely anything I want him to!'

Jayne gave Simon a mischievous grin. 'With help like that, who needs a husband?'

Simon made an attempt to recover his pride. 'There are *some* things he won't do, surely?'

'If there are, I haven't found them yet!'

The two women giggled conspiratorially but then the doorbell went and Cordelia went to answer it. She found Peter there, her own escort for the evening. He was the sort of handy fellow she kept in her address book to make up the numbers on occasions like this, on the understanding that he could do the same. They'd met at a wine-and-food fair, discovering a mutual interest in Middle Eastern gourmet cuisine so it had seemed a good idea to invite him.

'Cordelia!' He gave her a brotherly kiss on the cheek. 'What wonderful aromas coming from your kitchen! Smells as if you've been busy.'

'Oh, not me! I never have to do the cooking.'

'You don't?'

'Didn't I tell you? I always hire Ralph for my dinner parties. He will carry out my orders to the letter – so rare in hired help these days, don't you find?'

Peter knew she was playing some sort of game, but he didn't know what. Regarding her quizzically he said, 'And I had you down for a gourmet cook. Obviously I hardly know you at all, Cordelia.'

'Obviously! But come in and meet two of my other guests. Just tell Ralph what you'd like to drink and he'll mix it for you.'

'Ah, I shall test his knowledge of cocktails!'

Whether he passed the test or not she never discovered because soon after the doorbell went again and this time Karen stood there on the arm of a tall, dark stranger whom Cordelia presumed must be Lucien. His eyes ignited as they surveyed her exotic costume and she felt a warm shudder of arousal fizz through her. Something about the man was extraordinarily sexy, although as yet she didn't know what. A sense of danger, perhaps. Or some indecipherable pheromone signal that she was picking up at a subliminal level. If it was, indeed, chemistry it was certainly not the sort she'd learned at school!

He took her hand and kissed it, in Gallic fashion, his eyes never leaving her face. Cordelia felt herself blushing and giggling like a schoolgirl and hid her confusion by complimenting Karen on her outfit. Her friend's lush auburn hair was falling about her shoulders and making her heart-shaped face look very pretty, but it was obvious what all the males present would be looking at that evening: a minimal bra consisting of two silver cups joined by silver straps that hardly concealed any more than her nipples. Her perfect, apple-shaped breasts were virtually on full display, and the whole of her midriff and most of her belly were bare too. A jewelled girdle dipped towards her pussy and her loins were girt with black chiffon which barely concealed the dark shadow of her bush.

'You sexy thing!' Cordelia teased her, feeling somewhat upstaged. 'Come and meet the others – if you dare!'

With a few cocktails inside them and some party music on, things were soon going with a swing. By the time they moved next door to the sumptuous feast that Ralph had laid out, everyone was relaxed and happily anticipating the sensual delights of the meal – and who knew what else? Cordelia was already chalking up her 'Eastern Promise' dinner party as a success, and the way that Ralph had arranged the dining room was the icing on the cake.

Big velvet cushions were arranged in a semicircle around a low brass table that he had borrowed for the occasion. The air was filled with the scents of rose and jasmine, the music of the lute-like *oud* providing a quiet background to their excited chatter. In the corner was Ralph's triumph: a small fountain, electrically powered, that produced a charming tinkling note as the tiny jets of water splashed onto an arrangement of pebbles and plants in the bowl.

'Oh, how wonderful!' Karen exclaimed, arranging herself decorously on the cushion nearest the fountain. 'Cordelia, this is superb!'

'I have to thank Ralph for all this,' she smiled. 'He is such a treasure!'

'Where on earth did you find him?' Jayne asked.

'Oh, I picked him out of the gutter!'

Everyone laughed, the men slightly uneasily as they attempted to sit cross-legged on the cushions. Peter had the most difficulty, being rather portly, and compromised by putting his legs to one side. Cordelia took pride of place with Karen on her right hand and Lucien on her left. She felt keyed up, her pulses quivering eagerly and she knew it wasn't just the prospect of food that was making her so agitated.

No, it was the sexy brown eyes of the Frenchman who was staring at her minutely, taking in not only her facial features but also the voluptuous contours of her body as she lounged, in languid pose, on the big velvet cushion. She clapped her hands loudly and Ralph appeared, kneeling between her and Lucien as he took each small dish delicately off the tray and placed them on the low table.

'I have provided a selection of starters,' he explained in his low, soft voice, naming each dish in turn. 'Aubergine purée with yoghurt and meat balls, Tahina cream salad with almonds, Falafel, Dukkah, Taramasalata, fresh herbs, orange salad . . .'

'Oh, it all looks absolutely delicious!' Jayne gushed.

'Yes, you've done us proud, Cordelia,' Peter added.

'Not I – my little kitchen boy here.' She reached out and

caressed Ralph's rump through the thin satin trousers. 'He's been slaving away in the kitchen all day, haven't you, dear?'

Ralph nodded with a small, secretive smile, whispered, 'Enjoy!' then rose to leave the room.

'He's a bit of a strange fish, isn't he?' Karen said beneath her breath, but the others heard.

'We all have our little foibles, don't we?' Cordelia said, brightly. 'I know I do. Shall we begin?'

'One thing's for sure, he's a fantastic cook!' Simon declared, after just a few mouthfuls.

Ralph soon appeared again and, breaking the Arab taboo against alcohol, poured everyone a glass of cool Cypriot white wine. This time Cordelia caressed his hand in full view of everyone as he poured her glass, and was gratified when there was a sudden hiatus in the conversation. She moved her hand up to stroke his cheek. 'That will be all for now, thank you.'

There were knowing glances passing between the couples. Only Lucien stared at her with an intent and penetrating gaze that seemed to scrutinize her soul, making her uneasy. While the other guests now seemed to presume that she and Ralph were merely lovers, she sensed that the Frenchman was not convinced. He knew there was more to it than that.

The first course was finished and Cordelia summoned Ralph to clear the dishes, but this time Lucien insisted on rising to help him. Ignoring the protests of both chef and hostess, he took the serving dishes out to the kitchen before Ralph had time to collect the rest. For several minutes the two men were alone in the kitchen and Cordelia was racked with suspense. At last she could bear it no longer. Scrambling to her feet she excused herself from the company and went to see what the pair were up to behind the scenes.

She found them hunched over the stove, with Ralph explaining the intricacies of his cuisine while Lucien seemed to be equally engrossed in sharing his expertise. She stood at the door for a few seconds without either man noticing her, listening to their rival recipes for making a *roux*. It was somewhat bizarre to see the two men talking so earnestly about cooking, but the emotions that the scene was arousing in Cordelia were even stranger. It took her a minute or so to realize that what she was actually feeling was jealousy, but she couldn't quite work out which man she was jealous of. Why not both?

The idea was so ridiculous that she smothered a giggle and the ensuing snort drew their attention to her. Ralph, who had been in a fairly assertive pose, immediately assumed his habitual servile posture and Lucien noticed, his brows knitting slightly and his mouth twitching with thinly-veiled amusement. Cordelia strode up to the stove.

'What's this, distracting my chef?' she challenged Lucien. 'We're all waiting for the main course.'

'I'm sure no one is suffering hunger pangs,' the Frenchman said, wryly. 'Not after that magnificent feast of hors d'oeuvres. I just thought I'd glean a few tips from the *maestro*. No harm in that, surely?'

'I suppose not.'

Her reply was grudging. She turned to Ralph with her usual stern demeanour. 'Stop this slacking and get on with your work. We haven't got all night!'

Lucien looked slightly shocked. He stared from Cordelia's haughty face to Ralph's submissive stance and something clicked. He took hold of his hostess's bare arm and pulled her firmly towards the door, saying, 'Come, Cordelia, I think he will work much better if we leave him in peace. Besides, the others will be wondering what we are up to.'

She wanted to remonstrate with him but when she looked into his lucid dark brown eyes she saw something there that reduced her to jelly. A powerful confidence was beaming out at her, the confidence that comes of knowing one's own abilities and of understanding the weaknesses of others. The dark virility of the man was projecting itself into her soul, making her want him with the kind of yearning appetite that she had forgotten how to feel.

But he had come with Karen, and he would leave with Karen, she reminded herself. There was no point in hankering after what she couldn't have. Besides, she mustn't be greedy. Weren't two lovers enough for any woman? Her need to dominate and her need to be dominated were perfectly balanced in her, thanks to Nigel and Ralph, and there was no way she was going to let a chance encounter with a stranger upset that equilibrium.

But as they walked back to the fragrant dining room where the happy conversational hum was growing louder by the minute, Lucien's grip on her upper arm tightened, forcing her to a halt. She saw his eyes gleam at her in the dim hall light, saw the red fruit of his mouth open to show the pearly seeds of his teeth, and knew that she was doomed to desire him whatever the consequences.

He pulled her close, his mouth in her ear, and whispered, 'I want to fuck the arse off you!'

Chapter Nine

Throughout the rest of the dinner party Cordelia felt as if she were burning with inner fire. She was constantly aware of Lucien's dark eyes upon her, watching her like a hawk as she pretended to play the hostess, destroying all her carefully-laid plans. The exquisite Circassian chicken, accompanied by stuffed artichokes and leeks with tamarind, that Ralph had so diligently prepared seemed to her bland and tasteless, while the delicious little pastries stuffed with dates and almonds that he served with the coffee were like sawdust in her mouth.

She felt angry, disappointed and embarrassed by turns. The Frenchman was like a skeleton at the feast, ruining everything for her. When Ralph came and went she felt obliged to treat him like any other waiter hired for the occasion. If she'd played it as she'd intended it would have seemed like a shameful charade with Lucien's penetrating eyes on her all the time. If only Karen's lover had been able to come, everything would have been different, but this intrusive, presumptuous and thoroughly rude Frenchie had made it impossible for her to enjoy herself along with her guests.

What had he done? Said he wanted to fuck her, that's all. A sophisticated woman like her should have been able to handle that kind of verbal pass without freaking out. Yet she knew there was more to it, and it bothered her. Cordelia just couldn't dismiss the man's blunt overture from her mind. And when she had the urge to return to her script – to make some flippant remark about Ralph hinting at the nature of their relationship, to speak to him imperiously or touch him intimately in front of the others – she found she could no longer do it.

When the meal was over they continued to lounge on cushions while Ralph removed the low table and produced a hookah, filled with a mixture of tobacco and hashish, that they passed around, the mood growing languid as they grew increasingly bleary-eyed. Yet nothing seemed to affect Lucien. He was as alert and watchful as ever, an observer rather than a participant, even though he took a good draught on the hubble-bubble and sipped brandy on the side as well. His self-control was impressive but it also intrigued her. What would it take to reveal the man behind that complacent, knowing mask?

'Oh, I feel perfectly randy now!' Jayne said with a giggle, lying seductively on her side in the tight bikini-style top with her breasts almost popping out. She put a hand between her thighs and began to rub herself slowly.

'Don't mind us!' Karen smiled. 'I feel quite squiffy myself, actually.'

Peter, who was sitting next to her, was flirting shamelessly with her now, murmuring things into her ear and sneaking little kisses onto her neck while his roving hands caressed her shoulders. Cordelia glanced at Lucien, but he didn't seem to care. So Karen had been right in describing him as 'just a friend'. It looked as if the others were pairing off and Cordelia was in danger of being stuck with Lucien. That wouldn't do at all.

She clapped her hands vigorously and Ralph appeared. 'Belly dancing competition!' she declared loudly. 'Each of the women has to perform a belly dance and the men shall judge which of us can do it best. We'll draw lots to start. Ralph, put some spills into a hat or something, all different lengths, and get this hubble-bubble out of the way to make room.'

The other two women groaned in token protest but the men were enthusiastic. Cordelia livened up at the thought of some physical activity, hoping it would get that terrible sick longing out of her system. She was drawn last, with Jayne first. Well, she would know what the competition was like, at least.

Stoned as they were, both Jayne and Karen made an awkward mess of the dance although they looked undeniably sexy as they wiggled their hips exaggeratedly and did their best to roll their bellies around as they imagined the women of the harem would do. Karen contorted herself so much that she ended up overbalancing and falling on the floor amidst hysterical laughter. It was Peter who helped her up – helping himself to a good grope at the same time, Cordelia noticed.

Then it was her turn. *At least I've had some practice*, she thought, remembering the table dance she'd done for Nigel's colleague. Wishing she still had those sexy little balls inside urging her on, she rose and took up her stance, waiting for an opening in the music. For a split second she looked at Lucien, so still, dark and handsome on his embroidered cushion, and had the weird feeling that they belonged to a different time and place, that she had performed like this for him before. The idea took root in her imagination so that the scene before her became a real harem, and Lucien a real sultan. She must seduce him with her body tonight, make sure that she was the chosen one, to be honoured above all the other harem women. The fantasy took over as she swayed her hips to the music and she raised her arms slowly, stretching them out languidly until her wrists entwined above her head as if bound by invisible fetters.

Cordelia was relishing the prospect of making a slow beginning, leading up gradually to a passionate climax,

mirroring the act of love. The others had fallen silent, each
intent on the undulating curves of her body as she moved
belly, hips and pelvis in an easy rhythm that was making he
feel good. She had a faint smile on her face and a distant look
in her eyes as the spirit of the East took over, changing her
into a woman of finer sensibility and exotic sensuality, a
courtesan who knew how to use her body to elicit the most
exquisite pleasure, both for herself and her partner.

Her fingers fluttered out towards the circle of onlookers
in a gesture of entreaty that seemed to be saying, 'Choose
me, come to me, oh my love!' She could hear the impas-
sioned verses of the *Rubaiyat* echoing in her mind as she
danced, entranced.

With caressing movements she traced the shape of her hips
with her hands, moving up through the indentation of her
waist to her breasts, which felt full and ripe beneath the tight
bodice. She could feel the acorn-hard nipples beneath the
embroidered cloth, straining with barely-contained desire
and tingling hotly. Down below she was overheating too,
the subtle movements of her thighs and pelvis making her
wet and randy.

Her dance grew more suggestive as she plunged her joined
hands between her thighs and felt the friction on her clitoris,
pressing her breasts tightly together to increase the cleavage.
Now she was all woman, felt her own desirability in the eyes
of the men present and possibly the other women too. She
realized that the raw sexuality she was exuding would have an
elemental appeal, and her recent experience with Inez told her
that she could be attractive to her own sex, as well.

Through heavy-lidded eyes she could glimpse her guests
lounging on their cushions and the atmosphere was incredibly erotic. Simon and Jayne were blatantly kissing, Peter was
stroking Karen's bare arm. Only Lucien sat aloof, immobile,
but she could tell that even he was moved. His dark eyes were

in soft focus, lusting after her body, and his mobile, sensitive mouth was half-open, as if ready to be kissed. Her smile widened as their eyes met and his gaze smouldered at her, sending their unambiguous message of naked desire.

Part of her was asking 'Why not?' as she squeezed her hands between her thighs and rolled her pelvis more urgently, intensifying the pace and her own arousal. It would be so easy to throw herself into his arms and let him ravish her there and then, with the other guests ripe for the party to turn into an orgy.

Only the thought of Ralph stopped her. It wouldn't be fair to him, after his sterling work in the kitchen, to make love with a stranger in front of his eyes. She could see him hovering at the door, adoring her, wanting her to assert herself over him again, and knew she couldn't be such a bitch. He might thrive on humiliation, on being bossed around, but she had never yet given him cause for serious jealousy. That was why she had kept secret the true nature of her relationship to her boss, a relationship that she knew would seriously undermine her power over Ralph if he ever got to know about it.

And who knew what sex with Lucien might turn into, what particular kink might turn them both on if they engaged in sexual intimacy? The idea of it both excited and scared her. There was something foreign about his nature that could not be accounted for simply by his nationality. She sensed depths to his personality that possibly, not even he, had yet plumbed.

Stop this! she told herself, as the temptation to take him up on his offer grew almost irresistible. She directed her attentions towards Ralph instead, enjoying the rapt look that came over his face as she thrust her breasts in his direction and made a little pout with her red lips. Knowing that he wanted her constantly, achingly, was a kind of security that

she needed. Her life with Nigel was growing ever le:
predictable, and she needed the certainty of Ralph's devotio
more than ever. She just couldn't afford to do anything th;
would put it in jeopardy.

The spell of the dance had her in its grip, her and everyon
else in the room. She felt wicked, abandoned, wanting to d
something to shock. Slowly she felt behind her back for th
zipper of the bolero and began to pull it down.

'Yes!' she heard, barely a whisper, from Lucien. It almos
stopped her in her tracks, but then she thought, *Why not?* Sh
could torment him with her body, show him what he woul
never have. That would be a nice revenge for his presump
tion. Slowly she lifted the little top over the undersides of he
breasts, letting it lodge over her nipples. She could feel th
tension mounting as she gradually eased the material up an(
up, exposing her breasts entirely.

There was an unexpected round of applause from every
one except Lucien, who was just staring at her with eyes tha
were almost bored. Staring at him, Cordelia put a han(
down the front of her harem pants and felt the wetness o
her muff and the slipperiness of her quim. She pulled he:
hand out and, still staring at him, licked her fingers witl
relish. The others were starting to look a bit uncomfortable
she noticed.

She turned round and inched the elasticated waistban(
down over her buttocks, slowly again, until the trousers hun;
around her thighs and she was open to inspection in front. A
sidelong glance at Ralph made her think twice, however. H(
was looking scared that she might strip completely, migh
offer too much of herself and let things get out of hand. She
didn't want to upset him too much, so she pulled the pants up
just enough to cover her modesty and then turned around,
still swaying to the music.

Lucien looked disappointed. *Well, you can't please all oj*

the people all of the time, she thought wryly. It was time to bring the dance to a close.

With a flourish and a bow, Cordelia signed off to rapturous applause from four of her guests. Both Ralph and Lucien gave a few half-hearted claps and that was all. She gave each of them a special bow, then went up to Ralph and suggested that he might like to offer her guests more coffee. There was a general sense of anticlimax and she guessed that the offer of coffee might give her guests the excuse to draw the evening to a close.

It worked. Simon and Jayne were the first to rise, declining coffee and mumbling about the babysitter. Cordelia had completely forgotten they'd started a family, and it came as something of a shock. Perhaps her original plans for the evening had been inappropriate, she reflected. After all, she didn't know the couple that well. She had given them a wonderful gastronomic feast and a bit of naughty entertainment, so from their point of view the evening was probably a success.

And Lucien? She saw him look at his watch and rise too, murmuring something to Karen. In the end the four of them decided to leave together, which gave Cordelia an odd twinge that she identified as jealousy. At the door he mouthed some platitudes about a 'wonderful evening,' but as he bent forward to kiss her cheek she heard him whisper, 'I mean to have you, you know, sooner or later.'

She gave him a condescending smile, a look that said, 'No chance!' But her heart was battering wildly against her ribcage and she knew that theirs was to be a battle of wills. When the guests had gone and she was alone with Ralph she found she was trembling.

'Shall I run your bath, mistress?' he asked, sensing her agitation.

'Er . . . no, I'm rather tired. I'll go to bed now and shower in the morning.'

He looked disappointed. She threw him a smile that she hoped was reassuring and left him to clear up. Her bed was a haven, calling to her, but when she reached it and lay down to sleep she realized that she couldn't just blot out thoughts of Lucien. They would return to torment her all night long. She couldn't help wondering what sex would be like with him. It was a long time since she'd had straight sex. Would she find it boring? It was hard to imagine Lucien being boring. Maybe she would find the first time exciting, and the next. Maybe the thrill would even last a few months. But after a while the novelty would wear off and then she would want to be rid of him.

By then, she would probably have lost Ralph and maybe left her job as well. The thought of building up her life again from scratch was depressing. It took so much time and energy to train and be trained, so much to remember, and then the daily repetition, the constant watchfulness. Cordelia didn't think she could bear to go through it all again with one man, let alone two.

All day Sunday she was as nice as pie to Ralph, trying to reassure him, but by the evening she realized that it was herself she was trying to convince. Somehow Lucien had got his claws into her, penetrated her defences, and all she could hope for was that his memory faded as soon as possible.

At lunchtime on Monday Nigel gave her a special task. 'I want you to go out and buy some nice underwear,' he told her. 'Inez has a birthday this week. You're about her size. Get something sexy and don't count the cost.'

At first, Cordelia was quite pleased. It made a change from the daily tedium of being chained to the computer, and it gave her an excuse to go to one of those exclusive boutiques that sold French undies, all frills and lace in gorgeous colours and styles. There was one at the other end of the High Street.

The shop was empty when she arrived, the sales girl eager

to please. Cordelia lusted after a coffee-coloured set with half-cup bras and tanga briefs – but that was something she would choose for herself and she had a feeling Inez would find it too dull. Red was perhaps too obvious, but then she saw a set in primrose-yellow with white lace and was tempted. She was making a close inspection when the old-fashioned bell rang on the door and a man entered.

Looking round with some embarrassment, Cordelia was shocked to see Lucien's grinning face. 'A woman should never have to buy her own underwear,' he stated, his eyes flashing darkly at her, then looking from the dainty yellow bra to her breasts as if trying to imagine her wearing it. She felt a hot wave of desire between her thighs, making her pussy stream and her clitoris pulsate with lust.

'I'm buying it for my boss,' she said, coolly.

His brows lifted in amusement. 'Female, I hope?'

The suggestion that Nigel might be a cross-dresser made her giggle. 'For his girlfriend, I should say.'

'Ah!'

Cordelia turned to the assistant. 'I think she'd probably like something a little more colourful. Turquoise, maybe, or green.'

'We have a delightful set by Jacques Rivière in pale turquoise.'

'An excellent brand,' came Lucien's voice from behind. 'I've often bought his creations for my girlfriends and they've never been disappointed. Neither, for that matter, have I.'

Cordelia threw him a scornful look of dismissal. She had no idea how the man had tracked her down. Had he spotted her by chance, in passing? Or had he followed her all the way to the office, then lain in wait until she appeared again? If so, then he must be some kind of obsessive and she must avoid encouraging him at all costs. There were laws against stalking, and she wouldn't hesitate to inform the police if it became necessary.

He was talking to the sales girl now, charming her with his French accent and expressive eyes. Cordelia examined a pale blue bra, trying to concentrate on her task but finding it increasingly difficult to decide. Then Lucien began to look at the stock too, commenting loudly and putting her off even more.

'This purple one is rather *chic*, don't you think?'

Cordelia hoped he was addressing the girl but he tapped her arm to make it plain he was talking to her. She gave a non-committal shrug. 'Have you anything in orange?' she asked the girl.

'There's this one. Very bright, but beautifully made. And rather naughty, too,' she added, giving Lucien a nervous but excited glance.

He took the bra from her and poked his fingers through the peepholes intended for the nipples. He waggled them suggestively at Cordelia. 'Oh yes, I see what you mean! This would certainly set your boss's pulses racing, wouldn't it? He'd love this!'

'It's for his girlfriend,' she reiterated, coldly. She asked the girl, 'What about bright pink?'

'Well, I have this half-cup style in fuschia,' the girl said, an impatient note sneaking into her voice.

Cordelia decided she would have it even before it was out of its box. She had to get away from this pest of a Frenchman. And if he tried to follow her back to the office, Nigel would soon sort him out.

The deep pink half-cup bra and French knickers looked like the sort of thing Inez might wear. It was very expensive, but she paid from the sheaf of twenty-pound notes that Nigel had given her and prayed that the girl wouldn't take too long wrapping it. While she stood there Lucien kept showing her the orange underwear, trying to get an opinion out of her. In the end she snapped, 'It's all right if you like that sort of thing!'

'Don't you? I'd have thought this was just your style, judging by what I've seen you wearing before.' He grinned shamelessly at her and she knew he was referring to the gaudy top she'd worn at the dinner party. Her cheeks flushed, as much with anger as embarrassment.

'We have a quaint old English saying,' she told him, archly. 'Don't judge a book by the cover.'

'And *we* have a quaint old French saying,' he countered. '*C'est magnifique, mais ce n'est pas la guerre.* You'll have to do better than that if you want to offend me.'

She stared at him, hardly able to believe his cheek. In a dream she took her change and the carefully-wrapped parcel from the girl and turned to leave the shop. Behind her she heard Lucien say, pleasantly, 'I'll take this set please. Wrap it nicely, won't you?'

For the whole of the ten-minute walk back to the office Cordelia was looking over her shoulder, terrified that Lucien would follow her and find out where she worked. If he didn't know already. She felt paranoid, and not until she was safely back inside the office did she relax. Handing the packet to Nigel with a smile she said, 'I hope you and Mistress Inez will approve my choice, sir.'

'Can't tell until I see it on,' he replied, brusquely. 'Model it for me.'

'What . . . now?'

His fierce black brows beetled at her. 'Are you questioning me, Miss?'

'I'm sorry, I forgot myself.'

Cordelia went into the cloakroom to change. She'd become rather hot and bothered during her encounter with Lucien so she sprayed deodorant under her arms to disguise the fact, then slipped off her own underwear. The exquisite deep pink bra fitted her quite well and bolstered up her breasts to give her a provocative cleavage. She stepped into the French knickers, leaving her own on underneath for reasons of hygiene, and then put on the lacy suspender belt and half-slip. Feeling rather self-conscious, she stepped out into the office for Nigel's inspection.

'Hm, nice colour!' he began. 'And I like the bra style. What's under the slip?'

She lifted up the satiny skirt to show him her knickers. Her heart fell as he frowned and came closer. 'What kind of panties are these?'

'French knickers, sir.'

'Well, I don't like them. I want the briefest possible, practically a G-string. Those highlight the fact that your stomach sticks out.'

Humiliated, Cordelia walked back to the changing room. 'Take them back!' he called after her. 'See if they'll just change the pants. If they won't you'll have to choose something else.'

Wearily, she changed back into her own clothes. The prospect of returning to the shop was fraught with hazard. What if Lucien were still there, flirting with the pretty assistant? But she dared not delay. Nigel would expect her to hurry there and back again since she'd already wasted quite a bit of the working day. She hurried out of the office with the parcel under her arm and almost tripped over another parcel that had been left right outside the door.

Puzzled, she glanced at the label and found, to her horror, that it was addressed to her. She didn't have to open it to know what was in it: the orange lingerie set, left by the persistent Lucien. She opened it just a little, to confirm, and the saucy underwear peeped out cheekily at her. 'Damn the man!'

Well, she would take it right back. It was a good thing, in a way, that Nigel had not been satisfied with her choice or else she might not have got to this parcel first. She could imagine how suspicious her boss would be if he thought she had another admirer, and if he'd ordered her to open the parcel there and then and show him what was inside she would have had to obey. She thanked her lucky stars at her narrow escape.

The girl in the boutique was surprised to see her back so soon. Cordelia explained that they were the 'wrong sort of knickers' but there were no alternatives in that particular style so she had to go through the choices again. In the end she chose an emerald-green set with minute bikini pants that she hoped would meet with Nigel's approval.

'Er . . . and then there's these,' she began nervously, after the exchange had been made. 'That gentleman who was in here just now gave them to me, but I'm afraid I can't accept them. Could you possibly take them back?'

'Have you got the receipt?'

'Well, no, I didn't buy them, did I?'

'I'm sorry,' the girl said firmly, parroting the set response. 'No exchanges or refunds without a receipt. It's company policy.'

'Oh, I'm not asking for any money. I just don't want the stuff, that's all. It's a bit embarrassing . . . can't you just take them back and sell them again?'

The girl looked shocked. 'Oh no! They're shop-soiled now. They'd have to go back to the warehouse and I'd need a receipt for that. Why don't you ask the gentleman to let you have it? Say they're the wrong size, or something.'

'I don't think you understand. I don't really know the man. I've no idea where he lives. And I'm certainly not in the habit of accepting gifts from strangers.'

Now the girl was looking decidedly suspicious. 'I'm sorry,' she said, coldly. 'Why don't you give them away, if you don't want them? I'm sure any girl would be pleased to get a set of *Jacques Rivière* undies. I certainly would!'

Cordelia gave up the struggle, swallowed her pride and left with the two packages.

Fortunately, Nigel accepted her explanation that she'd bought something for herself as well, and he was enthusiasti about the new choice, rubbing her buttocks beneath the silk pants and her breasts beneath the uplifting bra. He went n further, though, although he made her wear the undies al through the afternoon.

'Inez will enjoy having your body odours on her under wear,' he told her. 'She fancies you something rotten, you know.' His dark eyes were scrutinizing her, watching he reaction. Helplessly Cordelia felt her cheeks redden. 'O course, she can't have you unless I say so. And after tha fiasco at Harley Grange she's in my bad books. But I shal forgive her on her birthday. Maybe you'd like to be part o her present?'

Cordelia didn't know what to say. She was tempted to explore lesbian love a little more with the voracious Inez, bu still afraid of the consequences for her relations with Nigel He saw her dilemma and laughed. 'All right, you don't have to choose. That's for me to decide, right? If I tell you I wan you to suck my mistress's pussy then you will, won't you?'

She nodded meekly. He patted her arm. 'Good girl. Now get on with those letters. You've wasted enough time today.'

She felt indignant but, as usual, let it go over her head. There was no point in feeling riled with her boss, since she was there to serve his every need and endure his every insult. It was part of their contract. Just lately, however, it had been harder than ever to knuckle under. Lucien was behind it, with his damnably knowing smile and blatant appetite for her. She had started to curse the day she'd met him.

When Cordelia arrived home that evening she went straight upstairs to her bedroom, telling Ralph that she wanted to be left alone for a while. This wasn't unusual. Sometimes, after a particularly gruelling day at the office, she needed a breathing space, time to lie down on her luxurious bed and unwind, gradually getting herself in the mood for giving orders after a day of taking them.

Tonight, though, she had a different motive. She opened the package of bright orange underwear and held up the garments, one by one. The peephole bra was blatantly sexy and now that she could inspect the panties more closely she saw that they were of the split-crotch variety. She might have known! Remembering that the assistant must also have known exactly what style they were, she heartily wished that she hadn't made such a fuss. It was all just too embarrassing!

There was a frilly suspender belt and a short slip with a slit up both sides. Slowly, she fingered the silky material, inspecting the perfect workmanship. Marks & Spencer undies were pretty and made to last, but only the French knew how to make *really* sexy underwear, she decided. The temptation to see how she looked in the ensemble was too great and soon she was stripping off her clothes.

As she had guessed, the image she presented in the bra and panties was wickedly sexy, her nipples peeking through the lacy holes and the opening in the briefs allowing the merest glimpse of her pussy lips. What if Lucien could see her now! She almost believed he could, by some weird telepathic means. Fastening on the suspender belt she found a clean pair of silk stockings from her underwear drawer and began to roll them carefully up her legs. She had just finished securing them when the bedside phone rang.

Casually, she answered it, thinking it was one of her girlfriends. But the low, seductive male voice was instantly recognizable by its slight accent. 'How do they look on you?'

'What?' She was tempted to slam down the phone, mostly

out of shock, but indignation soon took over and she snapped. 'How dare you!'

'What, give you that sexy lingerie? Or enquire how you look in it?'

'Both! And, for your information, I don't want your damned underwear.'

'But you can't deny that you tried it on, can you? No woman could resist it. I expect you're wearing it at this very moment, aren't you?'

'No, I certainly am not!' Cordelia lied. But she was trembling all over and her voice came out all of a quiver.

'Do your nipples peep through the holes nicely?' he went on. 'And what about your sweet little pussy, does it like to have the air circulating around it? So much more healthy, don't you think, than the conventional gusset.'

'I'm going to put this phone down right now!' she insisted, furious at being caught out. 'And don't you *dare* ring back again, because I shan't answer it!'

She slammed down the receiver and sat on the bed, trembling with fury and shame. How on earth had that bastard guessed? She suddenly rose and went to the window, fearful that he might be outside in his car, spying on her while he phoned from his mobile. But there were no strange vehicles in sight. No, he must have calculated the time it took her to return home, or even followed her to her door, and then guessed that she would try the undies on straight away. The idea that he knew her that well was uncanny, disturbing.

Angrily she stripped off the undies and threw them in the bottom of her wardrobe. Then she went to take a shower, as if she might wash off all contact with the man. Her skin felt contaminated by wearing his unwanted gift, and she scrubbed herself clean. But no matter how vigorously she shampooed her hair, she couldn't cleanse her mind of him. He lurked around her like a bad smell and she had a feeling that he was going to turn up again and again until she gave in to his desire, a desire that was dangerously mirrored in her own body and soul.

Chapter Ten

'I want you to take the present round to Inez.'

Cordelia wasn't sure she wanted to, but she knew she couldn't refuse. What little game was Nigel playing with her now? It was his mistress's birthday: he should be the one to deliver his gift. But was she to be part of the present too?

It seemed so, from what he said next. 'I want you to wear the undies,' he told her. 'I want to see her face when she undresses you.'

'You'll be there too?'

'Of course. Would I miss all the fun?'

She wasn't sure whether to feel reassured or not. Evidently Nigel had some scenario in mind and, as usual, she would be expected to go along with it. But Inez was unpredictable, temperamental. There was no knowing how she might react if the pair of them turned up on her doorstep.

Cordelia reminded herself of her contract with Nigel, but somehow it didn't seem as binding as before. He'd never told her that another woman was going to enter into the equation somewhere along the line. Then there was Ralph. She'd been out quite a lot lately in the evenings and he'd been looking sullenly neglected. She owed him some consideration, too.

'All right,' she said at last. 'But I must be home by midnight.'

'No problem.'

Her boss let her take the emerald lingerie home with her on Friday night, so she could put it on ready for the evening. It gave her a thrill to feel the sensual silk against her newly-washed skin, relishing the way the bra hugged her breasts in a smooth embrace and the pants sat snugly over her mound. She half-wished she had chosen it for herself – but then she thought of the even naughtier set that Lucien had bought her. It was still screwed up in a heap at the bottom of her wardrobe. A terrible waste of such beautiful underwear, but she still couldn't bring herself to wear it again after that shocking phone call.

Since then she'd heard nothing from him, and while half of her hoped he'd found some other object for his affection the vain part of her was miffed that he'd apparently dropped her.

Ralph looked forlorn when she went downstairs, so Cordelia decided to give him a nice task to keep him occupied till her return. She didn't want him to feel taken for granted.

'I want you to check all my clean underwear for any slight rips or loose stitches and sew them where necessary. Then you can go through my dirty linen and pick out the fragile undies for hand-washing. That should keep you busy, but if you've got any time after that you can go through my make-up case and wash any powder puffs, smooth the lipsticks into a nice pointy shape and make sure my mascara brushes aren't clogged. Got that?'

'Yes, madam,' he said, happily. Normally Ralph wasn't allowed anywhere near her underwear drawer, laundry or cosmetics. She kept such intimacies as rewards for special occasions and now it seemed right to reward him. He'd had a lot to put up with lately.

It was only when she was on her way to the Kensington address that Nigel had given her that it occurred to Cordelia that maybe she was spoiling Ralph to assuage her own guilt. It was true, she *had* been neglecting the poor boy lately and it was partly Lucien's fault. The effect of his brief appearance in her life had been to destabilize it, making her question whether or not she was happy with the status quo. It was horribly mean of the man to breeze into her life, sow the seeds of discontent and then breeze out again, but she'd get over it. She had to.

When the taxi dropped her off she saw Nigel's car at the kerb nearby. He was waiting for her, and the instant she appeared he got out of the vehicle, carrying a bunch of red roses, and escorted her towards the select block of flats where Inez lived. He said nothing as he propelled her by the elbow up to the door, which opened automatically when it recognized his voice. They took the lift to Inez's penthouse flat on the top floor, then he hid against the wall while she rang the bell.

Inez's face lit up when she saw her. 'Cordelia! What a nice surprise. Do come in.'

'Happy birthday!' Cordelia smiled back, pleased that Inez seemed to be in such a good mood for once. But then, it was her birthday.

Nigel appeared with his bouquet and there was much hugging and kissing before the three of them went inside. It was a luxuriously-furnished apartment with a balcony conservatory, where a fountain played amid exotic shrubs and with a view of London beyond. While Inez and Nigel kissed rapturously Cordelia wandered around, admiring the art and antiques. Then she heard her boss say, 'Cordelia has a very special present for you, darling. Want to see it?'

'Of course!' Inez, still in a good mood, beamed at the pair of them. 'But do let's open some champagne first. I have some in the fridge, ready.'

'What an excellent idea!' Nigel went into the kitchen to find it, and Inez came up and put her arm around Cordelia. She smelt of some exotic perfume. Her manner was so elated and her eyes so bright that Cordelia suspected she was high on something. Well, that was none of her concern. She was

there to do Nigel's bidding, that was all. He'd told her he
wanted her to perform a striptease for his mistress but she felt
rather self-conscious at the prospect. Perhaps the champagne
would help loosen her inhibitions.

Yet she couldn't help feeling excited at the thought of being
Inez's present, gift-wrapped in the sexy underwear that she
would then strip off to present herself in her 'birthday suit'.
She could see the Spanish woman eyeing her voraciously and
knew that she was in for a sensual treat of some kind,
although she didn't know what. But not knowing was half
the fun, after all.

'Cheers! Here's to my two lovely ladies!' Nigel announced,
entering with a tray of flûtes filled with sparkling, pale
yellow liquid.

As Cordelia drank she couldn't help making her own silent
toast, 'to my two lovely men!'

It was nice to have the feeling that she was 'off-duty' for
once. Neither Nigel nor his mistress seemed to be insisting on
her taking a submissive rôle in the proceedings, but were
treating her as their equal – their honoured guest, even.
Perhaps the idea of the threesome wasn't a bad one, after
all. They were so relaxed that it might just work, although
Nigel didn't seem to be in much of a hurry to move in
that direction.

Nevertheless it was obvious that Inez was impatient for the
action to begin. She seemed to have completely forgotten her
jealousy on the previous occasion when the three of them
were together. Obviously she was used to having her tan-
trums indulged. Cordelia finished the heady champagne and
took up her position in the middle of the white deep-
pile carpet as Nigel made for the hi-fi and put on the music
he had selected.

Once again Cordelia found herself having to perform
a seductive dance, but now she felt more practised and

confident. While Nigel and Inez lounged on the huge pink sofa, Nigel with his arm around Inez's shoulder and his hand down the front of her low-necked black velvet dress, Cordelia began to sway to the music and toy with the straps of her own green silk dress, chosen to match the underwear. She stretched her limbs like a cat, luxuriating in the sensual movements of her own body and the memory of how she looked in the erotic undies.

When she looked at Inez the woman's black eyes seemed to be drinking her in, undressing her mentally and no doubt fantasizing about what was in store. Cordelia pulled out all the stops, knowing she was turning the pair of them on. She was their puppet, their plaything, and she delighted in making them want her. Slowly she unzipped her dress and began to shimmy out of it, letting it fall in a pool of silk at her feet.

Inez gave a soft gasp when she saw the exquisite, sexy lingerie and Nigel whispered that it was to be hers. Cordelia acted like the models she'd seen on the catwalk, showing off the merchandise by stroking and fingering the fine material and twirling to show the effect from the back, her taut buttocks barely contained by the minuscule briefs that were already becoming damp with her juices.

On the sofa, Nigel had managed to unhook his mistress's dress and now the bodice hung down exposing her full breasts in their black bra, a rather boring garment compared to the one that Cordelia was currently flaunting. Soon she'd stripped off the half-slip to expose the suspender belt and panties. Inez groaned with scarcely-contained desire when she saw more of Cordelia's body and Nigel increased her arousal by playing roughly with her huge nipples, making them stick out provocatively.

To her surprise, Cordelia found that the attraction between her and Inez was mutual. The sight of the other woman's magnificent full breasts and outsize nipples was tantalizing her, making her wonder what it would be like to lick and suck at another woman's breasts and even her pussy. She knew she couldn't hope to match the excellent cunnilingus performance that Inez had put on for her when they were on stage together but, much to her surprise, for the first time she felt tempted to try.

A rush of hot adrenalin surged through her veins at the thought, and she found herself hoping that that was what Nigel had in mind. The lesbian videos she'd been watching lately had given her quite a few hints and tips as to how to set about it and there was no doubt that she was curious: curious to taste another woman's juices, to inspect her pussy at close quarters, to know how it felt to have her come beneath her tongue.

After taking off her high-heeled shoes, Cordelia lay down on the carpet and made a show of kicking her legs in the air. Then she took off her stockings, rolling them down slowly to display her well-shaped legs. She unhooked the suspender belt and tossed it aside, then began to writhe sexily on the carpet in time to the music, turning herself on more and more as she did so. She rolled over and rubbed her tingling mound against the floor, increasing the friction on her nipples and clitoris through the silk of the underwear. Faster and faster she moved in an orgy of self-frottage that had her breathless and gagging for it before long.

Inez could hardly restrain herself either. She was moaning in protest as Nigel held her firmly in place on the sofa, and when Cordelia managed to get a glimpse of her audience she saw that the pair of them were straining at the leash. The bulge in her boss's trousers was very obvious and Inez was encouraging his erection by squeezing it rhythmically with her left hand. Cordelia had a sudden vision of animals being kept in adjacent cages in the zoo while they were on heat, all straining to get at each other.

Slowly she got to her knees and began to slip the bra-straps down from her shoulders. She couldn't wait to remove the garment and get at her nipples, which were tormenting her with their longing to be stimulated more directly. Inez greeted the final revelation of her bosom with an 'Oh God! Those lovely tits!' and Cordelia knew she couldn't wait to get her hands on them too. Well, she would make her wait!

Slyly, Cordelia began to caress her own breasts, breathing a huge sigh of relief as she was able to pinch her aching nipples at last and give them the attention they craved. There was something extra-satisfying about stimulating herself in front of others, the mutual teasing and the building-up of their expectations being very titillating indeed. Her earlier shyness about performing in front of an audience had quite gone, and now she revelled in it. She squeezed her breasts together, stroked them all round, flicked and pinched her nipples, then lifted her tits up, one by one, to her mouth so that she could give them an experimental licking. And all the time she could see Inez becoming more and more frustrated at not being able to touch her.

At last she turned her attention to the final garment, putting her fingers down into the briefs and feeling her hotly throbbing pussy beneath the soft downy mound. She was wet, so wet! The gusset must be soaked with her musk. Pulling down the scrap of emerald silk she finally stood up and took it off altogether, then threw the smelly knickers directly at Inez who at once buried her face in them, breathing in the animal odours of a female on heat with evident relish.

'Spread your legs!' Nigel commanded her, abruptly. 'Let's see how turned on you are!'

Cordelia sat with her thighs as wide apart as they would go, exposing her pussy by drawing back her labia with her fingers. The temptation to do more was just too great, and soon she was working her clitoris rapidly with her fingertip, groaning with relief as the throbbing intensified to a warm steady buzz that she knew would soon end in a climax.

'Stop her!' she heard Inez exclaim, suddenly. 'She's *my* present. *I* want that pussy!'

'Go on, then.'

When Nigel released her, Inez came at Cordelia like a bat out of hell, kneeling down and letting her naked breasts flop onto the carpet in her eagerness to get her tongue into those well-oiled grooves. In the throes of extreme arousal, Cordelia didn't care how she got off right then and she uttered a huge sigh of relief as the expert tongue began its work, taking over where her finger had left off. She was dimly aware that Nigel was right behind his mistress, getting ready to plunge into her with his outsize cock while she performed cunnilingus, and the thought of all three of them climaxing together gave Cordelia such a buzz that it tipped her over the edge into a mind-blasting climax.

'Oh God, bloody hell!' she cried, as she bucked and rolled her way through the tide of gut-wrenching spasms like a surfer riding the crest of a wave. Something came right inside her – it felt like a fistful of fingers – prolonging her pleasure until it was almost agonizing, her stomach weak from the violence of the contractions.

Inez was face down on the carpet now as Nigel continued to slam into her from the rear, making her shudder and groan as her own orgasm approached. The pair came simultaneously, then Nigel collapsed onto her and rolled off so that, for a while, the trio lay prostrate on the deep, comforting carpet while their bodily functions slowly returned to normal.

'God, what a birthday!' Inez murmured, after a quiet five minutes or so, raising herself to a sitting position. She patted Cordelia's damp mound affectionately.

'You ain't seen nothin' yet!' Nigel promised her, dryly. 'Let's have more champagne. I'm sure there's more life in us still.'

While he refilled the glasses, Inez dragged Cordelia to her feet and took her over to the sofa. She lost no time in resuming foreplay, caressing her breasts with soft, tantalizing fingers until Cordelia felt her body hotting up and her insides starting to twitch impatiently again. But she didn't dare make any overtures to the woman in return.

Then Nigel appeared and handed them more champagne. 'Why don't you take that dress right off, darling?' he told Inez. 'It's getting creased, and I want to take you to dinner in it later.'

'Good idea!' she smiled, rising and disappearing into her bedroom where she could be heard removing a hanger from her wardrobe.

'Did you enjoy that girly stuff?' Nigel asked Cordelia, while they were temporarily alone.

She threw him a nervous smile. 'Of course. Couldn't you tell?'

'Mm. But we mustn't forget whose birthday it is, must we? Don't you think you should return the compliment?'

It was what Cordelia had been half-hoping for, but now that it was being put to her so bluntly she had misgivings. Inez had just given her a master class (or should that be 'mistress class'?) in lesbian sex, but she still doubted her abilities to satisfy the Spanish woman as thoroughly.

When Inez reappeared she was totally nude and Cordelia couldn't help staring at her voluptuous body, amazed to see the smooth, hairless vulva with its dark slit between the bulging, tumid lips. The blatant nakedness was very exciting, making the prospect of giving it a good licking even more inviting. She even found herself salivating at the thought of it.

Now only Nigel was wearing clothes. His tie was draped

around the open neck of his shirt and his cock jutted beneath, but he still had his socks on. The presence of a semi-undressed man seemed to increase the eroticism somehow, reminding Cordelia of that famous picture by Manet of two fully-clothed men picnicking with a naked woman.

Nigel soon took control of the proceedings. 'Sit down on the sofa, Inez, so Cordelia can get her head between your legs. It's time we acted out your favourite fantasy, don't you think?'

Inez's black eyes glowed like hot coals as her red mouth curved into a knowing smile. She didn't say a word but lay back languidly on the sofa, letting her great thighs flop open to display the wet interior of her vulva. Cordelia was surprised to see the size of her clitoris, which was rearing assertively from between the inner lips. It was bigger than hers and she felt a small pang of envy. But then, she reflected, amused, that if size was not supposed to matter to a man, then the same must be true of women.

'On your knees, slave!' Nigel said in his slave-master voice. Cordelia, recognizing the change of tone, slipped instantly into obedience. 'Now put your hands behind your back.'

He'd found a cord from somewhere and was binding her wrists, immobilizing her arms. Inez gave a knowing chuckle, making it plain that she knew the script. 'Now lick and suck those gorgeous nipples!' Nigel commanded her. 'I want to see you using those lips and tongue to good effect. I want to see her squirming on the sofa, creaming herself, do you hear?'

Cordelia nodded, the throb of new excitement growing in her pussy. The very act of doing what she was told was exciting, but as she neared the round, enticing globes of Inez's bosom she could feel her heartbeat clamouring in her ears, its rhythm echoed by the throbbing beat of her aroused clitoris. Carefully, to avoid toppling over, she edged her way on her knees, positioning herself between the outspread thighs until she could get her mouth near enough to the straining breasts to give the hungry nipples what they wanted.

As she moved in to lick at them with her tongue, Inez put her hands around her own breasts, making her gasp at the unexpected stimulus. She heard the woman crooning softly as she gently caressed her, and when Cordelia finally got to take one of her tumid nipples between her lips she heard a crescendo of approval coming from her lips, muttered phrases in Spanish that she was unable to decipher.

The mutual pleasuring of their breasts continued for quite a while until Cordelia felt herself growing weak with lust and wanted more. She could tell that Inez was in the same state, her thighs squeezing and tightening around her waist until it was quite painful. Without her hands to help her Cordelia was entirely reliant on her mouth to arouse the woman and she knew that soon she would be required to perform the same way down below. Still surprised at the ease with which she had taken to lesbian sex, she found she couldn't wait to taste that smooth, shaven pussy!

But then she heard a kind of growl coming from Nigel just behind, and something made the hairs prickle on the back of her neck. Her apprehension was justified when she heard her boss bark, 'Put more into it, slave! You're not giving it your best shot. Lick faster! Suck harder! Make her come just by using your mouth on her tits, or I'll give you what for!'

Inez was moaning out her frustration now and Cordelia was trying her best, but she knew it was a tall order to expect her to bring the woman to orgasm through stimulation of her breasts alone. She'd heard it was possible for some women to come that way but, although Inez was well turned on, the thought of keeping it up with her mouth for another hour or so was very daunting.

'Are you coming, my dear?' she heard Nigel ask as he sidled up to Inez on the sofa.

'Not yet.'

'Shall I motivate the slave to work harder for your pleasure?'

'Oh, yes!'

Inez was staring down at her with dark, malicious eyes and Cordelia realized that all her earlier pleasantness had been just a front. The bitch was determined to get her fun at Cordelia's expense and Nigel was in on the plot. Fearing the worst, she reapplied herself to sucking at Inez's huge red nipple in a desperate attempt to bring her to a climax before she was made to suffer.

But the woman seemed to be deliberately holding back. She was pinching Cordelia's nipples quite cruelly now and, as if that wasn't bad enough, Nigel began slapping her on the backside, exhorting her to 'make more of an effort' at the same time. Frantically she moved from one nipple to the other, licking and sucking by turns, but soon Inez wanted more direct stimulation. 'Down, down!' she gasped. 'Lower, lower!'

Cordelia shifted her knees back and, with her bottom stuck still further into the air – a perfect target for Nigel's punitive slaps – lowered her face to the open, musky vulva. The scent was a strange mixture of sweet and sour, but she didn't have the time or the inclination to analyse it. Nosing her way in through the swollen folds of Inez's labia she found the bulging bud of her clitoris without difficulty and began to press her wet tongue against it to cries of ecstasy from above.

Another stinging blow from the palm of Nigel's hand caught her unawares and jolted her head so that her bared teeth almost bit into the sensitive flesh. Inez yelped.

'Clumsy creature!' Nigel scolded, slapping her again. This time she was careful to keep her mouth soft and her tongue active. Inez settled back into it, her hands on her own tits now, fingering the nipples rapidly, moaning and writhing around so actively that Cordelia had trouble keeping her tongue on target.

She could feel Nigel spreading the cheeks of her bottom out now, and she wondered with some trepidation what he had in mind. 'Slut!' he murmured in her ear and she felt his cock rear against her thighs, exciting her unbearably. 'Cunt licker! Lezzy!'

The insulting, forbidden words had the effect of making her even more hot for whatever he intended to do to her. She felt him pinch her buttocks and then probe into her pussy with a greasy finger, opening her up and going some way further towards gratifying her urge for sensual experience. He pushed something hard into her – it felt like a dildo – and she squeezed her vaginal muscles in a fit of hungry lust, eager for him to fill her up and satisfy the gross appetite she was developing as a result of having to perform cunnilingus on another woman.

Putting out her tongue as far as it would go she reached right into Inez's gaping pussy and waggled the tip around, producing more cries of ecstasy. From then on she alternated her attention between the stiff, demanding clitoris and the streaming, open cunt. She began to develop more of a technique, using her whole tongue to lave over the hot wet tissues that surrounded the entrance to Inez's pussy, or using just the tip to penetrate right inside. The end of her tongue was useful for stroking the shaft of her clit, too, and she could also take it between her lips and roll it around, which Inez seemed to appreciate. She found she could suck at her whole vulva, as if it were a big juicy orange, or purse her lips and suck very gently and precisely at the stiff clitoris, breathing cool air over it – which Inez also seemed to like.

Her satisfaction in making a good job of it increased as she realized that there was a lot more to this cunnilingus business than she had at first imagined. It was also giving her ideas about how she might train Ralph to pleasure her more effectively. Soon the thought that she might give him his first lesson that night, when she got home, was spurring her on.

So engrossed was she in giving Inez pleasure that she was quite unprepared when Nigel began to turn push a dildo into her pussy and tickle around her anus at the same time, causing her to cry out involuntarily as the keen sensations caught her unawares.

'I'm gonna teach you a lesson, you fucking lez!' she heard him growl in her ear. 'I'm going to show you what a real man can do to a woman.'

'That's right!' Inez groaned her assent, but Cordelia was unable to tell whether she was addressing her or Nigel. She felt his huge cock entering between her thighs from behind and trembled as the glans engaged in her vagina, while he continued to tantalize her arse with his fingernails, making her ring tingle and itch with desire for more gratification. It was the most incredible feeling.

Now she had two people exhorting her. Nigel continued to talk dirty to her while she tried to keep up the pace with Inez who was swearing in Spanish, rubbing and squeezing her own breasts with a fierce concentration that suggested she was on the final ascent to orgasm. Cordelia realized she wasn't far off herself. Nigel had a hold on her tits too, squeezing them by turns with one big hand while his thumb rubbed over the turgid nipples. His cock was going in and out very slowly while he stimulated the sensitive skin around her nether opening. She felt so near to coming, and yet she was held in suspense by Nigel's infuriatingly slow progress.

It occurred to her that he was probably slowing her down deliberately, making sure that Inez came first. With that in mind she redoubled her efforts with her lips and tongue, desperate to get the woman off so that he would let her come too. Inez was keeping up a continual low moaning now and bucking her hips so that she was doing most of the work. All Cordelia had to do was make sure that she kept her tongue in direct contact with the swollen, throbbing clitoris. It was so hard to concentrate, though, with her own rear end being so thoroughly serviced, back and front, seducing her attention away from her task.

At last Inez gave a piercing cry and jerked her head back, uttering a stream of oaths as the climax hit her with extreme force. Almost before Cordelia realized what was happening Nigel increased the pace, and it took only a few rapid thrusts to get her into the same state. She fell forward with her face in the Spanish woman's lap, aware only of the ecstatic pulsations of her own flesh, and dimly heard Nigel repeating 'Dirty fucking lesbian!' as he shot into her.

For a while they lay in a stifling heap until Cordelia found herself struggling for breath and raised her head. She wriggled painfully, aware that her hands were still tied behind her back and she was quite unable to get to her feet. Inez caught her by the hair and, none too gently, lifted her face onto the cushion beside her, then got up off the sofa. Cordelia hoped she might have the decency to untie her but the Spanish woman stalked straight into the bathroom and shut the door. The noise of the shower could be heard soon after.

Cordelia moaned, trying to attract Nigel's attention, and eventually felt him levering himself off her and staggering to his feet. He noticed her bonds and untied them, helping her up. 'Time for you to go, I think,' he told her. 'Get your clothes on quick. I want you out of here by the time Inez has finished her shower.'

She felt resentment welling up in her. Didn't she deserve any thanks for giving up some of her free time to make Inez's birthday more of a special occasion? But Nigel was still in slave-master mode and when she hesitated he smacked her hard on the bottom, making her jump.

'Hurry up!' he snarled, walking towards the bathroom himself.

'Okay, I know when I'm not wanted!' Cordelia muttered crossly, picking up her green dress and putting it on without any underwear. Now that the *orgy à trois* was over she felt weary and disgruntled. Presumably she would have to phone for her own taxi. She picked up the receiver and dialled a number she knew. They told her she would have a twenty-minute wait. But she felt that she had to get out of the apartment as soon as possible. Picking up her jacket and bag, she slipped back into her shoes and left as quietly as she could, hurrying to the lift with the *swoosh* of the shower still ringing in her ears.

Chapter Eleven

Ralph was in seventh heaven. Left alone to explore the secret, enticing world of his mistress he scarcely knew where to begin. Sometimes he would sneak into her bedroom during the day in order to feel her underwear or smell her perfume, but he always felt guilty and feared that she might somehow know what he had been up to.

Now, though, he had licence to explore her feminine world to the full. He decided to start with her make-up and toilet bags, opening them up and spilling their contents out onto an old silk scarf that she had given him to use as a polishing cloth. He carefully sorted the objects into piles: seven lipsticks in various shades, four tubs of dusting powder, each with its own puff that needed washing, three deodorant sprays, two hair sprays . . . the scarf soon looked as if it were being prepared for some elaborate 'Kim's Game'.

When he had been a small boy Ralph had done just this with his mother's things, but he had never told Cordelia. Had she somehow looked into his heart, discerned the secrets of his soul? Sometimes he thought she had a sixth sense for what would turn him on. He opened a powder compact and raised it to his nostrils, instinctively closing his eyes as he took a long sniff. His nose would be put to good use tonight, as well as his other faculties.

After he had indulged himself for a while in looking and smelling he remembered what he had to do. The mascara brushes had to be cleaned and the lipsticks smoothed into nice points. He took the tiny brushes into the bathroom with the powder puffs and set to work as best he could, trying not to make too much of a mess. Then he put them over the radiator to dry and went back with a damp cloth to clean all the plastic casings of the cosmetics, trying to make them look as good as new. He hummed softly as he worked, becoming again the little boy who liked to clean the brass.

When he had done as much as he could to renovate the contents of Cordelia's make-up bag he turned to her jewellery. Taking the silver cloth he put a shine on all her bangles and bracelets, then went over the gold and jewelled items with a damp cloth. He laid them carefully in their velvet-lined boxes, then put them back in the bottom drawer of her dressing table, where they belonged.

As the evening progressed his sense of satisfaction deepened and he felt himself drifting into a kind of blissful trance. The house was so peaceful and quiet that the little tasks he found for himself took on something of the nature of a sacred trust. Ralph hadn't been quite so happy lately. Something was brooding in Cordelia, making her restless and unfairly sharp with him at times, and he was terribly afraid it might be going to affect him in some way. He didn't want anything to change: he was perfectly happy as he was, devoted to his mistress body and soul.

The warm thrill he was feeling deepened as he approached her underwear drawer and pulled it open to display the see-through plastic envelopes, each with a matching set of undies inside. One by one he took them out, opening them up and taking out the silky panties, the lacy bras, the frilly girdles, teddies, half-slips. Ralph examined them carefully, putting his hands into the cups and gussets to plump them out and make sure there were no tiny tears or caught stitches. One or two garments needed mending but on the whole they were in good condition. He set aside a black bra, a red satin slip and a pair of turquoise briefs for doing later.

The dirty-linen basket was kept on the landing. Ralph turned it out and gathered up armfuls of her discarded clothes, burying his face in the aroma, *her* aroma. He rubbed the soiled panties all over his face, revelling in their stale, slightly acidic scent, then sniffed the sides of her bras to smell the potent mix of underarm sweat and deodorant that reminded him of the many occasions when she'd raised her hand to him at the beginning of his training – days he was now starting to look back on with an acute sense of nostalgia.

It had been wonderful to discover gradually what pleased and displeased his mistress, to grow accustomed to every nuance of her expression, every tone of her voice so that he was able to serve her more devotedly. If only he could go through it all again! But now they understood each other so well, and the occasions when she needed to actually reprimand, let alone punish him were rare.

Sometimes he found himself thinking traitorous thoughts. Sometimes he longed to start all over again with a new mistress, just to regain that sense of danger, of living on a precipice, that he'd all but lost. It was gratifying to know that he could satisfy his mistress in so many different ways, but his life – no, *their* life – was in danger of becoming boring and predictable.

Was that why she had seemed distant with him lately, snappy one minute and over-indulgent the next? She had sometimes fallen short of the high standards he expected of her and that meant he couldn't give of *his* best, either. They had got into a cosy rut where it took great ingenuity to find ways of delivering that special excitement that had once been so easy to attain. Like addicts habituated to their drug, he and his mistress had simply become used to each other, and the highs and lows had evened out into what was becoming more and more like daily monotony.

'Rubbish!' Ralph suddenly scolded himself out loud. He was spoiling this delicious treat she'd laid on for him by his self-pitying maundering. Angry with himself, he picked up all the underwear that needed washing and took it into the bathroom where he proceeded to hand wash the garments in the basin with loving care, swirling the lacy pants in the water as if he were washing his mistress's soft hair, and squeezing the delicate bras as gently as he might squeeze her lovely breasts.

Cordelia got out of the taxi and paid the fare, then began walking slowly towards her front gate. It was scarcely eleven, still time for some fun and games before bed, and she was pretty sure Ralph would be in the mood after rummaging in her underwear drawer all evening. Lost in her plans, and filled with pleasurable anticipation, she failed to notice the figure lurking in the shadow of next door's hawthorn tree until it was too late.

'Cordelia!'

The urbane Gallic tones startled her but, even as she turned round to verify the source, she knew perfectly well who it was. 'Lucien! What the hell are you doing here?'

It was a mistake to let Karen bring a stranger to the party, she thought wildly. *Now he knows where I live he can lie in wait for me whenever I go out. He can stalk me . . .*

'I wanted to know if you liked the underwear I gave you.' She hadn't bothered to fasten her jacket and her braless breasts were visibly outlined beneath the clingy green fabric, the nipples aroused by the cool night air. His grin turned awry. 'Evidently you aren't wearing it tonight.'

'I shall never wear it!' she said venomously. 'It was presumptuous of you to buy it for me, but you've only wasted your money. Now go away and leave me alone!'

His expression seemed genuinely sad. 'That's a pity. I've

dreamed of seeing you in it, of kissing your nipples through the peepholes.'

'Dream on!' she said scornfully, turning towards her front gate.

He caught her arm and held her back. She tried to shrug him off but he drew her to him and planted a swift, totally unexpected kiss on her open mouth. Waves of heady adrenalin coursed through her, making her veins sing, but she fought the euphoria for all she was worth.

'You *will* come to me!' he told her vehemently, seeming to shrink back into the shadows again. 'But I can bide my time. As long as it takes, Cordelia.' He started to walk backwards looking like some movie hero of the Forties in his buff raincoat, wagging his finger at her. 'As long as it takes!'

'Get a life!' she called after him. Then, after opening the gate, she moved swiftly through it and up the path to her front door.

Afraid that he might come and hammer on it, causing a commotion, she got inside as quickly as she could. Then, still trembling with the shock of seeing Lucien, she went upstairs where Ralph was just laying out towels in the airing cupboard to spread her washed undies on. It was a relief to find him so calm and pleased to see her, but she didn't want to alarm him so she vowed to say nothing about the lurker outside.

'Have you had a nice evening?' she asked Ralph, pleasantly.

'Yes, thank you, madam. And you?'

'Very satisfying, thank you.'

She saw the slight waver in his expression, the hint of jealousy in his eyes and had to suppress an urge to be casually cruel. 'Have you finished in the bathroom?'

'Yes, madam. Do you wish to take a bath?'

She heard the eagerness in his voice and knew he wanted

to run it for her, help to wash her. Well, why not? It might put her in the mood for more, later. She wasn't sure whether she was up to retraining him in the fine art of cunnilingus tonight, but she wasn't going to dismiss it from the agenda entirely.

Soon she was wallowing in warm contentment, with Ralph on hand to scrub her back and do her bidding. But thoughts of Lucien continued to taunt her, hovering on the edge of her consciousness like the memory of a bad dream. What made it worse was that she was terribly tempted to give in to him. It had been so long since she'd had straight sex with another man – always assuming that 'straight sex' was what the Frenchman wanted from her.

Had he somehow guessed what kind of sexual world she inhabited? Was that what had drawn him to her? There were so many unanswered questions: the safest course would be to accept that she would never know, to rebuff him until he tired of the game. Yet Cordelia had never been one to resist a challenge. She was intrigued by what lay behind that knowing, penetrating gaze and something in her would not rest until she had at least tried to solve the mystery.

But she owed a debt of loyalty to Ralph, at least. Nigel she wasn't so sure about. By introducing his imperious mistress into the proceedings she felt he had somehow broken faith with her and she was annoyed. Perhaps she should look for another job.

'I'm thinking of looking for another job,' she said aloud.

Ralph faltered only slightly in his soaping of her arms. 'Yes, madam?'

'Somewhere nearer home, perhaps.' She gave him a glittering smile. 'So I can spend more time with you.'

His eyes lit up instantly. *How easy he is to please*, she thought, ashamed of the contempt she felt. But it was true: Ralph offered her no challenges any more.

That didn't mean she couldn't offer him one, though. When he'd finished washing her she stepped out into a warm, fluffy towel and then went through to the bedroom where she lay down for her massage. The long, slow process of arousal was always pleasant but tonight she was still fired up from her earlier encounter with Nigel and Inez, not to mention the sudden appearance of Lucien, so she reached a state of sensual tension far earlier.

Ralph's delicate massaging of her breasts and nipples was driving her into a frenzy. She could feel all her bodily functions gearing her up towards orgasm: the swelling of her labia, the moistening of her cleft, the steady throbbing of her clitoris as it thrust out firmly from beneath its little nook. She reached up and clutched at Ralph's golden, tousled hair.

'I want to lick me, down there. But you must do it exactly as I tell you.'

'Yes, madam.'

His slow ways were driving her mad, but she could see the smouldering desire in his eyes, the desire to please, and knew that he would do his best. His cheek brushed her belly as he moved down towards the hothouse of her sex, sending little anticipatory shivers right through her. At last he was parting her soft labia with his fingers, preparing to do whatever she wanted. Taking a deep breath, Cordelia began to give her orders. She had given him some hints and tips before, but never in such detail.

'Lick all along the outside of my pussy very lightly . . . ooh, yes! Then flick the tip of your tongue over my clit, back and forth . . . mm! Just keep doing that for a bit, lick and flick, lick and . . . Oh!'

Every so often she asked him to spread his tongue right over her fevered labia and waggle his head slightly so that every part of her vulva came into contact with the soft, wet coolness. Then she wanted him to venture inside her with his tongue-tip, lapping like a cat at her flowing juices. She taught him how to take the stiff bud of her clitoris between his lips and roll it, sucking at it all the time, making it tingle and throb. She had him thrust his tongue right into her as far as it would go, his lips twitching over her external organs, then she made him simulate the action of a cock by pushing his tongue in and out as rapidly as he could.

Whenever the pace got too hot she slowed him down and got him to make tiny, excruciatingly sensual movements of his lips and tongue to tease and torment her. That way she could make the blissful experience last far longer. Heedless of Ralph's tired tongue and aching jaws she made him service her without mercy and he put on a virtuoso performance of cunnilingus under her command.

Eventually, though, Cordelia knew she must come. She asked him to concentrate entirely on the swollen bud of pure sensation that was her clitoris, to use his tongue on it exclusively while his forefinger dabbled in the entrance to her cunt. The suspense was almost unbearable, her throbbing flesh aching for its consummation. When at last she felt the unstoppable rise towards orgasm begin she moaned, 'Stick it in! Stick your finger in!'

The minute he did so all her nerves exploded in a shattering series of spasms that had her writhing in ecstasy. She felt the fresh juice gush from her and was aware of Ralph taking it into his mouth, making her writhe and moan even louder with the suction.

It took a long while to come down again, and for some time she lay inert with her flesh pulsating, still glowing with warmth from the energy she had expended. Then she began to feel shivery and crawled beneath the duvet, alerting Ralph to the fact that it was gone midnight. After he'd tucked her up in bed, Ralph discreetly left the room. She lay for a while in a restless state, unable to drift into sleep as easily as she usually did after sex.

Although her body was thoroughly satiated her soul felt dissatisfied and she knew it was because Lucien had jumped out of the shadows at her earlier, upsetting her equilibrium. What would she do if she ran into him again? There was every chance she would. She had a feeling that he would not give up his pursuit of her lightly.

Perhaps the only thing that would satisfy him would be a one-night stand. Was that the answer? The thought of it sent tingling thrills right through her. One night with Lucien could do no harm, surely? She would make it a condition that he must leave her alone after that. Then Ralph would not get hurt and she wouldn't become involved. Sex, pure sex, was all he was after and she would give him a night to remember!

But I might have put him off tonight, she thought, surprised by the feeling of regret this produced in her. Now she was relishing the thought of one night of unfettered passion with a Frenchman. How complicated everything was becoming. For months her life had been coasting along quite happily but now she was thinking of finding a new job and contemplating having a fling with a new man. As sleep overtook her Cordelia was wondering what it would be like to have an ordinary office job and a normal relationship with her boss. It might be quite nice, for a change!

By the following Monday Cordelia was determined to start looking for a new post. She'd been with Nigel long enough, after all. The work was tedious and far below her capabilities, the only compensation being the extraordinary relationship that she had built up with her boss. He could hardly blame her for wanting to move on.

Even so, she thought better of telling him before she had secured another position, and after a dull day when he seemed to have run out of ideas for disciplining her, merely keeping her chained to her desk from nine to five, she was more convinced than ever that it was time for a change. Instead of going home, she bought a newspaper from a stand on a street corner and entered a nearby wine bar, intending to peruse the job pages.

Engrossed in the many ads for secretaries, both temporary and permanent, Cordelia took no notice of the man who sidled onto the tall stool next to her at the bar. When she picked up her glass of white wine and took a sip, however, she nearly spilled the lot down her front.

'Lucien! What the . . . ?'

'. . . devil am I doing here?' He finished her sentence with a wink. 'I followed you, my dear, of course. Did you think I'd give up that easily? I know where you work and where you live. It's not too difficult to catch you somewhere in between. Looking for a new job?'

Cordelia scarcely had time to draw breath. Her heart was on a wild trajectory of its own and she felt light-headed, a condition which had little to do with the one sip of alcohol she'd consumed. Remembering what she had contemplated last night she felt a flush rise in her cheeks. Now that the man was here in the flesh it was impossible to think rationally. A one-night stand: what on earth had made her think he would be content with that? From the way his eyes were devouring her body there was no way he'd be satisfied with a single encounter.

'I . . . I just thought I'd take a look at the jobs ads.'

'If you're serious, I know of a plum job going at an ad agency. Interested?'

She hesitated. The advertising world had always intrigued her, and once she'd fancied trying her hand as a copywriter. This could be the start of a whole new career. But were there strings attached?

Lucien interpreted her hesitation correctly. 'Don't worry, the firm is nothing to do with me. A friend of mine is leaving, that's all, and they haven't advertised her job yet. If you wrote pretending it was on the off chance you might be lucky.'

'This friend of yours . . .'

'A very close friend, called Kristina. And, because you're wondering, we are just good friends. She's a lesbian. Interested?'

His question shocked her, being so ambivalent. Could he possibly know about her recent session with Inez? She told herself there was no way he could possibly know about that. And yet she had this uncomfortable feeling that he knew absolutely everything about her, that he could read her soul.

'I might be,' she said, slowly. 'Advertising sounds fun. What does the job entail?'

'Mainly PA work, I believe. But you could meet Kristina and talk to her about it. I'll give her a ring now, if you like.'

Cordelia had the feeling that she was stuck on a fast-moving escalator that was taking her up to floor six when she only wanted floor three, but she nodded anyway. Hadn't she been wanting a change? The reckless part of her was prepared to go with the flow, despite her natural caution.

Lucien left her and went over to the public phone to make the call. While Cordelia finished her wine she found herself growing more and more elated. But was it just the idea of a new job that was exciting her or the thought of spending more time with Lucien, time that might well stretch to the rest of the night?

When he returned she slipped off her stool and he took her arm, guiding her through the growing crowd of after-work drinkers. 'We'll go in my car,' he said, his tone decisive. 'It's not far from here.'

She liked the way he took control of her, made all the decisions. Not like Nigel, who often made her do what she didn't want to do just to humiliate her, but more like a man who knows his own mind and assumes that women like men to take the lead. A sense of inevitability came over her as she followed him out of the wine bar and down the street to where his BMW was parked. The sleek silver lines of the automobile impressed her as her eyes took in the sexy curves of its body, and the soft leather upholstery caressed her behind as she slid in through the door.

'Nice car,' she murmured, as he took the wheel with his slender, confident hands.

'No point in not having the best.' He paused, waiting for her to turn and look at him before continuing, 'And that goes for sex, too. We only live once, let's have the best life we can.'

His philosophy seemed sound and his words were seductive, almost as seductive as the citrus scent of his *Cerruti* cologne which was making her feel very alert and energetic, as if she had the stamina for a long session of lovemaking. As the car moved smoothly into the traffic flow, she reflected that if Lucien initiated the proceedings she probably would be able to keep it up all night.

Cordelia glanced at his handsome profile and breathed in his essence. Already she felt she knew him intimately and her longing for him was gnawing at her womb, emphasizing the hollow emptiness she felt inside, a void that was clamouring to be filled. They turned off the main road and passed down a series of leafy side streets until he drew up outside a suburban house, not unlike the one Cordelia herself inhabited.

'You'll like Kristina,' he stated, reaching over to open her door from the inside. His forearm brushed her breasts, stimulating the nipples into instant, tingling life.

Cordelia followed him up to the house, from which low music was issuing. A woman dressed in a silver jumpsuit opened the door. She had curly blonde hair and bright blue eyes that seemed to be in a state of continuous amusement.

Lucien was right: she did like her. Except she wasn't the woman Cordelia thought she was.

'Come in, come in, the more the merrier!' she trilled, with just the trace of a Scandinavian accent. 'I'm Tasmin, by the way.'

Lucien introduced Cordelia and then Tasmin led the way down the hall, dancing almost, into the back room where a serious-looking brunette with generous clouds of hair and a huge bosom was sipping wine and swaying to rock music, her eyes closed in dreamy reverie. When they entered she opened them slowly, and soon a pair of tawny, leonine eyes were surveying Cordelia with frankly sexual interest.

Lucien said, 'Kristina, this is my new friend Cordelia. The one I told you about.'

Immediately Cordelia bristled, wondering what he'd been saying behind her back. But whatever it was Kristina was not put off. She advanced with a cool smile, the predatory eyes never leaving Cordelia's face as she offered her hand. 'Hi. Take a pew. Have some wine.'

She gestured towards a low table where there was a bottle of white wine in an ice-jacket and several glasses. Cordelia sat down in the only armchair. The room was sparsely furnished, with the air of a student dwelling, quite different from what she'd expected. She took the glass that Lucien poured for her

'I told Cordelia you were leaving and she's interested in your job,' he said bluntly.

Kristina stopped dancing and put her arm around Tasmin in an oddly self-conscious gesture, as if posing for a photograph. She made an ugly face. 'You don't want to work in that madhouse.'

'Really?' Cordelia smiled. 'You think it's any worse than the one I work in at the moment?'

'I wouldn't know. But if you don't mind crazy pressure and

a bunch of lunatics all giving you contradictory instructions then you're welcome!'

Cordelia shrugged. 'Sounds worth a try.'

'You see?' Lucien's grin passed from one to the other. 'I told you she was game for anything.'

Cordelia began to feel uncomfortable. The other three seemed to have a secret understanding and she was on the outside, looking in. Were they planning some kind of four-some for the evening? She wouldn't put anything past Lucien.

Kristina dropped her arm from her friend's shoulder and took her hand. Again they looked oddly posed, standing there hand in hand. 'Well,' she began, 'if you really want the job I'll put in a word with my super and he'll call you for interview. Better give me your home phone number. I presume you haven't told your present boss yet?'

'Oh no!'

'Quite. Best to leave your options open, I always say.' She gave Tasmin a brief smile, then kissed her full on the lips for several seconds.

Cordelia felt uncomfortable and turned away, only to meet Lucien's amused gaze. His darkly handsome face was watching her intently, with an expression of calm curiosity. She had the weird feeling she was being put to the test in some way.

'Tell her a bit more about your work, Kristina,' he said, his tone faintly reproving. 'After all, that's what she's come for.'

'Really? I thought . . . oh well, never mind. Come on, Cordelia. It's best if I show you. My work is upstairs.'

Awkward as she felt going upstairs with the voluptuous brunette, Cordelia was relieved to be out of Lucien's presence for a while. She followed Kristina's substantial rump up the stairs and into the room at the front of the house which she soon realized had been converted into a workroom. A desk with a businesslike lamp stood in one corner and there was a computer workstation in the other. Piles of books, disks, files and papers were everywhere. It looked chaotic, but on closer inspection it was obvious that everything was carefully arranged in some kind of order.

'We are a medium-sized agency,' Kristina began, then gave a sigh. 'Listen to me, talk about corporate woman! *They* are a medium-sized agency. Doing pretty well, as a matter of fact. I'm just a glorified dogsbody doing general office work most of the time, but I do get to do some layouts and sometimes a bit of editing. This is one of mine.' She showed her a stylish mock-up of an advert for a sports watch. 'That went in *GQ*.'

'Hm. Impressive!'

Kristina was regarding Cordelia strangely with those feline eyes, igniting a trail of fire down her spine. In a voice that was little more than a husky whisper she asked, 'Do you swing both ways?'

The urbane question, with its presumption that she knew the score, shocked her. Cordelia realized that, locked in her cosy world of sub-dom with Nigel and Ralph, she was not nearly so sexually sophisticated as she liked to think. It was only recently that she'd had her first lesbian experience, and now this virtual stranger was asking her an intimate question about her sexual preferences that she simply didn't know how to answer.

'Isn't that a bit . . . er . . . personal?' she faltered.

Kristina's full mouth curved prettily into a smile. She was gorgeous when her habitual sullen expression lifted, Cordelia decided. But dangerous. Definitely dangerous!

'I mean, I hardly know you,' Cordelia added, timidly.

There was only a second or two of dawning realization and by then it was too late. Cordelia found herself being pulled strongly into Kristina's embrace and her mouth was instantly covered with those luscious, taunting lips. She let loose a little gasp of surprise but made no attempt to pull away. Instead she felt her whole body relax into the kiss, milking it for as much as it was worth. Their tongues locked and Cordelia felt her guts melt with lust, wanting this strangely alluring female and yet afraid of what the consequences might be.

Just as suddenly she found herself thrust back again, standing dazed while Kristina turned back to her desk as if nothing significant had happened. 'Don't worry, I know you're hung up on Lucien right now. But when you're tired of him, I'll still be around. Now how about this? I did this list of clients last week. You can see exactly who we . . . there I go again! Who *Parton and Davis* work for, I should say. Take a look!'

The transition from personal to business had taken place seamlessly, leaving Cordelia gaping in bewilderment. The presumption that she was 'hung up' (whatever that meant) on Lucien annoyed her, but it seemed too late to protest so she let it pass. The feeling of being taken for granted deepened when Kristina put her arm around Cordelia as she bent over the desk to look at the list of clients, and at that moment Lucien entered.

'Hands off, Kristina!' he smiled, good-naturedly. 'If you've finished your business I'll take her away now. I want her all to myself – for tonight, at least.'

Cordelia swung round, pushing Kristina away as she did so. Indignation was blazing in her as she approached Lucien, jabbing her finger in his direction. 'Well, excuse me! Has anyone thought to find out what *I* might feel about the way you two are behaving?'

He smiled with infuriating nonchalance and held up his hands in a gesture of mock surrender. 'Don't worry, Cordelia. I just want to make sure Kristina isn't trying to mix business with pleasure, that's all. Now, will you let me take you to dinner?'

'Only if you promise to behave yourself.'

'I always behave myself. No point in trying to make anyone else behave, is there?'

Kristina giggled behind her back, infuriating Cordelia further. She tried to brush past Lucien and exit through the door, but he caught her arm and held her back with a strong grip. His mouth was very close to hers as he whispered, 'There's no point in trying to escape me, you know. If it's not tonight it will be some other night. I will have you in the end.'

'I think you're ridiculously presumptuous!' she hissed. But her wet pussy and erect nipples were telling another story, and her heart was pounding a wild denial in her ears.

'Join the club!' he smiled.

Chapter Twelve

Lucien took her to a restaurant that specialized in Thai cuisine, the most delicious Cordelia had ever tasted. By the time they left at around ten-thirty all her senses had been aroused: by the scent of fresh lemongrass, the taste of subtle spices, the tinkling notes of Oriental music, the sight of the handsome Frenchman's dark eyes undressing her all through the meal, and the light touch of his hand on her bare arm as he helped her on with her jacket.

'I don't live far from here,' he told her as they walked the few paces to his BMW.

There was no need to say more. Both of them knew that she was going to spend the night at his place. She had already phoned Ralph from the restaurant to say that she was with a friend and felt too tired to make the long journey home that night. It was the kind of white lie she'd been telling often lately to save his pride, but for once she didn't feel guilty. This night with Lucien was written in the stars, so who was she to try and avoid it?

At last she knew where he lived: a decaying mansion in Notting Hill whose exterior belied the spacious luxury within. As she entered his apartment Cordelia had the instant impression that here was a man of culture. There were books, for one thing, shelf upon shelf of them, plus a baby grand piano, several small bronze statuettes that looked extremely valuable and a print on the wall that might just have been a Matisse.

'Can I get you anything?' he asked, removing her jacket from her shoulders. 'A drink? Coffee?'

'A brandy would be nice.'

The room smelled masculine. Cigars had been smoked in it, fine wines consumed and something else – an animal aroma, leather or fur. Cordelia sank into the plush grey leather of the sofa and watched him switch on a living-flame gas fire before going to pour her drink. The sensual warmth soon reached her skin, making her feel relaxed to the point of drowsiness.

Lucien returned with two brandy glasses. He gave Cordelia hers and put his on the low coffee table in front of them. Then, to her surprise, he curled up at her feet and rested his head on her knee. It was not the kind of behaviour she would have expected from him and she was instantly suspicious but, cheap trick or not, it endeared him to her all the same.

She began to stroke the luxuriant dark hair, letting her fingers weave through the strands which caressed her silkily. He sighed and picked up his glass, taking sips from it. Cordelia stretched and yawned as a warm indolence spread through her.

'This is almost cosy!' she said, wryly. 'Look at us, like a couple of old cats by the fire.'

'Not what you expected, is it?' He turned around to grin at her. 'But don't worry, this is the calm before the storm. I'm just getting you used to me, making sure you're off your guard when I pounce.'

'I'm not a mouse. I'm not sure I want to be pounced upon.'

'What you want is immaterial, my dear. I shall have you any way I want, and you will love it, whatever I do. For example, this . . .'

Slowly he removed her right shoe and began to massage her foot, his thumbs pressing into her instep where the tensions of the day were lodged. Cordelia sighed and relaxed, letting her head loll against the sofa back. He took off her other shoe and gave her left foot the same treatment, smoothing away all the stress. His palms moved up her shins to her knees, then on up her thighs until he found her suspenders which he flicked open. Then he began to roll her stockings down until her legs were bare.

Lucien pressed his lips to her knees while he continued to massage her feet. She caressed his hair again, feeling the slow burn of desire kindling in the pit of her stomach. He certainly knew how to make her feel good. The thorough treatment he was giving to her feet was overcoming all her resistance, making her soft and pliable, affecting her whole body. Was he some kind of magician, she wondered idly, that he could get her into such a state of willing compliance just by stroking her feet?

The gentle, sensual touch of his hands had reached above her knees now but she didn't want him to stop. While his palms moved with slow insinuation up the insides of her thighs he was kissing her toes beautifully, bestowing his benediction on them, one by one. A part of her could see how he was manipulating her, lulling her with one gesture while arousing her with another, but she just didn't care. She was in a delicious, trance-like state of bliss. Like a subject under hypnosis she believed she could snap out of it in a moment if she wanted to, but the fact was that she didn't want to. She was perfectly happy for him to do whatever he liked to her.

Lucien's questing fingers found the leg of her pants and, to her surprise, went in under them. She'd thought he would take longer to get there, but now the digits were on course for her pussy like heat-seeking missiles. With a slight moan she shifted her position to allow him more access, taking in a sharp breath as her labia opened to admit him and she immediately felt a flood of warm secretions stream out of her, bathing his fingertips.

He withdrew them again slowly and, with a sly grin, put the ends of his fingers into his mouth and sucked them with relish. 'Nectar!' he murmured, moving up on his knees to take her in his arms. He kissed her tenderly, then as their mutual need took hold his kiss became searching, rapacious. Cordelia felt limp in his arms, her head reeling as she submitted to the overwhelming force of his passion. She thought of him boring into her and her insides convulsed. The urge to touch him, to feel the hard solidity of his prick was overwhelming.

But when she tried to reach his fly he caught her hand and prevented her. She was soon distracted by the way he was nuzzling at her neck, his fingers working their way up underneath her cotton-knit top to find her bra. In seconds he'd freed one nipple and was rolling it between his finger and thumb, making the other one jealous. Cordelia wriggled and moaned with longing, her breasts straining so hard she was afraid they might burst the bra. She reached behind her back and released the fastening, feeling the relief as her bosom was freed from its constriction.

Lucien gave a soft moan and dived beneath her top, pushing up her bra until her breasts were revealed. His mouth travelled eagerly from one to the other, sucking gently at her nipples and kissing the taut flesh surrounding them until they were hot and pulsating, notching up her libido and making her desire for him keen. Her curiosity about his penis deepened and she tried not to speculate about how it would feel inside her, whether it would fill her, satisfy her.

He had both hands on her tits now, squeezing and fondling them with rapt attention. Cordelia was dying to get her hands on some part of his anatomy and found she could get beneath the rear waistband of his trousers, so she contented herself with sliding her fingers down the smooth curves of his buttocks, then digging her nails in, urging him on. His lips returned to hers with ferocious hunger and, for a few seconds, their tongues duelled wildly.

Then Lucien withdrew from her and, for a moment, Cordelia was afraid he had changed his mind, that he was going to be a clit-tease. She stared up at him from the sofa, knowing her doubt was clearly visible in her eyes, and he gave a slow, almost regretful, smile.

'Are you sure you really want me, Cordelia?'

She nodded, dumbly, her senses reeling from the sudden end to their stimulation: she felt as giddy as if she'd just stepped off a roundabout. His smile widened and her eyes searched his face anxiously for signs of mockery, but found none.

'Then I think we might be more comfortable on the floor, in front of the fire.'

Relief swept through her, accompanied by such an upsurge of lust that she was knocked back onto the sofa when she tried to rise. He helped her up and tossed the sofa cushions down, covering them with a throw and some scatter cushions from another settee. Then he unbuttoned his shirt. Cordelia had a glimpse of his lightly tanned, muscled chest with his dark brown nipples stiffened into points and she reached out to stroke it. He pressed her palm to his heart. 'Hear it beating?'

'Mine too,' she smiled, provocatively. He pulled off her cotton jumper and the dangling bra then gave a deep sigh of pleasure as his hands moved freely over the heavy curves of her breasts. Cordelia's head went back in a gesture of surrender, loving the erotic caress of his fingers on her warm, naked skin, his hands brushing lightly across her erect nipples. He lifted her tits and pushed them together, plunging his face into the deep cleavage he'd created, breathing in the scent of her.

His tongue began to lick down the ravine, exciting her even more. She clutched at Lucien's hair, willing him to move lower, but his mouth returned to her nipples and sucked gently, sending powerful streams of energy down her spine and making her back arch in a long feline stretch. His hands moved slowly down her sides, his thumbs brushing the edges of her breasts, then rested at the sleek indentation of her waist for a few seconds before finding the zipper of her skirt and sliding it down.

Cordelia helped him divest her of her lower garments, but he stopped short of removing her panties and turned his attention to his own clothing. When he'd stripped off his shirt and trousers she could see the tent-pole effect that his erection made in the front of his pants. It looked very promising, but still he kept his cock under wraps. Despite the fact that they were both crazy for each other Lucien was evidently a man used to taking his time. Cordelia was faintly surprised. After the importunate way he'd pursued her she'd expected to be practically raped, but this slow foreplay was wonderful.

Now his fingers were tickling at her clitoris through the thin cloth of her knickers, feeling the hard nub of her desire for him grow even more stiff and eager for gratification. She tried to touch his prick again but he gently removed her hand as before and she had to content herself with stroking the smooth expanse of his back as he bent over her or slipping down to feel his rotund, taut buttocks. She eased a finger into his crack and felt his sphincter contract over it.

'Later,' he murmured. 'Now turn over.'

Lucien made it clear that he wanted her on her knees and elbows, with her rump stuck in the air. He pulled the panties down at the back and began to plant small kisses all over her bottom while his fingers found their way into her vulva from behind. Cordelia wriggled and moaned in delight when the other hand sneaked under her and began to play with her dangling breasts, pulling the long nipples and scratching at the areolae gently with his nails. She could feel herself opening up to him, both arse and cunt, front and back.

Although she felt vulnerable she also trusted him, and it came as a shock to realize that she didn't trust Nigel any more. She felt betrayed, but she had no such fears about Lucien. Somehow she sensed that he cared about her feelings, as well as lusted after her, and she had stopped believing that of her boss.

Now Lucien was stroking around her anus with his fingertip, something she found exquisitely titillating. She felt him doing something, reaching out for something, and soon a well-oiled finger was penetrating her there, very gradually stretching her ring so that she felt hardly any pain.

'Relax!' he whispered. 'This is going to be good.'

Cordelia rested on her elbows and let him ease his way in past the taut ring of muscle until she could feel him gently moving his finger inside her. The initial pain faded and a raw, delicious pleasure took over, familiar and unfamiliar at the same time. Gradually she lost her inhibitions and responded with enthusiasm to the heightened sensitivity of her back passage.

At the same time he began to lick her pussy from beneath, his long tongue reaching up to gather moisture from the entrance to her cunt and then going higher until she felt him anoint her yearning clitoris with her own liquid. Ready for him now, she breathed a long sigh of relief as he fumbled with his underwear and she knew that, at last, he was preparing to come inside her. She could feel herself expanding, pulsating, eagerly anticipating the moment when that solid shaft would enter the void of her longing and fill her need completely.

But she never expected him to choose her rear entrance. At first Cordelia was shocked and rather afraid. What if he injured her? As the slippery glans began to meld with the oiled skin around her anus, inching forward only a millimetre at a time, she had to make a conscious effort to relax. He was moving very slowly, stretching her gradually, which reassured her that he knew what he was doing. She decided to make the most of what was, for her, a novel experience.

Lucien didn't come in all the way. She could tell, even without looking, that his cock was far too big for her tight little arse to accommodate. But the sensations that his gentle probing produced in her were vivid and exciting so that she revelled in the novelty. When the aching need within her empty pussy became unbearable he sensed it and slowly introduced first one finger and then a couple more into her. She moaned and clasped onto him with all her muscles, tightening up front and back.

'Good girl!' he whispered, his breath hot on the back of her neck. He began to kiss her there with tickling brushes of his lips that made the skin of her back and shoulders prickle with delight. She bent down lower, feeling her anus open up all the more, and another centimetre or so slipped in, making her more confident that she could enjoy the experience without fear of harm. The thick pad of his thumb found her clitoral nub and began to circle over it with slight pressure, taking her further towards orgasm.

But Cordelia didn't want to come yet. She was savouring it all too much, wondering at the novel sensations that his anal penetration of her was producing. It was strange to feel his fingers moving against his prick, with just the wall of her cunt in between. Was that good for him, too? She squeezed him again, experimentally, and he groaned aloud. *Don't come yet*, she thought. *Not before I do*.

She sensed a new need dawning in him, signalled by the urgency of his tiny bites on the back of her neck, on her earlobes. Soon he had her turning onto her side, carefully so that his cock remained within her rear, and he was bending his head towards her pussy. It was awkward at first until they found a comfortable compromise, and then Cordelia relaxed again with a long sigh of contentment as she felt his tongue on her fiery clitoris. He began to lick and suck at her in earnest in an effort to satisfy her completely.

Now there was no need to hold back, and she began to squeeze his prick with her anus while she revelled in the good licking he was giving her, with his fingers still probing her cunt. She felt the wild flurries of her approaching orgasm and groaned with abandon as the onslaught hit her, fiercely spasming through her lower regions and then passing throughout her whole body until she was reduced to one heaving, quivering mass of fleshly delight. She could hear Lucien making little guttural noises, expressing his satisfaction in her pleasure, while her climax went on and on and she extracted every nuance of sensual rapture from it.

Afterwards, spreading herself out fully on the cushions, Cordelia continued to enjoy the blissful contentment that enveloped her as her body vibrated at a higher frequency, the afterglow taking a long, long time to fade. She was aware that Lucien was still caressing her, his hands sweeping down her spine and over the switchback of her buttocks, then softly on the sensitive backs of her thighs. He continued to massage her with a delicate touch, prolonging the sweetness of their lovemaking as she lay inert, utterly happy and satisfied.

Then he snuggled up beside her for a while and they drifted into a half-sleep, all warm and dreamy, the fire replacing the heat that their bodies had expended. Cordelia was awakened by his kisses on her neck and she turned over languidly to feel the silky nakedness of him against her, his prick semi-erect. It was a good one, long and thick the way she liked them, and the shaft was a pleasing biscuit colour with a dusky pink glans.

'I think I took your virginity tonight,' he whispered.

'Mm?' She caught his drift and giggled. 'Oh, that!'

'Yes, that. Did you enjoy it?'

'I never thought I would. Never fancied it, even. But I surprised myself – or rather, you surprised me.'

'I told you I wanted to fuck the arse off you.'

She laughed. 'I never realized you meant it literally.'

'Neither did I, until tonight.'

She looked deep into his brown eyes and thought she recognized urges lurking there that she had felt herself. An overriding desire to be completely open with someone, and open *to* them. A Biblical phrase sprang to mind: 'Then shall I know even as also I am known.' No more hiding in the dark places of the soul.

'I'd like to take a warm bath with you, then go to bed,' he said.

Lucien had a large whirlpool bath, plenty big enough for the two of them. It was blissful to lie there wallowing in his gentle, soapy caresses while the bubbles soothed her aching muscles. Cordelia suddenly caught herself thinking *I don't want this to end* – but the thought was followed by a stab of panic. Just what had she got herself into? Lying neck-deep in the foaming water the symbolism was obvious.

'What's the matter?' Somehow Lucien had sensed her change of mood.

'Oh, nothing. Just . . . you know, complications.'

'Ralph?'

'Mm. I don't want him to be hurt, Lucien.'

'I rather thought that was what he enjoyed.'

She threw the soap at him crossly. 'You know what I mean!'

'Not exactly. Perhaps you'd better explain.'

Cordelia struggled to her feet and, brushing aside his restraining hand, stepped out of the tub and grabbed a towel.

'I don't want to talk about it now. It would spoil things.'

He got out too, dripping everywhere. She threw him another towel.

'I think you're right,' he said, 'and I'd hate to spoil things. But it's a funny thing about sexual attraction. Sometimes you just know the chemistry is right and when that happens it's very difficult to stop yourself. That's how I felt about you, the minute I met you.'

'I think that's why I found you attractive too, knowing you wanted me in that uncompromising way. I'm not used to being desired so . . . completely.'

The conversation was growing dangerous. Cordelia finished drying herself and left Lucien in the bathroom while she went off to explore. His bedroom was a delight. The colour scheme was silver and blue, with a vast bed dominating the room and a huge vase of lilies on a table in the corner. She was sniffing them when Lucien entered and caught her round the waist.

'Sensual woman! Come to bed, please?'

He flung back the pretty embroidered coverlet to reveal pristine white sheets. She wondered if he'd made a special effort because he'd planned to seduce her or whether he always lived like that.

'Mrs Reynolds, my housekeeper, looks after everything,' he told her, reading her mind. 'And one thing I insist on is clean sheets every day.'

'More than you get in some hotels these days,' she commented, smoothing her hand over the cool pillow. She got into the bed and laid there while Lucien finished drying himself. Then he slipped in beside her and Cordelia stretched voluptuously at the thought of more love-making. She didn't feel in the least tired, she noted with amazement.

The instant he began kissing her she was filled with new desires. This time she wanted his prick, first in her hand then in her cunt, to feel its hard flesh sliding in and out of her and bringing her the total fulfilment she craved. When he began kissing her breasts she moaned aloud, her thighs restless beneath the sheets, her hands reaching for his growing erection. She caught the sleek length of it against her palm and enclosed it gently, making him sigh with bliss. Her fingers played with it, rubbing the ball of her thumb over the sticky glans then delicately massaging the skin of the shaft, feeling the iron core within.

'If you do that, I won't last long!' he warned her, catching his breath as she squeezed it softly. 'Do you want me in your pussy now?'

'Yes, now!' she breathed, delighted.

Lucien turned and found a condom in the bedside drawer. He rolled the sheath on carefully, then positioned himself on his knees above her. Neither of them wanted to wait. He plunged straight towards her ready quim, pausing at her entrance for a while until she was entirely loosened up inside and could accommodate the full girth of him. Cordelia felt as if she were drawing him in with her vaginal muscles. She twitched her cunny walls and her entrance mouthed first at his glans, then the rest of his shaft, inching further and further in until she felt the root clash against her pubic bone and the glans lock against her cervix.

Then she giggled and murmured, 'Gotcha!'

'Oh yes, you have, haven't you?' He gazed down at her fondly, his face shadowed in the dim light from the bedside lamp. Then he began shafting her slowly, sensually, both of them deriving the utmost gratification from the way their moist flesh melded in the most intimate of caresses. Cordelia felt a climax approaching and, when it came, it was infinitely gentle and erotic, filling her with sweetness.

Scarcely had the faint tremors died away than Lucien increased the pace, giving his cock its head. He rammed into her with heedless strength, bent on his own goal, and as the pace quickened she felt another orgasm on the way. This time it blasted through her with a fierce, raw energy that matched his. For a split second she saw her lover's face distorted with the extremity of his passion before she, too, succumbed and was hurled into blissful oblivion.

Panting and drenched with sweat, the pair clung to each other through the long seconds as their mutual climax shuddered through to its conclusion, then they sank back into each other's arms and fell asleep almost instantly, spent and sated.

Waking early, Cordelia took a few seconds to reorientate herself. When she remembered the events that had led to her being in Lucien's bed a whole slew of conflicting emotions overtook her. But the one that motivated her to creep out of bed without disturbing her heavily sleeping lover was guilt. She had to get back to Ralph, to reassure him that she was still his beloved mistress. Glancing at the bedside clock she saw that it was only five forty-five, but that was even better. If she could manage to get indoors and into bed without disturbing Ralph then he could wake her at seven with a cup of tea, his usual routine on a weekday. The day could then start like any normal one, and order would soon be restored.

Her plan worked and by nine Cordelia was in the office, preparing herself for Nigel but with more trepidation than usual because she had decided to tell him she was looking for another post. She owed him a clean break, she'd decided, with honest reasons for her departure and fair warning. That way she could pursue Kristina's job with a clear conscience.

Her boss arrived in a distant mood as if he had other things on his mind, and Cordelia was tempted to postpone her news. Emotionally she was in turmoil, wondering if she would ever see Lucien again, fearing that she might not. But the need to sort out her working life was some kind of refuge from the chaos in her heart and she wanted to make the change as soon as possible.

The problem was, how to choose her moment? She soon fell foul of her boss because, with her mind preoccupied with other things, she made several mistakes in a special letter and presented it to him for his signature without checking it thoroughly.

'You sloppy cow!' he yelled at her, throwing the offensive sheet in her face. 'How dare you compromise my standards? You need to be taught a lesson. Come here!'

She was wearing a leather bikini top and hot pants with a panel across the buttocks secured by a Velcro strip. He cleared a space on his desk and she knew what was to follow.

'Bend over my desk!' he snarled.

As she did so Nigel ripped open the Velcro and she felt the air circulating around her exposed bottom. Knowing she was in for a beating Cordelia felt the familiar mix of excitement and apprehension kick in, gearing her up for what was to follow. She heard her boss go to his cupboard where he spent some time deliberating over which instrument to use, increasing her fear that this time he might punish her too severely. He was in a strange mood and she had the oddest feeling that he had somehow guessed that she was going to give in her notice.

Cordelia could feel her thighs trembling as he approached, making swishing sounds as he tried out the whip he had selected. She wanted to remain humble, to take her punishment well, but a traitorous voice was whispering in her ear, *Why should I take this shit? Why not walk out on the bastard, right now?*

But she needed a good reference. Common sense warned her that now was not the time to rock the boat. He would find out soon enough that she was capable of standing up to him.

'Are you ready to submit to the lash, slave?'

She nodded, dumbly, bracing herself on her arms to take the first blow. It came with stinging force, almost knocking her off her feet. The second made her wince and hot tears came into her eyes as the pain lingered on, raw and undiminished, making her dread the next.

This was to be no token chastisement, she realized. A sense of outrage took over as she reflected that the severity of the discipline was out of proportion to the offence. Was he fed up with Inez and taking it out on her? Could be possibly be annoyed at the way his mistress had intruded on his relationship with his secretary, and vice versa? The idea that the situation had got out of control, and that Nigel was actually feeling similar emotions to hers, put a different slant on things. But it didn't excuse the way he was slashing at her rear end as if he was the one totally out of control.

'Bitch!' he muttered, delivering another lash so forceful that it made her cry out in pain. That seemed to bring him to his senses.

Cordelia slumped over his desk in agony, her bottom throbbing and her knees weak.

'Go and sort yourself out in the bathroom!' he snapped.

It was rare for Nigel to be so callous. Whenever he'd had to punish her physically he had always been most solicitous afterwards, often rubbing in some soothing cream and, on a few memorable occasions, that had led on to other, far sweeter activities. Today Cordelia felt affronted by his offhandedness.

Nevertheless she held her tongue and went into the bathroom, where she found some antiseptic cream in the first-aid box. When she looked at her bare bottom in the mirror she was shocked to see red weals. Nigel had never whipped her so ferociously before. Her determination to leave his employ grew as she applied the stinging ointment to her cuts, and she felt she could no longer bottle it up. She must go right back in there and tell him, whatever the consequences.

Instead of putting the leather outfit back on she dressed in the clothes she had arrived in, reasoning that they would be kinder to her damaged skin. The silk of her pants and matching slip soothed her as she walked into Nigel's office. He looked up, his eyes widening with a combination of surprise and disapproval as he saw how she was dressed.

'Why aren't you in your office clothes? I told you to wear the leather today.'

'It's too uncomfortable,' she replied, calmly. 'You've given me a very sore bottom.'

'I'll give you an even worse one if you talk to me like that! How dare you lift your eyes to me and talk back in that insolent manner? Isn't one beating enough for you?'

'More than enough. In fact, you might say it's one beating too far. I'm leaving you, Nigel. I'm looking for another job. It's something I've been contemplating for quite a while.'

'What?' He rose from his chair and swept round the desk, glowering at her. All Cordelia's pluck seemed to desert her as she met his dark, threatening gaze and she cowered before him.

'I . . . I just wanted to give in my no – tice,' she stammered.

'But you can't! I mean, I need you Cordelia. You can't just leave me in the lurch like this.'

'I'm not. I've giving you a month's notice. It's what we agreed, remember?'

An agonized, panicky look shot across his face as he realized that his hold over her had been illusory and that she was simply an employee, with rights like any other. His manner changed and he began pleading with her.

'Cordelia, where will I ever find another girl like you?' His expression brightened a little. 'Come to that, where will you find another boss like me? We're perfect for each other. We understand each other so well. Imagine having to go through all that training again . . .'

'Maybe I wouldn't want to. People change, you know, Nigel.'

He looked flabbergasted. 'Not you! I know exactly what you need, how you want to be treated.' Slowly he was regaining his confidence. He reached out and stroked her cheek. 'What is it, Cordelia, have I overstepped the mark? If so, I'm truly sorry and it won't happen again.'

'It's not what you've done or not done, Nigel. I just feel I need a change.'

'Is it because of Inez? Is that why?' He saw her flinch. 'That's it, isn't it?' He sounded triumphant. 'You feel used, abused by her. I knew it was risky, letting her in on the act. But I was right about you having secret lesbian tendencies, you can't deny that.'

Cordelia felt trapped by his logic, his determination to maintain his hold over her. And by her own sense of loyalty. Perhaps she was being unfair, after all. Maybe she should reconsider.

But then she thought of Lucien and knew that it would never work.

'I'll serve my month out,' she told him. 'I owe you that, at least. But I really do feel it's time to move on.'

He stared at her, his eyes wild and empty. The pact by which his power over her had been sustained through mutual consent had come to an end and he suddenly appeared devastated, emasculated even. But although Cordelia felt guilty she'd meant what she said: it was over.

Chapter Thirteen

Cordelia was behaving weirdly. Ralph had known her act strangely before but never like this, and it was worrying him. When she came home from work on Tuesday she was in a black mood and only picked at the exquisite corn-fed chicken breast steamed to perfection on a bed of mixed herbs with a tomato-and-olive coulis and buttered saffron rice. She asked him if there had been any phone calls, not once but three times, and every time a car drew up in the road outside she leapt to the window as if she was expecting someone.

There were no visitors, however, and as the evening wore on he could see that she was still as jumpy as a cat and had little interest in him. He offered her drinks, a massage, a hot bath, but she refused them all and eventually snapped, 'Oh, stop bothering me! When I want something I'll tell you. Now get out of my sight!'

Later she relented and came into the kitchen to apologize. 'I didn't mean to upset you, Ralph,' she said contritely. 'It's nothing you've done. It's just . . .'

Then, to his horror, she burst into tears. He could never remember this happening before, and as he tore off sheets of kitchen roll and helped to wipe her eyes and nose Ralph couldn't help wondering if this was the beginning of the end of the world as they knew it. Cordelia blew her nose loudly, then asked him to make her a hot chocolate with brandy.

'I need something comforting,' she confessed. 'I've had a hard day.'

'Trouble at work, madam?' he enquired, relieved that the awful tension had been broken.

'You could say that. I handed in my notice today, and my boss didn't take it too well.'

'I'm sure he will be very sorry to lose you, madam.'

It was on the tip of Ralph's tongue to confess how upset *he* would be if she ever dismissed him from her service, but he couldn't bring himself to mention it. There was a very real possibility of that very situation materializing now. If she were changing jobs she might move to another part of the country and want to start a new life, a life that held no room for him. Just lately that had become a recurrent nightmare of his.

She smiled sweetly at him as he handed her the steaming mug of chocolate, and Ralph was reminded that once he would have done anything to induce that smile. Now he was not so sure. It came as a shock to realize that there were limits to his devotion, his servitude. Her recent behaviour seemed to have broken a pact between them, one that said she would never act unfairly or quixotically towards him. What was even more worrying was that he had no idea what was behind it.

Was she leaving her job because she'd been having an affair with her boss, and it had all gone wrong? Once the idea hit him it wouldn't let him go and he sat in the kitchen pondering long after Cordelia had returned to the sitting room. He was aware that sometimes his mistress indulged herself sexually with other men. There was nothing in their agreement to prevent that, and he did not feel dogged by any inappropriate feelings of jealousy. But whatever had been going on during the past week or so had started to affect her domestic life.

She had spent a night away from home on Monday. It had happened before on the weekend, but to sleep at a 'friend's house' on a weekday, when there was work in the morning, was unheard of. And then to come home from the office in such a jittery condition – well, that was extraordinary, too. Ralph liked routine and order, not surprises and chaos. If life in Cordelia's household was going to lose its basic discipline then he couldn't tolerate it. He would have to leave.

Next morning Cordelia woke filled with trepidation and knew that she was afraid to go to work. It reminded her of being a schoolgirl and having exams to face, that queasiness in the stomach and dread of the unknown. Her nervousness communicated itself to Ralph as she refused all but a black coffee and left in a hurry, eager to be out of the house and away from his bewildered, faintly accusing gaze. She knew that she wasn't being fair on him, yet in her present state it was impossible to take on the rôle of dominatrix with any conviction so she preferred to avoid him altogether.

But the real cause of her distress was something she could scarcely bring herself to admit to herself, let alone to Ralph. Behind her superficial anxiety about facing Nigel lay a far deeper worry. She was afraid that she would never see Lucien again.

The Frenchman had got into her blood and bones, had taken vacant possession of her heart and was so vividly present in her memory and imagination that she could hardly concentrate on anything else. She kept reminding herself that it was only a couple of days since she'd seen him, but it was no consolation when he knew exactly where she lived and, only a week or so ago, had been prepared to lurk in the bushes just to grab a sneaky kiss from her. Why hadn't he got in touch again?

Had Lucien's passion for her cooled now that he'd had his wicked way with her? That was the ugly question that had been tormenting her day and night, making her feel rash and foolish for succumbing to his charms, taunting her with the thought that he might have set his sights on another prey already. Was he the archetypal Don Juan, interested only in seduction and deflowering? The evidence for that seemed overwhelming. He'd taken her virginity in the only way he could, and she'd not seen hide nor hair of him since.

Miserably, Cordelia drove to work, and by the time she reached the office her thoughts were all of Lucien and whether she should go round to his flat after work and confront him. She was still wondering whether that would be a big mistake as she entered the office and headed for the bathroom. Then she stopped in her tracks.

'Good morning, Cordelia!'

Sitting behind Nigel's desk, as if she had a perfect right to be there, was Inez. She gave Cordelia a broad, beckoning smile. 'I know you didn't expect to see me, but I wanted us to have a little chat. Pull up a chair.'

She gestured towards one of the leather armchairs that Cordelia never normally got to sit in as they were meant for guests. Somehow she guessed that this was a business meeting – but what was the nature of the business? Warily she eyed the Spanish woman as she sat on the edge of the leather cushion with her thighs tightly pressed together, hands clasped in her lap.

'Relax, dear, I won't bite.'

'Does Nigel know you're here?'

'He has some other business to attend to and won't be in until ten-thirty today, so you needn't worry that he will walk in on our conversation. Would you like a coffee?'

It was strange to waited on by Inez. Cordelia sat stiffly, watching her work the coffee machine that was normally her province, wondering what this was all about. Nothing seemed normal any more, so she was prepared for almost anything. She was handed her coffee cup with a smile and then the two women were sitting face to face again, with a gulf the size of the Grand Canyon between them.

Inez did her best to look and sound friendly and informal, but it was about as convincing as the Queen chatting to New Age travellers. Cordelia squirmed in her seat as the woman said, with studied casualness. 'Nigel tells me you're thinking of moving on.'

'That's right. I haven't given in my notice formally yet, but . . .'

'Then perhaps I can persuade you to change your mind.'

'You?' Cordelia frowned at her. 'Why? I don't get it. Why should you want me to stay?'

Inez gave a rather sad smile. 'You probably think it's because I'm after your pussy, but you'd be wrong. It's pretty obvious that you don't want me to interfere in your relationship with Nigel, and the main reason I'm here today is to convince you that I have no such intentions. All I want is for the status quo to be maintained.'

'You haven't answered my question.'

'Haven't I?' Inez sighed. 'Let me fill you in on some history. Before you came Nigel had a string of secretaries, and most of them he fucked. Then things would go sour and they would leave, another girl would take her place and . . . well, you get the picture. It was very bad for Nigel. It made him swing between euphoria and depression – he's a bit manic, you know – and it was sheer hell for me. But when you arrived he calmed down: everything went smoothly. You were his 'office slave' and I was his mistress, the lines were clearly drawn. I liked that.'

'Well, I can't stay just because *you* want me to. I have needs and ambitions of my own.'

'Is it the salary? Nigel has authorized me to say he will give you a pay rise if you agree to stay on for a minimum of six months.'

Cordelia regarded her contemptuously. 'No, it's not the money.'

'Is it the way he treats you, then? I know he can be heavy-handed at times, but I thought you had an understanding. After all the training you've been through no one knows your secret desires better than Nigel, surely?' Her expression became sly, cajoling. 'We all know how much you love to be restrained. It turns you on, doesn't it, that helplessness? And to be told what to do in that sharp voice of his, to be under his control. He knows so well what a satisfaction that can be because, well, he's been through it, too.'

'Nigel has?'

In a flash Cordelia realized that Inez had the upper hand over him in more ways than she imagined. Just as she switched from one rôle at home to the opposite at work, so did he. The realization hit her with sudden clarity, making sense of the strange undercurrents she had detected in him whenever he was with his mistress. Of course, they wouldn't act it out fully in front of her, but the clues had been there and she was a fool not to have put two and two together.

'So you see,' Inez went on smoothly, 'it would be in everyone's interests for us to remain exactly as we are. Don't you agree?'

Cordelia took a deep breath. 'No, I don't. Even if I agreed to stay on for another six months I'd still want to leave at the end of it, and I'd only be all the more frustrated in the meantime.'

'Is there nothing that would induce you to stay, then?'

'No, I have to go. For . . . several reasons.'

'You disappoint me.'

Inez pouted, lighting up a stinking Spanish cigarette without bothering to ask if Cordelia minded. She felt annoyed. Now there was a new tension in the air, the pique of a jilted lover. Inez was staring coldly at her through eyes that had narrowed to black slits.

'Nigel will be disappointed too, and you know what he's like when he's angry.'

'He'd better not try it on. Not like yesterday.'

'Yesterday was a mistake, he freely admits it. And he's anxious to make amends, to make it up to you. He's even offering to let *you* administer punishment to *him*. Would you like that?'

She grimaced. 'Not particularly.'

Inez came to kneel beside Cordelia's chair, blowing smoke into the air around her. She spoke in a low, insinuating tone that grated on her nerves. 'Oh, I think you would. You know, between us, you and I could devise some pretty fiendish punishments for that man. I have a few old scores to settle too, you know.'

'I'll bet you have!'

Cordelia rose impatiently from her seat. She was sick and tired of listening to this bitch and anxious to get down to some work before Nigel arrived. The four weeks of servitude that she still had to endure had begun to seem a very long time indeed.

'I can see you want me to leave, but I promised Nigel I would stay until he came. Another coffee?'

'No, thanks. I'd like to get on with some letters now.'

'Ever the perfect secretary!' Inez taunted her. She walked off with a pout, blowing smoke everywhere, and poured herself another black coffee.

Cordelia went through into her office and calmly switched on the computer, but she was fuming inside. Angry not so much with Inez as with Nigel, for getting his mistress to do his dirty work for him. What a worm he was, after all! How could she ever have admired him, thought him so full of authority and presence? He'd been under the thumb of that

Spanish hussy all the while and she'd been laughing at his little 'office slave' behind her back.

It sickened her that she'd let Inez make love to her, enjoyed it even. She wanted to be rid of the pair of them but she knew if she just walked out she would never get a decent reference. Oh, why hadn't she thought about all this before? Mixing her private fantasy world with her working world had been a big mistake and now she was paying for it.

Soon after half-past ten Nigel arrived. Sensing the atmosphere was not exactly one of sweetness and light, he came into Cordelia's office wearing a frown.

'Good morning, Cordelia. I presume you and Inez have had your little chat?'

Her eyes never left the screen. 'Mm.'

'I see. Well, if bribes won't work perhaps we should try other methods. Inez!'

His mistress was soon at his side. Cordelia turned in alarm but was not quick enough to evade the handcuffs that Inez swiftly clipped around her wrists, securing her hands in front of her.

'Now we have you exactly how we want you,' Nigel smiled.

'You're crazy! If you think you can coerce me into playing your crazy games . . .'

'Coerce? I don't think that will be necessary. We all know how you love to be manhandled, especially by another woman. Now you're going to find out exactly how persuasive Inez can be.'

'She's not dressed for work properly, is she?' Inez said with a smile. 'I think you'd better strip her and we'll find her something more appropriate to wear.'

Cordelia felt chilled. She was powerless to prevent her boss from undoing her skirt and pulling it down over her hips. Her bottom was almost healed but as his fingers brushed her bruised skin she felt a faint twinge. God help her if he took it into his head to thrash her again.

'Now her stockings and panties,' she heard Inez say. 'I want to see how her *derrière* looks after that punishment you gave it. Perhaps it needs some creaming.'

Cordelia was caught in the maelstrom of conflicting emotions. Was this to be an erotic encounter? Were they seeking to prove that they could satisfy her as only they knew how? The trouble was, she was vulnerable to such an approach and they knew it. The adrenalin rush of fear was very addictive when mixed with sexual desire.

Soon Cordelia's lower half was completely naked and she could feel Inez's inquisitive fingers caressing the tense buttock globes. 'Not too bad,' she heard her say. 'Relax, dear. I'm not going to hurt you. Not if you behave yourself, anyway. Fetch me the antiseptic cream, Nigel.'

While he was in the bathroom Inez began fondling Cordelia's breasts as she whispered in her ear, 'You are so luscious, I can hardly keep my hands off you!' Soon her nipples were tweaked to sharp points, clearly visible even beneath her blouse and bra. When Nigel returned Inez stepped back, leaving her breasts tingling and hungry for more stimulation.

The smell of the medicinal cream reached Cordelia's nostrils as the tube was opened and Inez took a generous amount onto her palm. 'It will be easier if you bend over,' Inez said.

Cordelia rested her elbows on her desk and lowered her head, submissive because it was easier to fall into the old routine than to resist. She reminded herself that she only had a few more weeks of this to endure – but the euphoria she should have felt at the thought of freedom was absent. When she'd told Nigel she wanted to leave she had been full of dreams for the future, dreams that included Lucien. Since he had failed to contact her she was having second thoughts. Perhaps what Inez had said to her made sense, after all.

And the sensual caresses that the woman was now administering to her bottom were extremely pleasant, making her languid and voluptuous, slowly awakening her desire for more of the erotic treatment. Surreptitiously she enclosed both her nipples between her thumbs and forefingers, giving them a squeeze and heightening her arousal. Inez was smoothing her palm over both buttocks now, and Nigel was repositioning her legs, pushing them further apart so that she was now open to more intimate intrusion.

Inez soon took advantage of the new possibilities for access. First her creamed finger toyed with Cordelia's anus, teasing the sensitive puckered skin and making her groan with augmented lust. After its penetration by Lucien her arse had developed desires of its own. While the insinuating finger worked its way round and round in exquisitely tormenting circles she could feel Nigel unbuttoning her blouse at the back and then unfastening her bra.

'Shall I remove these?' he asked Inez.

'If you can. We'll get her kitted out later.'

The Spanish woman's voice was guttural with suppressed excitement. Nigel managed to pull down Cordelia's blouse until it lay coiled in a rope around her waist, out of the way of the activity that was going on behind. The bra, conveniently enough, was designed to have optional shoulder straps, halter-neck style or strapless, so Nigel was able to unclip the straps and remove the garment altogether. His hands clutched at her naked breasts and she could feel his hot breath on her neck as he kneaded them, sending her libido into overdrive.

'Get down on your knees!' Inez ordered.

At first Cordelia thought she meant her, but it was Nigel who clumsily pushed himself between her and the desk on all fours, then thrust his head up towards her open pussy.

'Now get licking. I want her good and wet, back and front.'

Cordelia felt shudders of lust pass through her, and at the same time something was probing her back passage. 'Hm, nice and open,' Inez commented as the nose of something smooth and round pushed into her. 'She can take a dildo better now. I wonder if anyone's been knocking at the tradesman's entrance lately?'

Almost before the words registered a fresh attack was made on Cordelia's overstretched nerve endings as Nigel's tongue found its way into the fleshy folds of her vulva. She groaned again, helplessly caught between the two of them, her clitoris and empty cunt crying out for some action. They didn't have to wait long. Nigel's assault on them both was eager and assured, his tongue lapping constantly at the jutting button while his fingers slid easily in and out of her well-lubricated quim.

It didn't take her more than a few seconds to come, sprawled in an ungainly fashion across the desk with her breasts squashed beneath her, helplessly caught in the spasms of wild ecstasy that were zipping through her body from dizzy head to trembling toe.

They left her there to recover, and soon Cordelia's joints were feeling stiff, her wrists chafing against the metal that bound them. She turned round and was surprised to find that she was alone, although noises were coming from Nigel's office next door. Curiously she crept to the opening between the two rooms and saw the pair of them hard at it on the carpet. Nigel was lying on his back with his trousers around his knees and Inez was bouncing up and down on him, her fingers inside her blouse so that she could stimulate her own breasts.

Cordelia didn't know what to do, since they were completely ignoring her. Now that the sexual heat had diminished she felt jaded, resentful. They wanted her as their plaything, but she wasn't going to play their silly games any more. She would quit right now, as soon as she could get out of these stupid handcuffs . . .

Then she remembered that she needed a reference and her mood grew sombre. She contemplated simply coming clean with her potential employers, telling them that she and her previous boss hadn't seen eye to eye, but how would that reflect on her? She wouldn't put it past Nigel to give her a damning reference either. Caught in a cleft stick, she moodily accepted that she would have to serve out her notice if she wanted a good chance of another job.

The pair in the next room came noisily and Cordelia resumed her position leaning over the desk, awaiting the next phase of their plan for her. After a few long minutes Inez entered carrying a black leather bustier and thigh boots, which she proceeded to dress Cordelia in, once she had removed the steel cuffs. Then she stood back and admired her handiwork.

'There, that's better! Now you can carry out your office duties with more enthusiasm, I'm sure. And you *will* consider what I suggested, won't you, Cordelia? Staying on for another six months, I mean. I'm sure it would be to everyone's advantage, perhaps yours most of all. Now I really must go. Be good!'

Inez blew her a mocking kiss, then turned on her high heels and departed without so much as a word to Nigel. Cordelia sat at her desk and reviewed her workload for the day. She was in the middle of some typing when her boss appeared, looking rather the worse for wear.

'That woman!' he commented, shaking his head with a bemused frown. 'A real man-eater, wouldn't you say? Trouble is, she's a woman-eater, too!'

Cordelia appreciated his attempt to lighten the atmosphere, which continued through the day. He seemed more inclined to open up to her and talked about Inez quite a lot.

'Reason tells me I should get shot of her, but somehow I can't,' he confessed, as they drank afternoon tea together. 'She has me firmly by the balls, that one.'

'Maybe it was a mistake to let her ever set foot in this office,' Cordelia suggested.

Nigel sighed. 'You're right, of course. But she can be awfully persuasive, you know. If she can only manage to persuade you to stay . . .'

'It's no good, it wouldn't work out.' He looked so crestfallen that Cordelia put out a reassuring hand. 'You could train another girl. Put an ad in one of those sexy magazines, or something.'

'But that would take ages. And I'd never find anyone like you, Cordelia. We know each other so well by now.'

'Then maybe we know each other *too* well and it really is time for me to move on.'

'I'm trying to resign myself to the prospect of you leaving, but it's very hard. Perhaps you could see me sometimes afterwards – you know, as a social thing. Just once in a while.'

He looked wistful. She rose and kissed his cheek. 'Maybe, but I'm not making any promises.'

It was strange, having that heart-to-heart with her boss. The immediate result was a further weakening of his power over her, a shattering of the illusion that he was the strong and she the weak one, but paradoxically his opening up to her had increased her sympathy for him. Now that she understood what a hold Inez had over him Cordelia felt a new bond of understanding between them. She still wasn't ready to tell him about Ralph but maybe one day, when she felt secure in her new job, they might meet and she would reveal all. Maybe.

Before she went home that day Cordelia typed out three copies of her curriculum vitae.

*   *   *

Ralph was performing a magical act. He'd always believed in magic in a half-hearted way, but now he reasoned that if there really was anything in it he had need of it, and fast. Alone in his darkened room, with an hour to spare before he had to put the final touches to the evening meal, he was standing naked before his favourite photo of Cordelia in the nude, around which were placed four green candles in copper holders. The air was heavy with rose incense.

'Oh Goddess of Love,' he murmured, swaying slightly as he knelt with his eyes closed and his mind firmly focused on the image of his beloved. 'Bring her back to me like a homing pigeon to her nest. Rekindle the warm fire of her attachment to me and may I increase in my devotion to her. Help me, Venus, to serve my mistress with a pure heart and soul, so that I may once again be indispensable to her . . .'

His hands moved down to the stirring organ between his thighs and he squeezed it gently, feeling the erection thicken and lengthen in the hollow of his palm. He opened his eyes and gazed fixedly at the photograph of his mistress, taking in the proud beauty of her naturally uplifted breasts and the dark triangle of hair that guarded the inner sanctum of her sexual being. He recalled the scent and taste of her pussy, so rare and delicious a treat for him that it seemed like some sacred sacrament to be held in great reverence. His cock grew lively, pushing against his hand in its urge to be free.

Ralph's breath was coming in rapid bursts as his desire increased, aided by the regular stimulation of his shaft as he gave it a firm, rhythmic hand. He could feel the essence oozing out of his glans, lubricating his organ so that the skin moved more smoothly and his task was made easier. The delightful prickles of sensation were intensifying into sharp, exquisite pangs that enlivened his belly and spread up to his chest, causing his nipples to grow erect and tingling too.

Still he stared at the picture of his mistress, her skin and eyes glowing in the candlelight as they might in the flesh, and his lust for her was ennobled into something approaching goddess worship. As his arousal grew his feelings expanded into something timeless, elemental, and the despair that he'd been feeling lately was transformed into a euphoric hope, a certainty that this act of devotion would bring about the desired result and draw Cordelia closer to him.

He remembered how it had been for him in the beginning when, drunk with passion, he had discovered so many new things about his secret nature, things she had drawn out of him with an instinctive skill that she'd probably not even suspected she possessed. How he had adored her then! It was different now, the thrill of novelty harder to achieve but her intimate knowledge of him more than compensating. It made him feel safe, knowing that she knew exactly what made him tick. Which was why he must keep that precious sense of security intact.

He was at full cock now, his organ straining for release as the glans secreted more of his juice and his fingers grew sticky with the residue. Ralph felt the last urgent ascent towards orgasm commence, and he concentrated his mind on drawing his mistress closer to him, thought he could see the imperious expression in the image of her face, the look that told him she was getting turned on by making him execute her bidding. He was turning her into an archetype, no longer Cordelia with her human foibles and contradictions, but the perfect image of the Dominatrix, the Controlling Mother, the Dark Goddess of Pleasure and Pain.

She, above all women, knew what was meant by the quote, 'I must be cruel only to be kind.' She was his *Belle Dame Sans Merci* . . .

The jism spurted out of him in a wide arc, spattering the glass in the photo frame and almost putting out one of the candles that sputtered and fizzled in its struggle to remain alight. Ralph snatched a tissue from the box on the floor and wrapped it around his still-throbbing dick, minimizing the mess. Even in the throes of orgasm he could never quite renounce his rôle as house-husband.

Getting up from his knees with difficulty, Ralph blew out the candles and drew the curtains to let in enough light to see by. He took the photo frame into the bathroom and gave it a good cleaning, then took a quick shower. Returning to his room he cleared away the remnants of his devotions and dressed in one of Cordelia's favourite uniforms, a black latex job with zippers in all kinds of unexpected places. Then he lay down on his bed with his hands behind his head for a short rest.

He'd hoped that a spot of magical ritual would make him feel more at ease, but something still nagged at him with a painful, sneaking intensity. With a shock he realized that the 'something' was plain old-fashioned jealousy, and the man he was jealous of was Cordelia's boss. He'd never met him, never even heard his name, but he now knew exactly where the bugger worked and if he wanted to he could bloody well go there and confront him.

The idea sent zig-zag waves of energy dancing through him, rousing him in a way that was almost sexual again. It was a dangerous idea, sure enough. If Cordelia found out he'd been sneaking round behind her back it would make matters worse, not better. But the thought of easing his frustrated impotence by doing something, however futile, about the situation was reassuring. Even if he didn't get to see the man but just spied on him a little, kept watch to see if the pair of them went off together, it would be worth it.

The idea of playing detective took hold with the powerful allure of a fantasy. Tomorrow he would go, just for an hour or two in the middle of the day. There would be plenty of time for him to return home and perform his duties before Cordelia returned. Talking of which . . .

Ralph glanced at the bedside clock, then sprang off the bed. Tonight there was roast guinea fowl with a redcurrant sauce, glazed baby turnips and broccoli with slivered almonds on the menu . . .

Chapter Fourteen

Cordelia had been nice to him for once. So nice that Ralph felt ashamed of his urge to follow her to the office and sniff out her boss. After complimenting him on his cooking she had let him bathe her and then pleasure her with a new double-probe dildo that she had acquired. Seeing the thing boring into both her front and back passages had turned him on a treat and she had graciously allowed him to ease his frustration by relieving himself over her gorgeous naked breasts.

Quite why she had come home in such a good mood had not much bothered him at the time, since his mind and body were fully occupied with more pleasant concerns. Now, however, it was a different matter. Lying in bed and reflecting on the evening's entertainment Ralph grew convinced that she was only happy because of her boss. Had they kissed and made up after a quarrel? He fondled his balls absently as he cogitated, his mind veering this way and that as he wondered what, if anything, to do about it.

The safest course was obviously to stay at home and keep his nose as clean as the house – but then his curiosity would never be satisfied. At last he hit on a compromise: he would go to her office and lie in wait, without showing himself. He could probably find a place to use as a lookout. A café perhaps, or a pub, somewhere with a convenient window. There was no need for either Cordelia or her anonymous boss to know anything about it.

Once his mistress had left next morning Ralph dashed around like a whirlwind, clearing and washing up, dusting and hoovering, laundering and gardening. By half-eleven he was exhausted and glad to grab a sandwich and coffee before preparing to leave for the centre of town. He got into his little VW Golf and followed the route he had taken when he was acting as Cordelia's chauffeur. It seemed ages ago. Wistfully, he reflected that things had seemed better then, more normal.

Before he got too near to her place of work Ralph parked the car in an inconspicuous place in a side street and made the rest of the journey on foot. As he approached the block where her office was he scanned the neighbourhood for convenient lookout spots and found a bookie's almost opposite. It would do for a while, he decided. Entering with as casual an air as he could muster, he grabbed a handful of betting slips and walked over to the window, near a shelf from which a Biro dangled on a piece of string. Someone had left a newspaper there, which he opened at the racing pages and pretended to read, frowning as if he were seriously studying form. There were about half a dozen men in there and two girls behind the desk, but none of them paid him much attention after his entrance. The punters were gathering around the TV screen at the far end, waiting for the next race to begin.

Outside it was a mellow autumn day, the golden shafts of sunlight falling full on the windows opposite. Ralph stared into them but it was impossible to see very much, with the light reflected back into the street. A female figure did appear for a few seconds at one of the windows, making his heart race as wildly as the horses on the screen, but it was not Cordelia. A sense of unreality took hold of him, making him wonder just what he was doing there.

Suddenly, just before one, he saw Cordelia emerge from the building, clutching her bag. She looked like she was in a hurry, as if she had some shopping to do in her lunch hour.

Or maybe she was on some errand for her boss. He watched her cross the road and disappear into the shopping mall further down the street. What to do now? Ralph decided to leave the betting shop and find another vantage point while he had the chance.

There was a café right next to the office block, with tables set out on the pavement. It would be risky, but he still had the newspaper to cover his face and, besides, he quite fancied a bit of excitement. More to the point, he also fancied a beer and another sandwich. Edgily, he made his way across the road and approached the only table with a vacant seat. When he asked the couple of tourists if he could join them they waved him into the seat cheerily, saying, 'Oh no, not at all! Please be our guest!' in thick East European accents. *Good*, he thought, *they can be my cover*.

Cordelia reappeared before he had finished either his beer or his sandwich, this time clutching a carrier bag as well as her handbag. She looked in a hurry to get back to the office, so Ralph was in a quandary. He waved the waiter over and paid his bill, then, after seeing her disappear into the building, decided to follow.

Inside there were two lifts and she was already halfway up in one of them. He got into the other one and pressed the button for the top floor. By peering through a small window it was possible to see out of the lift shaft as it went up through the floors and he was counting on being able to spot Cordelia before she disappeared into her office.

Once again he was in luck. As his lift glided past the third floor he could see her getting out of the other one and making for a door with a distinctive sign on it, one he thought he might remember if he came back later. At the top of the building he got out, spent a few seconds admiring the view over the London rooftops, then took the stairs down to the third floor where he soon recognized the door he had seen. Close to, the notice read: *Nigel Willoughby, Financier. Meetings by appointment only.*

Walking slowly back towards the stairwell, Ralph considered his options. This Willoughby was probably in the phone book, although he might be ex-directory in which case Ralph might have to do some detective work at home to find the number. Getting Willoughby's private number might be even harder. Alternatively, he could stick a note under his door, but that was risky. Suppose Cordelia got there first? He shuddered to think of the consequences if she found out he'd been spying on her and her boss. Then he thought of the Internet. That might be the best route of all.

Ralph looked at his watch. He really ought to be getting back. Reluctantly he left the building and returned to his car. Well, at least he now knew her boss's name and the location of his office. Maybe sometime in the future he'd find himself needing some financial advice . . .

Although it was a damp and cloudy September day, Cordelia was skipping along the street like a kid let out of school early. It was her lunch hour, but this was no ordinary, workaday lunch hour. She was on her way to meet Lucien at a small restaurant just round the corner from where she worked, called La Margarita.

She'd told Nigel she was meeting an old friend for lunch, and he had looked instantly suspicious, as if she were sneaking off for a job interview, but she'd already done that. Kristina had put in a good word at the ad agency and they'd agreed to see her at six on Thursday. They'd rung her at home on Monday evening to tell her she had the job. Minutes later, as if by special arrangement, Lucien had phoned too.

Now she felt as if everything was falling neatly into place. Reminding herself not to chide Lucien for leaving her in suspense for almost two weeks, Cordelia entered the small, exclusive restaurant and found him already at their table. The way his eyes lit up when she entered made it seem worth the wait.

'Cordelia!' His voice and eyes caressed her even before his fingers and lips did, a gentle touch of greeting that made her want to scream for more except that she knew it was not the done thing to make such an exhibition of herself in a posh restaurant in the middle of the day. He seemed to sense what she was going through all the same, to share it, even.

'I've longed so much to see you again,' he whispered in her ear as the waiter came over to hand her a menu. She bit back the sarcastic remark that leapt into her mind and concentrated on the menu. 'I had to go back to France for a family funeral,' he explained, making her glad she hadn't said anything.

'Oh dear – no one close, I hope?'

'My sister.'

'My God, I'm so sorry!'

'It was expected. She'd had leukaemia for some time. But let's choose from the menu, shall we? They do a rather good *aoli provençal* here, so I've heard.'

'I don't think I'd be in a fit state to go back to work if I had that!'

'Doesn't your boss appreciate the stinking rose, then?'

She stared at him blankly, then giggled as the penny dropped. 'Oh, you mean garlic! In his food, yes, I'm sure. He just wouldn't want the whole office reeking of it. The wild mushroom pâté sounds nice.'

They ate in companionable silence for a while, savouring the delicate flavours that the young, fashionable chef had managed to coax out of his ingredients. But then Lucien started to talk about himself. He had come to England ten years ago to make a new start after a failed marriage and since then had done rather well for himself on the Stock Exchange.

He admitted that his visit to France seemed to have reminded him of less happy times, however. 'I couldn't wait to see you, Cordelia,' he said. 'I want to think of the future, not the past. But listen to me, talking about myself all the time. Did you go after Kristina's job?'

'Yes, and I got it! I start in just over two weeks.'

'Hey, this calls for a celebration!'

She could see he was about to signal to the waiter, but she put a restraining hand on his arm. 'Wait, Lucien. This is the middle of the day, remember? I'm not exactly free to celebrate right now . . .'

'Tonight, then?'

His eyes were seducing her, as they had at the beginning over her own deliciously-laden table, making it impossible for her to refuse. 'I'd love to. But . . .'

'Ralph is expecting you? Ring him. Tell him you've been invited out for the evening.'

'I'm not sure, I . . .'

Lucien took her hand, caressing the fingers as he spoke and sending shock waves of desire ricocheting through her system. 'Look, Cordelia, I'm not the type to go chasing a woman forever. If you want me, then show it. If you don't, forget it. Okay?'

His words might have sounded brutal without that soft Gallic accent and without the look of soft adoration in his brown eyes. She smiled at him, saying in a low voice, 'Of course I want you, idiot! I'll make that call now.'

She left a lettuce leaf, all that remained of her starter, for the waiter to collect and went to the phone near the cloakroom. Ralph sounded nervous when he recognized her voice and, for a moment, she felt a pang of misgiving. 'Oh . . . er . . . I'm ringing to let you know that I won't be home for dinner tonight, Ralph. I've been invited out. Don't wait up for me.'

'That's perfectly all right, madam,' he replied, but she heard the strain in his voice. 'The food I've bought will keep until tomorrow in the refrigerator.'

He's trying to make me feel guilty, she thought, which only strengthened her resolve. 'Right, then. I probably won't be coming home tonight. I'll go straight to work from wherever I end up. Hopefully it won't be in Cardboard City!'

Her attempt to lighten the proceedings fell dismally flat and she was left with a worrying feeling that Ralph was going to be miserable for the rest of the day. Still, she wasn't responsible for the state of his soul. Perhaps once, near the beginning, she'd believed she might have been, but she had grown up since then. The games they played were just that, games, and if he was taking them too seriously it might be time to throw in the towel.

Lucien saw her face as she returned to the table and gave her a shrewd look. But he refrained from commenting and soon she was being distracted by his questions about her new job. She was excited at the prospect and glad to talk about it, but when he asked what her present boss felt about her leaving she shut up like a clam.

'He's not happy, huh?' Lucien persisted.

'Let me put it this way. I think he's grown quite dependent on me during the time we've been together.'

Cordelia realized as she spoke that she was telling the truth. He was, in some strange way, more dependent on her than she was on him, although that had not been the case at the start. The balance of power must have made its subtle shift somewhere along the line.

'I can imagine that being a rather comfortable state to be in, dependent on you,' Lucien mused, a teasing grin on his face. 'I'd like to try it, sometime.'

She looked at her watch: time was flying, and if she got back any later than two Nigel would devise some punishment for her. They had called an uneasy truce over the past few days, with her boss seeming to finally accept that she was leaving. Their office routine now was more a matter of going through the motions as he attempted to distance himself from her. But she knew there was still a lot of pent-up aggression in him that only needed a small excuse to unleash itself upon her.

The meal was delicious but Cordelia couldn't do it justice. She had to get back and, at ten to two, rose abruptly with a quarter of the food still on her plate.

'It's no good, Lucien,' she said apologetically. 'It's wonderful food, but I can't eat any more. I really must get back.'

'Your boss won't mind if you're a few minutes late, surely?'

'You don't know him!' Her reply was vehement and she saw a hint of suspicion dawn in Lucien's eye. Cursing herself for the indiscretion she tried to cover it up. 'It's just that we've a rush job on right now and he only let me out of the office if I promised to get back on the stroke of two. Anyway, I'm seeing you tonight, aren't I?' she ended, cheerily.

But as she left the restaurant she was haunted by the mixture of doubt and curiosity she saw in Lucien's eyes.

Cordelia heard a clock strike two as she entered the street and her heart sank. There was no way she could avoid a punishment session now. She had been very careful not to put a foot wrong lately, fearing that Nigel might go over the top again, and now she'd slipped up – thanks to Lucien. It seemed ironic. She hurried along the pavement and dashed into the office building, stabbing the lift button impatiently until it arrived. By the time she got to Nigel's door it was almost five past two.

Perhaps he won't notice, she thought as she let herself in. But it was a futile hope: her boss was already looking at his watch as she entered.

'You're late!' he said, with a satisfied smirk that made Cordelia furious.

'I'm really sorry. I did try to get back on time, but I was held up.'

'It's just not good enough, is it?' Nigel rose and walked slowly around the desk, his expression thoughtful. 'I've been wondering what to do about it. I mean, we can't tolerate slackers, can we?'

She lowered her eyes. 'No, sir.'

I have the new job now, she thought, although she wasn't sure if they'd taken up her references yet. That was the whole trouble. If she knew she was in the clear she would pack her bags and leave straight away, but she couldn't risk it. Not today. Oh, why hadn't she been able to hold out a bit longer before making such a stupid mistake?

Nigel told her to strip. For a moment Cordelia hesitated, knowing that once she had submitted to him there would be no going back. The familiar tensions were growing inside her, the automatic urge to obey vying with the urge to defy, the strange appetite for shame and humiliation mixed with the fear of pain. Yet now everything was subtly different. He had Inez and she had Lucien, as well as Ralph. The old order had changed, irrevocably.

'I don't see why I should,' she said.

Nigel's black brows glowered at her. 'Disobedience? This is intolerable! Strip at once.'

She giggled. 'I will if you will. If you will, so will I!'

To her horror he gave her a slap on the cheek. She stared at him while rubbing the sore spot, stunned into temporary silence.

'That will teach you to defy me and make silly jokes!' he snarled. 'Now are you going to get undressed, or do I have to strip you myself?'

'If you lay your hand on me again I shall walk straight out of here,' she told him. 'I've got the job I wanted.'

'If you leave without working out your notice I shall have no hesitation in suing you.'

She knew he meant it. Some people knew to their cost that he was of a litigious disposition. Although she quailed at the prospect she decided to beat him at his own game. 'And if you physically abuse me *I* shall have no hesitation in suing *you*. I still have the bruises from last time.'

'You're playing a dangerous game, Cordelia.'

'Am I? I should imagine that some of your clients might take their custom elsewhere if they found out that you were in the habit of whiplashing your secretary.'

Nigel gave her a contemptuous look and turned his back on her, going into the bathroom. She went through to her desk and began to look through the work she had been doing before lunch. Although she was outwardly calm her heartbeat had practically doubled and her ears were on full alert. She heard the toilet flush and then the soft tread of Nigel's shoes on the carpet. The hairs began to prickle on the nape of her neck as she realized that he was standing at the entrance to her part of the office, watching her.

'All right, I accept that things are not going to be as they were,' she heard him say quietly. 'But can we at least be friends, Cordelia?'

She looked round at last and, seeing how crestfallen he looked, was shocked to find that she felt really sorry for him. But her guard was up and she didn't trust her reaction.

'What do you want from me now, Nigel?'

He shrugged, palms up. 'Nothing except a good day's work, I guess. I'm sorry things can't be as they were. I thought we might have some fun for the last couple of weeks. But if you're not into it there's no point.'

'It's just . . . well, I'm afraid I don't trust you any more. Maybe it's because of Inez, I don't know. Anyway, of course we can be friends. For the next two weeks, at least!'

Cordelia smiled brightly at him but his dark eyes looked pained and haunted as he turned away and returned to his desk. The thrill she felt at standing up to him faded abruptly.

Only the thought of seeing Lucien again kept her going through the afternoon, yet even that made her feel guilty. It was because of him that she had betrayed both Nigel and Ralph. She'd not been straightforward with either of them, taking on a new lover behind their backs and then behaving out of character – or, at least, out of the character she pretended to be when she was with them.

But it had become harder and harder to go on as before, playing sub to Nigel's dom and dom to Ralph's sub. With Lucien she was just . . . herself. She had begun to wonder who that was, and now Lucien was beginning to show her, to let her find herself again. It was a quest that, once begun, could not be lightly abandoned.

Among the various outfits that Nigel kept for her in the office were one or two less outrageous dresses. When he went into the bathroom again she opened the cupboard and grabbed one of them: a sleek blue silk dress with spaghetti straps holding up a boned bodice that made the most of her tits. *Lucien will love this*, she thought, as she rolled it up and stuffed it into the shopping bag she kept in the office. She planned to slip into the Ladies at the department store down the street and change into it, doing her hair and make-up at the same time. Then she would slink along to the wine bar in time to meet her lover.

When Nigel finally dismissed her at five, Cordelia put her plan into operation. Fortunately the store was fairly empty at that time of day, so she was able to get into the Ladies more or less unnoticed and found only one other customer washing her hands before departing. Going into one of the cubicles, she hastily swapped her office blouse and skirt for the glamorous dress, hoping that it wouldn't look too odd beneath her leather jacket. Then she emerged and touched up first her eyes, applying a purplish-blue shadow that enhanced their size, then her lipstick, making a pretty pink mouth with a glossy sheen. A squirt of her favourite perfume completed the transformation.

Feeling feminine and sexy, Cordelia left the cloakroom and went down in the lift as if she had a perfect right to be there. Heads turned as she ventured forth into the street, however, and she enjoyed the swish of the silk around her knees as she walked along in her high heels, making male eyes goggle. Knowing that she would turn Lucien on the instant he saw her was a real plus, doing wonders for her morale after the sober reflections of that afternoon.

She was early, it seemed. There was no sign of Lucien and as she casually walked up to the bar and slid onto one of the stools Cordelia did her best to quell the uneasy doubt that was making her pulse erratic and her palms sweat a little. What if he didn't show? Here she was, dressed to the nines, and a prey for any man who might fancy chatting her up. She tried to look cool as she ordered a dry martini, but inside she was quaking.

The barman was chatting pleasantly, doing his best to make her feel at ease, when she was tapped on the bare shoulder and turned to see Lucien smiling down at her.

'You look good enough to eat in that dress!'

She sparkled at him, relief flooding through her veins like champagne. 'You're not bad-looking either!' she grinned.

He leaned towards her with an answering smile, wafting a delicious aroma of some French cologne into her nostrils. 'I don't want us to be in public like this for much longer. I want to do things to you that might get me arrested! Let's go to my place, shall we?'

Much as Cordelia would have enjoyed flaunting herself on the arm of such a handsome man in some classy nightclub, the allure of his body was far too strong. She nodded and he led her out of the bar and round the corner to where his car was parked. As soon as they were seated inside he took her face between his hands and planted a long, lingering kiss on her mouth. She responded wholeheartedly, feeling the first aching hunger for him fill her pussy, squeezing her thighs hard together so that the throbbing itch in her clitoris was temporarily eased.

Lucien drew away, first from Cordelia and then from the kerb, smoothly joining the London traffic. After a few minutes he asked her, 'Did your boss give you a hard time for being late this afternoon?'

'He tried to!'

'He sounds pretty strict. Or is it you who keeps him under control?'

Lucien was giving her a sidelong glance, watching her reactions. Cordelia considered telling all, but decided to wait until a more opportune moment. 'Mm . . . he likes to think he's the boss, but I reckon he's going to be pretty lost without me.'

'You mean, he won't know how to work the coffee machine?'

She giggled. 'And the rest!'

As she'd hoped, he let it drop after that, going on to talk about a new painting he'd bought while he was in Paris. Cordelia felt excited at the prospect of getting to know this man. There were so many sides to him and she wanted to have at least a glimpse of them all. He sounded as if he were an art expert and he even dropped a hint that he might take her to Paris when he next visited the private gallery where he made most of his purchases.

She warned herself not to hope for too much. There was something precarious about her current lifestyle and she knew that if she were too reckless and extravagant she might lose all three of her lovers. The spectre of loneliness was too much to risk. Cordelia had always lived for the moment but there had been times in the past when moments had stretched to long, lonely weeks and she dreaded returning to that feeling of isolation.

But there was no danger of that right now, she reminded herself cheerfully as they reached the now-familiar area where Lucien lived. He helped her out of the car and into his flat in a matter of seconds, and once she was safely inside pressed her to the wall with a passionate and relentless kiss that had all her senses reeling and the straps of her gown falling down from her shoulders.

Avidly he lifted the double swell of her breasts to his lips and buried his nose in her cleavage. Cordelia wanted him to take her there and then against the wall, just the way Mickey Rourke took Kim Basinger in that wet alley in *9½ Weeks*. Lucien sensed her need, his hands lifting up the silken folds of her dress and exposing her brief, lacy knickers above the stocking tops. She could feel his hot breath on her breasts, making her nipples stiffen and tingle, as his fingers sought to free her pussy from its flimsy pouch.

Impatiently he tugged at the scrap of lace until she heard it tear and gave a gasp. 'Don't worry, I'll buy you a dozen new pairs!' he grunted, fumbling with his fly.

Cordelia thought of the orange underwear he'd given her and felt her libido rise dramatically, fuelled by adrenalin, as she realized that he was about to plunge into her without any preliminaries. Soon his sturdy cock was nosing at her entrance and she could feel the welcome juices flowing, readying her for instant penetration. Lucien pushed into her hard and strong, filling her up at first thrust and making her gasp with sudden ecstasy.

'If you knew how much I've been wanting to fuck you like this,' he murmured as he lifted her thighs. She wound her legs around his waist then crossed her ankles, her body still hard pressed against the wall. He rammed into her again and again, supporting her with his hands and grunting with the exertion. Cordelia loved the sheer male energy of the man. She was high on his pheromones, driven wild by his testosterone, drunk on this new cocktail called 'Lucien's Love Liquor'.

Her eyes were open, staring into his, as her climax approached. She was still staring into the dark depths of his soul as the first flurries of sensation took her and shook her, turning her flesh into liquid bliss. Fierce electric spasms followed, making her clutch at her lover's neck to bring him close, so close, his body hard against her and his cock hard within her. She felt consumed by him, and when the hot spurt of his seed fountained into her she felt complete, satiated, and collapsed into his arms with a long, faint 'Aah!' of utter contentment.

He carried her as if she were a doll, staggering a little but holding her safe, through to his bedroom where he deposited her gently on his big bed. Then he lay beside her and took her in his arms again. Cordelia snuggled up to him as he murmured in her ear, 'That's just for starters. There are several more courses on the menu in this love feast. Do you feel up to them?'

'Just give me a few minutes . . .' she responded, still lost in the drowsy afterglow.

'That's okay, you don't have to do a thing for now.'

He began to strip the gown off her, then unclasped her stockings from her suspenders and rolled them down her legs. Naked save for the push-up bra, she felt him gently massaging her feet with some sensuous oil, sending a voluptuous warmth spreading upward throughout her body. Relaxed and happy she let him do whatever he wanted, his slow fingers doing a good job of awakening her desire for him again.

When Lucien at last lifted her thighs over his shoulders and came to lick at her overheated vulva she was in seventh heaven. His tongue kept up a steady rhythm and a delicate touch while both hands were busily occupied, his right forefinger making gentle inroads into her puckered anus while his left was dabbling at the opening of her cunt, moving in and out like a youth joyriding on a waterslide. Cordelia gasped and moaned as a second orgasm took her almost by surprise, flushing through her with a fierce erotic energy that left her panting.

'God, Lucien, you are one hell of a lover!' she exclaimed when the cataclysm had passed. She could feel his erection still nudging against her thigh as he lay beside her.

'It takes real inspiration to be a good lover,' he commented. 'And you inspire me like no other woman I've ever known, Cordelia. So much so that I have the horrible suspicion I might be falling in love with you.'

Chapter Fifteen

'Willoughby, Willoughby, N. Willoughby . . . aha, gotcha!'

Ralph was leafing through the financial section of the yellow pages and at last he found the name of Cordelia's boss. It wasn't a boxed ad, just a single-line entry, but the address and phone code were right for the area. Now all he had to do was work out the best approach. Perhaps he might ask him for investment advice. That seemed to be what he was there for. But what if Cordelia answered the phone?

He thought about using the Internet – but what if Cordelia went through her boss's e-mail as well as his snail mail? It was frustrating to know nothing about her work. In the end he decided to phone, but to use the 141 number so the call couldn't be traced. If a woman's voice answered he would replace the receiver immediately.

He decided to risk it and was relieved when a man's voice answered. Ralph had his story worked out but he began nervously, saying Willoughby had been recommended to him by a friend of a friend. At first this aroused suspicion. Willoughby said he didn't give his expert advice to 'just anyone off the street' but after Ralph had dropped a few of the names he'd picked up off the Internet, Willoughby sounded mollified.

'I could meet you for a drink tonight, after work,' he suggested. 'But it can't be for long. I have a couple of other clients to see this evening.'

When he put the receiver down Ralph was triumphant. Cordelia had already told him that she wouldn't be back that night – it was becoming a common occurrence, he reflected ruefully – so there would be no problem about him going out for a few hours. The only difficulty was how to get Willoughby off the subject of finance and onto Cordelia in the few minutes at his disposal. In between boning up on the markets through the Internet, he spent most of the rest of the day thinking about how to approach his mistress's boss.

By the time he entered the wine bar, just around the corner from Willoughby's office, Ralph was feeling horribly on edge. He hadn't come to any conclusion about how to bring the conversation round to what he really wanted to talk about. His instructions were to ask the barman to point Willoughby out, and he did so full of trepidation, afraid that this meeting might get reported to Cordelia and he might end up in hot water.

The man gave him a superficially amiable greeting, although Ralph sensed at once that it wouldn't do to get on the wrong side of him. Tall and dark, with saturnine good looks, he was dressed in an impeccably tailored suit and sipping a glass of white burgundy from a bottle which he offered to share. The two men sat down at the discreet corner table while the bar filled up all around them with City types and their secretaries or girlfriends. Ralph was painfully reminded that, in Willoughby's case, Cordelia probably served both functions.

The thought spurred him into action and he decided to place his cards on the table. After some preliminary chat about trading via the Internet, Ralph admitted that that wasn't what he wanted to talk about. 'Forgive me if I seem to have got you here under false pretences,' he began, defensively, 'but I really wanted to talk to you about your secretary, Cordelia Blane.'

Willoughby's face changed dramatically, and Ralph was terribly afraid that his upfront approach had backfired on him. 'Soon to be my ex-secretary,' the man muttered. His tone grew sarcastic. 'Why, do you want the bitch?'

Although it rankled to hear his beloved mistress so described, Ralph managed to keep his feelings in check. 'I'm living with her,' he said, quietly.

'Good God! You're not! You mean – as her lover?'

As Willoughby looked him up and down he felt a flush of shame heat his pale cheeks. He nodded, unwilling to describe himself as her servant in case that invoked yet another shocked reaction. Well, anyway, he *did* love her, he told himself in self-defence. More than this complacent prick could ever understand.

'And I look after the house for her. Do the cooking and stuff.'

'What's this got to do with me?' Willoughby went on, rather tetchily. 'I know nothing about her private life, and I don't want to either.'

It was all going badly. Ralph sipped his wine anxiously. He felt intimidated by this man and, he had to admit, jealous of him too. He'd always been jealous of her boss.

'I'm . . . er, sorry to have got you here under false pretences,' he said at last.

'Are you wasting my time?' Ralph found the question odd. But Willoughby looked thoughtful. He continued, 'I must say I was knocked for six when Cordelia gave in her notice. Perhaps you have some light to throw on that. If you have, I'd be glad to hear it.'

'I think she's seeing someone else. Someone who is affecting her in strange ways. I thought maybe it was . . . well, I wondered if she was having a relationship with her boss. I mean, it's a bit of cliché isn't it, boss and secretary kind of thing . . .'

He tailed off awkwardly, but Willoughby didn't seem put off. He looked thoughtful. 'Now that *is* interesting. Of course, I'd noticed a strangeness about her recently, but I'd put it down to . . . other factors. A third man in her life, eh?'

'A *third*?' Ralph was startled, then surprised to see that it was her boss's turn to look embarrassed.

'I suppose you could say that Cordelia and I had a special relationship, something more than the usual boss-secretary one. She is a very special woman, as I'm sure you know. I shall be very sorry indeed to lose her.'

'I'm afraid I might lose her too,' Ralph admitted, miserably. It was one thing to think such a thing but another to say it, and to a stranger. It made the possibility seem all the more horribly real.

Willoughby gave a wry smile. 'So we have something in common after all, a fear of losing Cordelia. In my case I fear it's too late, since she's already given in her notice. I gather she has another job lined up. But a new lover, now that's something I hadn't thought of. Do you have any proof?'

'Not exactly. I mean, she's had a few flings from time to time but none of them came to anything. I have a feeling this one is more serious, though. She stays out late, sometimes the whole night, and she's never done that before.'

'Mm. So what do you think I might be able to do about it, given that she'll be in my employ for less than two weeks now? I presume that you need information, is that it?'

'I can probably get that. Quite honestly, I'm not sure what I did hope to gain from meeting you. I'm . . . well, I'm at the end of my tether, really, not knowing what to do.'

'Have you thought of simply confronting her, asking her what's going on?'

Ralph shrank back. 'Oh, I couldn't possible do that!'

'Why? What kind of a wimp are you?'

The flush spread over Ralph's cheeks again and this time Willoughby grew suspicious. 'Wimp, eh? Is that how she likes her men when she's off duty?' His mind was almost visibly racing ahead, making his eyes gleam with the excitement of the chase. 'What a thought! Cordelia the submissive secretary becomes Cordelia the strict mistress at home. Is that how it is, eh?'

Ralph nodded again, lowering his eyes. Willoughby gave a low chuckle. 'Well, well! You have to hand it to the girl, she's found out how to have her cake and eat it! But what about this mystery lover, what can he have to offer her that she doesn't get out of us two, I wonder?'

'I don't know. I wish I did.'

'Have you any idea of the man's identity?'

'I'm not sure. It could be one of the guests at a party she gave a while back.'

Ralph remembered the Frenchman. That was the only candidate he could come up with, unless it was someone altogether unknown to him, which seemed less likely. He recalled the look that the Frenchie had given him with distaste. It was as if he knew how utterly he depended on Cordelia and was determined to break the bond between them. He shuddered to think of it.

At least he now seemed to have an ally. But how much did Willoughby care, now that Cordelia was leaving him? Ralph decided this conversation had gone as far as it was going to. He'd found out that Cordelia's relations with her boss had been more than strictly business, but that was all. Perhaps it was time to leave and sort things out as best he could by himself. He downed his wine and put his glass back on the table with an air of finality.

Willoughby picked up his briefcase. 'If you find out who he is for sure, let me know. Perhaps we can warn him off. Seems to me that things were going rather well before and if I can persuade her to continue seeing me occasionally while she continues to live with you then we'll all be happy. Am I right?'

Ralph quickly calculated the score. Perhaps he could continue to live with one rival. It seemed that all the time he had known Cordelia she'd been leading this double life, playing one rôle in the office and another at home. But this new lover was a destabilizing influence that could not be tolerated. With Willoughby's help he might be able to eliminate him, and then their little love triangle could be restored to its former happy equilibrium.

Before they parted, Willoughby gave Ralph his private phone number with instructions to let him know as soon as he had established the 'third man's' identity for sure. 'Then we'll know exactly what kind of animal we're dealing with,' he ended, with a grim smile and a handshake. Ralph watched him go, wishing he had the man's self-assurance. He could quite see why Cordelia had been attracted to him.

After he'd left, Ralph stayed on in the bar, finishing the rather fine burgundy and musing about how he was going to set about the detective task. It would not be difficult to turn his suspicions into hard evidence, he was pretty sure of that. The difficult part would be deciding just what to do about it.

Cordelia sat curled up on her big sofa in front of the television and stretched languorously. It was nice to have a night in, for a change. Since her affair with Lucien had begun in earnest she'd scarcely had a moment to herself. Talk about a whirlwind romance! But perhaps it was time to sit back and take stock. She switched off the TV, which she hadn't really been watching anyway, and drifted into pensive mode.

Ever since Lucien had mentioned that taboo four-letter word, 'love', Cordelia had been in something of a turmoil although she gave no hint of it to him. Long ago she had decided that she would run her love life as a game, not for real, and that commitment was something she wouldn't risk. Not after she had given her heart to that shallow creep when she was eighteen and been taken for a ride. But now she knew that she would have to face it again, that stomach-churning emotion she had always tried to avoid.

Because – it was a funny thing – if someone said they loved you it was quite hard to resist feeling the same way about them. If you were as attracted to them as she was to Lucien, that was. Things had been different with Nigel and Ralph. The rôles she played with them had strict rules and the erotic feelings were carefully controlled, on both sides. She had no doubt that Ralph loved her in his way, but it was with a doglike devotion that sometimes got on her nerves and although she was fond of him he didn't move her like Lucien did.

In the same way she had felt attached to Nigel, although the ill-timed introduction of Inez had diminished her loyalty to him so that now she was relieved to be leaving him. But what if Lucien demanded her exclusive love? She had never promised herself to one man since that disastrous episode of the broken engagement. And what would happen to poor Ralph if she slung him out?

She told herself that she was worrying unduly, that she should cross those bridges if and when she came to them. For the moment she should be content to remember her last wonderful evening with Lucien and look forward to the next one. He had introduced her to new heights of sensuality in the few short weeks since they'd met and she was amazed that there were still new things to learn, new sensations to experience. After the ritualized sex she had enjoyed with Nigel and Ralph this new lover had the power to surprise and astound her, to take her to places she had never before imagined.

It was going on for eleven and Cordelia decided to take a bath. She didn't bother Ralph, she wanted to be alone. That way she could better explore the strange new feelings that were taking her over as she thought about Lucien. She ran herself a scented bath and was soon soaking in it, thinking about last night. They had spent the first part of the night at a club in Soho where the cabaret had consisted of a white girl and a black girl making lesbian love.

'Does this turn you on?' Lucien had enquired, as she watched the performance with frank curiosity. When she nodded he'd asked, 'Have you ever made love to another woman?'

'Mm – hm,' she'd replied, non-committally.

Back at his flat he'd made her talk about it. Cordelia didn't let on that Inez was the mistress of her boss but pretended they had met at a party. It was strange at first, talking about it, but she soon found herself becoming aroused both by the memory and by Lucien's rapt attention. He explained that he wanted to know about it in case the pleasure she'd derived from her lesbian experience had been greater than when she'd made love with him.

'Of course not!' she'd laughed, but he seemed only half convinced.

'Tell me exactly what she did and how she did it.'

So she'd gone into detail about the act of cunnilingus that Inez had performed upon her. Thinking about it now, she grew aroused again. Her fingers moved between her thighs under the bathwater, seeking out the hard button of her clitoris, and she stroked the slippery nub of flesh until she felt the sharp tingling rise in her, spreading beyond her vulva down her thighs and up her stomach. With the other hand she smoothed soapy lather over her breasts and nipples. The keen pleasure coursed through her, making her long for a climax.

She finished washing quickly and stepped out of the bath, picking up a bottle of body oil. Lying down on the thick bath mat she smoothed the oil all over her breasts and stomach, her flesh quivering in anticipation as she reached her thighs. Parting the soft lips of her labia she burrowed her way inside with her finger and was soon frigging herself again, bringing herself close to orgasm. It didn't take long.

Soon she was writhing in ecstasy all over the bathroom floor, moaning softly as she climaxed with a couple of fingers in her pussy, imagining that it was Lucien's cock inside her. Afterwards she lay there, hot and panting, wishing that she could have been with him that night instead of masturbating alone.

But she would see him again soon, maybe tomorrow. He'd said he'd ring. She found herself starting to resent the time he had to spend with other people, starting to want to be with him all the time. It was frightening, this urge to share his life completely. Who knew where it might lead?

Eventually Cordelia rose and towelled herself dry, then put on her robe and went into the bedroom. She was surprised to find Ralph in there, standing by her dressing table with something in his hand. He started guiltily and she realized that he was holding her diary.

'What are you doing?' she frowned. 'Give me that!' Sheepishly he handed it over. 'Were you daring to read my private diary?' she thundered.

Ralph shook his head but she could see he was scared stiff. Good. It was about time she disciplined him again. She snatched the leather-bound book from him and threw it on the bed.

'I . . . I came in her to make sure everything was in order before you went to bed,' he told her, his eyes darting wildly around the room. 'And when I saw your diary on the dressing table I thought it should go by the phone. In case . . . in case you wanted to make an appointment.'

'Liar! You were reading it. Take your trousers down and lean over the bed. I'll teach you to snoop when my back is turned!'

She fetched the cane that she kept in her wardrobe. It was not an implement she used very often, but she enjoyed swishing it through the air and feeling its supple strength. Seeing Ralph's pink behind exposed and rotund before her brought out all the old feelings, and yet they had changed subtly. Cordelia was aware that she was going through the motions, that she was doing it more for him than for herself. Perhaps that had always been the case.

She raised the cane in the air and brought it down smartly on Ralph's naked buttocks. He winced, but withstood the blow well. She gave him another stroke, and another, but then decided that enough was enough. If he was going to derive any gratification from the whipping he must have done so by now. And her initial anger at finding him with her diary had subsided. She didn't suppose that he had discovered anything particularly secret.

Replacing the cane in the wardrobe Cordelia came back to find Ralph still slumped over the bed. She gave his rump a few resounding slaps, enjoying the feel of his hot flesh beneath her palm. 'All right, you can get up now,' she told him, when she'd finished.

He turned round and looked up at her, but she was disturbed to see something other than the usual expression of abject devotion in his face. This time he looked wary, resentful even. Cordelia gave an uncertain smile. 'Now you're excused. I'd like a brandy, for a nightcap. Bring it to me in bed.'

She'd intended to grant him some favour to make up for the beating, a chance to caress her breasts perhaps, or even to place his cock between them and jack off. Something not too strenuous as far as she was concerned, anyway, since she felt tired. But when he reappeared bearing the brandy glass on a silver tray his face still looked sullen and his movements were strained as he placed the tray on the bedside table.

'Thank you, Ralph,' she said pleasantly, patting the side of the bed. 'You may sit here for a while and chat to me. Is everything all right?'

'Perfectly, madam,' he muttered. But there was a sarcastic ring to his tone that set her on alert again.

'Are you quite sure?' The feeling that he knew more than he was letting on grew in her. 'Did you see anything in my diary that disturbed you?' she added, on a hunch.

His eyes flickered guiltily. 'No, madam. I did not read it.'

'I find that hard to believe. You are curious about the life I lead outside the home, aren't you?' He remained stubbornly silent. She poked his upper arm, quite hard. 'Aren't you?'

He shrugged. 'Not particularly.'

Suddenly Cordelia tired of him. There was such a difference between the formalized way she behaved with Ralph and the way she was with Lucien, so open and carefree. 'You may go!' she told him. 'But don't forget, if I find you prying among my things in future you can expect a more severe punishment. Goodnight.'

'Goodnight, madam,' he mumbled, still in that disrespectful tone. But she let it pass and he shuffled out of her bedroom.

Maybe soon I'll have a heart-to-heart with him, she thought, *tell him what's going on*. But it was not going to be easy. Cordelia knew that she had a responsibility towards Ralph, one that she had not been discharging properly since she met Lucien. This state of affairs could not go on for much longer.

When Lucien phoned next morning, however, all thoughts of anyone else promptly left Cordelia's head. He rang early and she was still in bed, picking up her bedside phone with a bleary-eyed 'Hello?'

'I love the way you sound when you're sleepy,' Lucien purred. 'Did you sleep well, *ma chère*? Did you have sweet dreams – of me?'

'Mm! But I'd rather see you in the flesh.'

'My own preference entirely. How do you fancy a weekend in the country, just you and me?'

'Really?' She was wide awake now. 'That sounds wonderful!'

'A friend of mine is lending us his cottage in Berkshire. It's near the Thames, awfully pretty. With a few smart restaurants nearby. If the weather's fine we might even try a spot of boating.'

'Sounds like heaven!'

'I'll meet you in our usual wine bar at six, then. Bring your country casuals, but something a bit dressy too. I can't wait to see you again, darling!'

'Me too.'

Cordelia replaced the receiver and lay back on the pillow, dreaming. A whole weekend with Lucien! Time to really get to know each other on long walks, communing with nature. It sounded perfect.

Then she heard the familiar sounds of Ralph switching on the coffee grinder in the kitchen and a shadow passed over her heart. He would be upset that she was going away yet again, this time for the whole weekend. She knew he had probably already planned his menus and shopping lists. Still, perhaps he could be persuaded to visit his sister in Brighton, then she wouldn't feel so bad about abandoning him.

By the time he entered with her coffee Cordelia was dozing again. She sat up brightly and took the tray on her knee, trying to sound casual as she said, 'By the way, I shall be going away tonight and not getting back until sometime on Sunday. Do feel free to visit your sister, if you wish.'

Ralph stared at her dully, looking as if he'd heard the words but couldn't fathom the meaning. She took a sip of coffee. 'Thank you. That will be all for now.'

'Going away for the weekend . . .' he repeated.

She snapped at him. 'Yes. Don't worry about my clothes, I'll sort and pack them. You just prepare my muesli. I'll be down in ten minutes.'

He slunk out and she sprang from the bed and into the bathroom, where she took a rapid, invigorating shower. When she entered the kitchen in her bathrobe Ralph was sitting moodily, drinking a mug of tea, and for a few seconds he appeared not to notice her. When he did, he got up off his stool but not in the prompt manner with which he usually sprang to attention. He just slid off it, sloppily. A reprimand was on Cordelia's lips but she decided to bite her tongue. It wouldn't do to antagonize Ralph any more than she'd already done.

When she arrived at the office Nigel was already there. He raised his brows when he saw her suitcase. 'Going away for the weekend?'

Cordelia recalled the 'conference' she had attended with her boss. That was what had started all the trouble between them, with Inez getting involved. But it all seemed a long time ago now that Lucien had come into her life.

'Yes,' she answered coolly, taking the case through to the cloakroom. She turned back, once she had deposited it, to see Nigel still staring after her. 'What did you want me to wear for you today, sir?'

'It doesn't matter. Stay as you are.'

He sounded bitter and Cordelia felt a pang of guilt. She reminded herself that it was guilt that was keeping her on here when she might just as well take her leave. After all, she could have gone off to Paris with Lucien for a week, then come back ready and refreshed to start her new job. She was sure he would have jumped at the chance. Instead she chose, out of loyalty, to work out her notice with Nigel. She had nothing to reproach herself with, she decided.

'Well, what do you want me to do, sir?'

'Later this morning you will be inducting your replacement. Until then you can deal with the mail.'

Cordelia was stunned. Of course, she knew there would have to be a replacement for her but she had no idea Nigel had chosen her already. She was filled with an excited anticipation. What kind of girl would he have chosen, and did he intend to 'train' her successor the way he'd trained her? Although she sat down and worked steadily through the mail, outwardly calm, inside Cordelia was seething with suppressed excitement.

Promptly at eleven the new girl arrived. Cordelia answered the door and introduced herself with a handshake, taking in the salient features of the woman as she did so. Pamela Ransom was a petite, attractive blonde with massed curls, big blue eyes and a pink rosebud mouth. She had a prominent bosom, shown off to good effect in the tight-fitting double-breasted jacket, and a slim waist and hips. It struck Cordelia at once that Pamela's looks were the very antithesis of hers.

'Ah, Pamela – very prompt!' Nigel said, coming towards the door with his hand outstretched. 'Cordelia, make us all a coffee, would you?'

There was a dreamlike quality to the next half-hour, with the three of them chatting politely while all kinds of undercurrents were going on beneath the surface. Cordelia sensed that Pamela was wondering what kind of relationship she had with her boss, wondering whether it was a sexual one. She was also aware of the chemical sparks flying between Pamela and Nigel. Their attraction to each other made her absurdly jealous.

'Why should I care?' she asked herself. But she couldn't deny that she did.

After a while she was left to put Pamela through her paces on the computer. The girl was pleasant, and quick to pick things up, but Cordelia sensed a tension between them that she couldn't quite understand. Had Nigel said anything to her about their 'special relationship'? She wondered when he'd found time to take interviews, then recalled that he'd been absent from the office several times that week. He must have used another room in the building.

'I'm going to leave you two lovely ladies together for a few minutes,' Nigel announced, looking in on them. 'Don't gossip about me behind my back, now, will you?'

His dark eyes bored into Cordelia with a warning glint but she smiled sweetly at him and turned her attention back to the screen. The instant he left the office, however, Pamela's manner changed completely. She turned all girly and giggly, her blue eyes dancing as she said in a low voice, 'Okay, now you can dish the dirt on your sexy boss. Does he do it in office hours?'

Cordelia pretended to be affronted. 'I beg your pardon?'

'Oh, you don't have to pretend with me. It's obvious that he's a randy pervert and he chose me because he thought I'd come across. That's okay, I'm used to it. My last boss used to chase me all over the office, and when he caught me, he liked to mega-ram me over the computer keyboard.'

'Is that why you left?'

'Sort of. It got boring after a while and I thought I'd find something a bit more kinky, if you know what I mean. What's Nigel into?'

'Maybe you should find out from his girlfriend.'

'He's got a mistress too, has he? Is she up for three-somes?'

'Don't ask me.'

Cordelia wouldn't put it past her boss to be testing her out, setting a trap through this frank-talking floozy. She was determined to remain discreet, even though Pamela was giving her arch looks. 'I *am* asking you.'

'I wouldn't know.'

'Are you saying you never let your boss fuck you, then?'

Cordelia shrugged. 'I'm not saying anything, one way or the other. Now, do you want to look at these spreadsheets or not?'

Pamela pouted. 'I can learn about them any time, but we may only have a few minutes left to swap more interesting information. Be a sport, Cordelia. Let me know what to expect. You know what they say, "Forewarned is forearmed." '

Cordelia couldn't resist the pun. 'You need to be fourarmed all right, with Nigel around. And four-eyed would help, too. Not to mention four-legged.'

Pamela let out a scream when she got the joke. 'Likes it doggy fashion, then, does he?'

'Oh ha, ha!'

'But, seriously for a minute, have you enjoyed working for him?'

The clear blue eyes had turned earnest and Cordelia felt she owed her a fair assessment. 'Nigel has certain . . . idiosyncrasies. If you can cater to them he'll be a good boss. I imagine he chose you because he thought you would fit in. How did he find you, by the way?'

Pamela's eyes sparkled wickedly. 'Through the pages of a rather select magazine, actually.'

'Which one?'

'*Super-Sexy Secs.*'

'Oh, I see. Well, in that case, I should imagine you would suit him very well indeed.'

'He's got to suit me as well. I'm on a month's trial with one week's notice, either side.'

'Yes, I remember. Those were the same terms . . .'

'Intimate terms, that's what you mean, isn't it? You were on intimate terms.' Pamela sighed, pushing up from the desk with straight arms so that her ample breasts were outlined even more pertly. Then she said in a low, seductive drawl, 'I can't wait to step into your thigh-length leather boots, Miss Cordelia. I just can't wait!'

Chapter Sixteen

'She's going away for the weekend, and I know it's with *him*!'

Ralph had managed to get word to Nigel before Cordelia arrived at the office that morning, but Willoughby sounded fed up. 'Damn! I've got the new girl coming in today, and I was planning to take her out to dinner afterwards, but that will have to wait. It's more important to nail this bugger, I'm sure you'll agree. Any idea what time he's picking her up?'

'Six. At the wine bar they use. The same one we went to. I saw it in her diary.'

'Oh, you have been a busy little bee, haven't you?'

The sarcasm ran off Ralph like water over oil. He was used to being mocked and, sometimes, he liked it. The thought that Nigel was annoyed at having to put up with such a wimp for an ally amused him. He would show that poser that he knew what he was talking about. They would follow the pair to their country cottage and spy on them, gaining the final proof they needed that Cordelia was knocking off the Frenchie. Then he'd see Willoughby smiling on the other side of his face!

Ralph drove to the centre of town in a hired car. He was pleased he'd thought of that. Cordelia would recognize his car and, presumably, her boss's too, so it was best to be on the safe side. By five-thirty he was parked opposite the entrance to Willoughby's office block, an area which by now had become rather familiar to him. He enjoyed playing detective. It appealed to the schoolboy sneak in him that loved to nose out secrets and then, at the moment of maximum damage, leak them to the right person.

Still, the thought of taking his revenge on his mistress filled him with contrary feelings. He owed her some loyalty, but he felt she'd broken her bond and therefore his own obligation to her was limited. Besides, it was possible, with a little effort, to imagine that she had been unfairly seduced away from him by Lucien Le Frog. He imagined that her boss might take a similar view. Whether it would be possible to restore the previous happy arrangement was doubtful, but at least he and Willoughby would be doing something instead of just putting up with the situation.

Ralph had agreed to park nearby and keep watch so he'd provided himself with a newspaper to hide behind, just like in the movies. Peering around the edge he saw Cordelia on the arm of her paramour. They must have bumped into each other en route, and now she was laughing and joking with him. Incensed, Ralph watched them stroll into the wine bar like an established courting couple. *They've only known each other a matter of weeks*, he told himself sourly. Such sudden infatuation was bound to end in tears.

Her boss was a while appearing, but at last he came along cautiously on the other side of the road. Ralph gave him a honk and wave from the shelter of his car and eventually Willoughby spotted him and came over.

'Get in,' Ralph invited him. 'We're better off keeping watch from the car, then we can get going as soon as they appear.'

'They're inside?' Willoughby glanced towards the lighted windows of the wine bar, a wistful expression on his face. Ralph nodded, feeling almost sorry for his rival. Amazing how having a common enemy formed bonds between men who had cause to hate each other before.

The couple didn't stay long in the bar, but soon emerged clutching a magnum of champagne, then walked back along the pavement towards a side street. Ralph started the engine, which gave a discreet cough, then moved slowly along the main road in the stream of traffic. He waited a while to turn right, hoping he wouldn't miss them, but by the time he caught up with the couple they were getting into a sleek BMW.

'Don't know how you're going to keep up with that thing,' Willoughby moaned. 'It'll be hell on the motorway.'

But Ralph had his trump card. 'It doesn't matter, because I know where they're going.'

'You do?'

'Yes. Diary again. I have the address and the phone number of the house they're staying in near Pangbourne.'

'Good Lord!'

Ralph found Willoughby's look of admiration most gratifying.

They were soon on the A4 with Willoughby navigating, but by the time they turned off at junction twelve Cordelia and Lucien had gone zooming ahead in the fast lane. Not that Ralph cared. If they got to the place first the chances were they'd be *in flagrante delicto* by the time they arrived to spy on them. He had no doubt that spying was Willoughby's bag. He seemed just the type.

When they arrived at the charming cottage near the river it was dark and there was only a faint orange glow coming from an upper-floor window, looking more like the light from a lamp or candle. Ralph let the car's engine die away at some distance from the house and then they made their way on foot, walking on the grass verge instead of the gravel to minimize the noise of their footsteps.

'What the hell do we do now?' Willoughby wanted to know, when they were within a stone's throw of the front door.

'You stay here while I do a recce,' Ralph suggested.

He could tell that Willoughby wasn't the sort to take orders but Ralph found, much to his surprise, that he rather liked dishing them out. It made him feel manly to be taking charge of the situation. He walked stealthily up to the front door and gave the handle a try but it was firmly locked, so he went round to the back of the cottage, which was in utter darkness. He tried the back door but that was locked too. Then he found some steps leading down to a cellar. To his surprise the door at the bottom, which was old and rotten, opened grudgingly on rusted hinges.

Taking his torch from his pocket Ralph entered the musty cellar and shone the light on a flight of steps in the corner. He overcame his fear of rats in order to ascend the steps and try the door to the house at the top. To his amazement, it could be opened.

He hurried back to where he'd left Willoughby and took him round to the back of the house again. Carefully they picked their way over the rubbish-strewn floor and up the steps. The door to the house creaked a little, and they waited in the dark to make quite sure the coast was clear before proceeding.

The hall had an oak staircase that led past a stained-glass window to the rooms upstairs. Ralph began to climb, slowly and cautiously, wincing and pausing at every creak of a stair, with Willoughby following behind. He had the impression that the man was impatient and would have preferred to storm the place, but Ralph wanted to be sure of taking the couple completely by surprise.

There were faint murmurs coming from one of the bedrooms, the one with the glow beneath the door, so they knew which room to aim for. Ralph tiptoed over the runner on the landing and took hold of the brass door handle, turning it very slowly by degrees. Soon he was able to push open the door until a crack of light shone out and, putting his eye to it, he had a good view of the bed.

Cordelia was lying back against a bank of fancy pillows with her knees up as if she were about to give birth. Between her thighs crouched the French bastard, busily licking away. In the lamplight the sweat on her breasts and face gleamed and her eyes were closed, her mouth soft and open in an expression of blissful enjoyment.

'What's going on?' Willoughby whispered hoarsely, pressing close to him. 'Let me see!'

Reluctant as he was to draw his eyes away from the terrible scene before him Ralph moved his head for the other man to get a view. He felt a tight knot of hatred in his stomach, making him want to rush in and attack the usurper, but he settled for clenching his fists – for the time being, at least.

'What are we going to do?' Willoughby whispered again, his face contorted with disgust.

Ralph took the handcuffs out of his pocket. He'd brought them along as a precaution. Ironically they were the ones his mistress had used on him. He dangled them before Willoughby. 'I'll put these on Cordelia while you grab hold of the Frenchie. You're bigger than I am. I think we should teach them both a lesson, don't you?'

'Agreed. Let's do it. We can decide how to proceed once we have the pair of them at our mercy.'

As the two men burst into the room Cordelia opened her eyes, suddenly projected out of the state of bliss she'd been wallowing in and disoriented by the sight of what she thought at first were two robbers or madmen, perhaps even the owner of the cottage. Various possibilities rushed through her head before she became aware of their identity, and the shock of realizing that her other lovers had broken in on her and Lucien, made her scream with alarm.

'What the hell are you doing?' she gasped, as Ralph grabbed her arms and pulled them behind her, securing her wrists with handcuffs. 'Are you crazy?'

He said nothing, just went to aid Nigel who was struggling to prevent Lucien from doing him some serious damage. The pair of them forced the Frenchman to the ground and ended up sitting on his back and legs to keep him down.

Cordelia felt fury rise in her as she realized that two of her lovers were ganging up on the third in a most ruthless and undignified manner. *How dare they barge in here like that!* She heaved herself off the bed and went over to give Nigel a hefty kick, but he caught her foot and she crashed to the ground so that all four of them were in a tangled heap on the carpet.

'This is bloody ridiculous!' she protested. 'What are you two doing here?'

'I was going to ask you and this French fucker the same question,' Nigel replied, a dull anger visible in the dark depths of his eyes. 'Except it was bloody obvious!'

'You've no right to do this.' She remembered catching Ralph with her diary and turned on him furiously. 'Did you put him up to this?'

Ralph was looking at her with smug assurance and she wanted to punch him, but the painful bite of the cuffs into her wrists reminded her that she could do very little. Beneath her anger was a growing fear that they would do something very nasty to Lucien. She would never forgive herself if anything happened to him on her account.

'We're in it together,' Ralph mumbled. He wouldn't look her in the eye – she wasn't surprised.

'What do you want, then?' she asked, wearily. 'You know I'm seeing someone else. So what? I never had an exclusive agreement with either of you.'

'Cordelia!' It was Lucien's turn to speak. He twisted his head round to look at her and she saw the resignation in his eyes. And something else: amusement, perhaps? For a moment she felt as if she were the dupe of some practical joke with the three men in league against her. Then he said, 'Let them enjoy their jealousy if they want to. They're entitled to it.'

It wasn't what she'd expected to hear. She felt as if she were in the middle of some bizarre dream. The biochemical high that had been filling her with ecstasy seconds ago was turning sour in her blood, filling her with poison, and she wanted revenge on her two lovers for spoiling her fun. 'They're not entitled to burst in on us like this. No one is.'

'Cordelia!' Nigel was using his office voice on her and, try as she might to resist its insidious appeal, she felt herself succumbing to that note of authority. 'Get away from us and let us get on with what we have to do. Ralph, fetch that dressing-gown belt. We'll immobilize this bastard.'

She watched helplessly as Ralph went over to the dressing gown hanging behind the door and removed the cord. The pair of them then trussed Lucien like a young steer, tying his hands and feet up together so that his body was bent like a bow. He suffered it with an ironic smile on his face that made her angry. Why didn't he fight them, for heaven's sake? It irked her to see him going along with it all, like a lamb to the slaughter.

'Right!' Nigel stood up, panting, and so did Ralph, leaving Lucien on the floor. 'I imagine he won't give us too much trouble now.'

'I don't know what you hope to gain by this,' Cordelia said to him, coldly. She turned to Ralph. He at least might still be amenable. 'Ralph, can't you see how silly this is? I'm very disappointed in you. I thought you'd have more sense than to get mixed up in some ridiculous revenge plot.'

'I'm sorry, but you cheated on me. And on your boss, too.'

'Cheated? I'll remind you that nowhere in our agreement did I sign an exclusivity clause. Come to think of it, neither did you. For all I know you could have been knocking off anyone during the day while I was at work.'

'Never!' Ralph sounded shocked. 'I would never betray you.'

'Hm. So reading my diary, spying on me, causing me and my lover harm and distress . . . none of that counts as betrayal, does it?'

Ralph had the grace to look ashamed. He blushed and hung his head, so that Nigel was obliged to take over. 'This is sheer impertinence! You have been caught betraying the pair of us and you still talk as if you are not to blame. I think this calls for punishment. Ralph, you will administer the chastisement. It's time you learned how to give discipline as well as receive it.'

Despite herself, Cordelia found herself responding with an illicit thrill to the scenario that was unfolding. She had three men vying with each other for her attention, and although the strange reversal of rôles that was taking place was confusing to her, it was still oddly exciting. She was hot and ready for anything, even though she mistrusted their motives.

Nigel came up and led Cordelia over to the bed. He forced her to kneel beside it and bend forward until her face was half buried in the duvet with her bare bottom stuck out and her hands still cuffed behind her back. The excitement of being naked and vulnerable was getting to her once more and she couldn't help being aware of the renewed throbbing between her labia and the heat spreading over her throat and chest that was making her nipples tingle.

'Ever spanked a woman with your bare hand?' she heard Nigel ask.

'N–no,' came Ralph's murmured response.

'About time, then. This is the woman you revered, the woman you worshipped, and she's been playing around with a bloody Frog. Doesn't that make you mad as hell?'

'Y–yes.'

'Go to it, then. Give her a good trouncing! She's beaten you often enough, I dare say. Now give her a taste of her own medicine.'

Cordelia knew how hard it would be for Ralph to raise his hand against her. There was a long, silent pause. Then she felt the feeble impact of a palm on her left buttock and she knew that he had screwed up the courage to smack her. That first slap seemed to encourage him more because he was soon at it in earnest, making her buns wobble and smart with the relentless rhythm of his palms.

She heard Nigel egging him on from the sidelines. 'That's the style! Give her a good whacking – she deserves it!'

At last the buffeting stopped and Cordelia felt her flesh throb hotly, making her feel both sore and randy. Her mons was pressed hard against the side of the bed and the friction involved whenever he'd thrashed her had stimulated her halfway to a climax. Now she was more concerned about relieving her frustration than she was about easing the pain of the beating.

'That's taught her a lesson she won't forget in a hurry!' Nigel declared, his smug tone getting on her nerves. 'But what about Froggie here? Froggie would a-wooing go, wouldn't he? So he's been a naughty boy too, and must be punished. What's the best way to set about it, would you say, Ralph?'

Cordelia's heart sank with dread. She would be mortified if Lucien were subjected to any kind of humiliation. More than he'd suffered already, of course, which was bad enough. What if they used physical violence on him? She couldn't imagine Ralph taking part in anything like that but she wouldn't put it past Nigel.

She turned her head to see Nigel walking in rings around the still-prostrate Lucien, with Ralph looking on nervously. To see all three of her lovers together was still a novelty and she had to admit that at some level she found it very exciting. It was easy to imagine them all making love to her at once, monopolizing her senses and bringing her to a sensational climax. An erotic shudder passed through her womb as she visualized being fucked in her pussy, arse and mouth at the same time.

'I know!' Nigel's voice brought her back to the harsh reality of the present. 'We'll make the bugger feel jealous, just like he's made us feel. What do you say to that, Ralph?'

'What? You mean . . .'

He had his scared-rabbit look, the one that Cordelia used to despise. Now she found it peculiarly touching. He was out of his depth, being made to play a rôle he wasn't suited to, and she wanted to protect him against that bully Nigel.

'Don't make him do anything he doesn't want to!' she called.

Nigel came striding up. 'You don't have a say in this. *I'm* calling the shots now, and what I say goes. Get up off your knees and lie down on the bed, the way you were with *him* . . .' He pointed in disdain to Lucien, who was not grinning quite so widely now.

When Cordelia hesitated she was pushed backwards onto the bed and her thighs were roughly pulled apart so that she had no option but to resume the position she'd been in when Lucien was performing cunnilingus on her. Her arms ached from being pulled back and her wrists were beginning to feel the strain too. Yet her body was still aroused and yearning, her breasts taut with the nipples high and hard, and the throbbing of her clitoris was intense.

'Now, Ralph, I'm sure your mistress must have granted you this favour before, hasn't she?' Nigel said in a horrible, condescending tone. Cordelia saw him nod, but he was flushing beetroot. 'But not often enough, I dare say. Well, now is your big chance to show us what you can do in the lip-service department. Go to it, man! Make the bitch scream with pleasure and the Frog scream with torment!'

Nigel was going over the top, obviously enjoying himself enormously, no doubt aware that he was tormenting Ralph as much as anyone. Cordelia knew just what her slave was going through. His shame and embarrassment were acute as he looked towards the bed, seeking some reassurance from her, but all she could do was shrug and give a wry grin.

'Go on!' With an impatient shove Nigel pushed Ralph onto the bed. He crawled up between her legs, his eyes lowered and his face red. Cordelia guessed that he was secretly revelling in his humiliation just as she was in hers, but he dared not show it. The exhilarating mixture of lust and disgust that was keeping her on the edge was holding him in thrall, too.

She gasped as Ralph's warm mouth fastened around the damp cleft between her labia, his tongue delicately probing until he found her erect nub. His technique was hesitant at first, evidence of his shyness in performing before an audience. But the musky juices soon did their work in releasing his inhibitions and he began to tongue her with gusto.

Aware that Lucien was being made to witness the scene, Cordelia tried her best to appear unmoved by the action of her slave. She didn't want to upset her new lover, but Ralph's ministrations were growing increasingly enthusiastic and she could feel herself responding with an automatic rise in her libido. Her breath came in short gasps as the tinglings in her clitoris intensified, taking her into a steady upward climb towards orgasm. Soon she was helpless to resist the rising tide and, throwing her head back in abandon, she gave herself up to the voluptuous feelings that were rocketing through her.

'Oh God!' she cried, as the fierceness of her climax caught her unawares in its maelstrom.

'*Mon Dieu!*' she heard Lucien echo, knowing how hurt he must be feeling at seeing his woman in the throes of an orgasm induced by another man.

But then, to her amazement, she heard applause. It was Nigel, walking towards the bed with a mocking smile on his face. 'Very good, the pair of you! Don't you think so, Froggie?'

'Beast!' Cordelia yelled, wishing her hands were free so she could throw a pillow at his sneering, handsome face.

Nigel came up and sat on the other side of the bed to Ralph. He pushed a strand of her damp hair back from her eyes and stroked her cheek. 'Did you enjoy that, Cordelia?' he enquired, in a soft, insinuating voice.

'He made me come. That was all.'

'Well, maybe we can make you come again. I'm sure you'd like that.'

'Why can't you leave me alone?'

'Oh, we can't do that, can we, Ralph old chap? We're both infatuated with you, dear Cordelia. Both of us, in our different ways. And I dare say old Frenchie here is, too. Doesn't that make you feel wonderful, to have three men flinging themselves at your feet and telling you they can't live without you?'

'Don't!' Ralph muttered. 'Please don't!'

'Am I embarrassing you? Don't tell me you're ashamed of being her slave. But of course you are. That's what you get off on, isn't it, being ashamed?'

'Leave him alone!' Cordelia snapped. 'He's done nothing to you.'

'All right.' He turned to Ralph. 'Go over by the Frog, and make sure he's watching. I don't want him to miss a thing.'

Cordelia watched helplessly as Nigel began to undo his belt. Ralph did as he was told, sliding off the bed and going to kneel beside the prostrate figure of Lucien who was still behaving with a calm dignity that did him credit. She longed to go over and comfort him, to tell him that neither Nigel nor Ralph moved her as he did, that she didn't love either of them, only him, Lucien. But she knew that to do so would be to court severe punishment and then her lover would be even more upset than he already was.

Nigel was lifting his shirt out of his trousers now, filling her with trepidation. He unzipped his fly and pulled the waistband down to reveal his Calvin Klein underpants. A cold dread filled Cordelia's veins as she watched him slowly remove his large, erect cock from the pants and stroke it with possessive pride until the shiny pink head was rearing aggressively.

'Right!' he said, turning slightly so that Lucien had a good view of his organ. 'I'm going to show you one of the many duties Cordelia performed for me in the office. I'm sure you'll both be interested to see exactly what her job entailed.' He reached forward and pulled her head down towards his rampant penis.

Knowing she had no alternative but to do as she was told, Cordelia opened her mouth and took the musky glans between her lips. With her tongue she swept across the smooth tip, tasting the drop of acrid-tasting semen that the groove was already secreting. He thrust against her mouth until he had found his way in through her lips, pushing against the roof of her mouth as he entered her like some rough explorer, eager for spoil and devoid of respect. She almost gagged as the glans pressed against her soft palate, but managed to control herself and let her throat open to him, accommodating the length and girth of him more easily.

'That's better!' he commented smugly, looking down on her.

She just hoped it would be over as soon as possible. Yet, once they had a rhythm going, with Nigel thrusting and her sucking, she knew that she wanted it to last. There was something enormously satisfying about the meaty taste of his prick in her mouth, the salty fluid teasing her taste buds. She wanted him to spurt so she could drink him down, drink the essence of him and take in some of his male arrogance, his spunk.

'See what a good girl she is!' Nigel said, his tone growing harsh and guttural as he approached his climax. 'She gives fantastic head. I don't suppose she's done it for you very often, has she Ralph? If at all. But I bet she eats you practically every night, Froggie. I bet you feast off each other, the pair of you, munching away on each others' parts, sixty-nine style. Well, now it's my turn to get the munchies and I can tell you, it's bloody good. She certainly knows how to . . . get . . . a . . . man . . . go . . . ing!'

He ended on a long, low moan as the seed spilled out of him and Cordelia kept pumping him with her mouth, alternately swallowing and sucking until she had drunk him dry. It was all she could do by way of retaliation, to drain him like a closed tap and leave him spent and empty. She knew he wanted to pull away but she kept a tight hold on him with her lips and created a vacuum with her mouth so that he was locked inside it, unable to free himself without causing himself pain.

'Let me go, bitch!' he snarled at last.

She released him slowly, feeling the spent organ pop out of her mouth with an ignominious dribble of semen drooling from it. Nigel was staring at her angrily. She had somehow managed to turn his display of masculine aggression into a parody of male pride, making the act of enforced fellatio seem more shameful to him than it did to her.

Somehow Lucien picked up on this. 'Bravo, Cordelia!' he murmured when she looked in his direction. His dark eyes seemed to be telling her that he knew exactly what was going on and that once these tiresome creatures finished their childish games they could get back to what they'd been doing before they had been so rudely interrupted.

But Nigel wasn't finished with her yet. He turned her abruptly and pushed her shoulders down, making her gasp as the air was knocked out of her lungs. Then he slapped her roundly on the buttocks, several times. 'This is the way to treat horny bitches like her!' she heard him say to Lucien. 'Give them a good hiding, then they'll do anything you want.'

Cordelia glanced up and saw Ralph looking at her disgustedly. She realized that the image of herself she had carefully nurtured for his benefit over the past months had now been ruined forever, and a deep shame ran through her. How he could respect her after this? Her fear of losing all her lovers at once returned to her and it now seemed all too probable. Surely not even tolerant, understanding Lucien could take much more of this?

But when she glanced at him he winked at her. It looked so comic, with him lying there trussed like an oven-ready chicken that she couldn't help giggling. That was fatal.

'You dare to make fun of me?' Nigel snapped, shaking her roughly by the shoulders. He turned her round and slapped across her breasts, making them wobble and smart. The nipples stood out proud and defiant, but inside she was quailing. What further torments did he have planned for her or, heaven forbid, for Lucien?

Nigel looked at Ralph and a slow smile spread across his face. 'Hey, Ralph, you'd like your mistress to suck you off, wouldn't you, like you just saw her doing to me?'

A look of utter horror passed over Ralph's features and she knew that Nigel couldn't have chosen a more distressing option. She had never lowered herself to perform fellatio on her slave and he would never have wanted her to. The favours she'd granted him were all designed to pleasure *her*, not him. This was an uncomfortable reversal of their rôles and Nigel knew it, the bastard!

'All right, get your kit off and come over here!' he barked.

Ralph hesitated and Cordelia could see he was trembling. She wanted to give him a sympathetic smile but he couldn't bring himself to look at her. A deep flush was rising from his neck into his face, hiding his usual pallor, and she felt really sorry for him. Nigel went up and roughly pulled down his trousers and pants to expose his dangling penis.

'Not up to much, are you?' he sneered.

'Hey, that's below the belt!' Lucien called.

Cordelia wasn't sure whether the pun was intended or not, whether Lucien was trying to lighten the proceedings, but they all giggled, including the shamefaced Ralph.

'All right, Cordelia, see what you can do with this apology for a penis,' Nigel ordered, taking her by the scruff of the neck and pushing her forward on her knees.

She looked up and caught a glimpse of Ralph's terrified expression. She gave him a wink, murmuring, 'It's okay, don't worry,' but he was in such a zombie-like state that she wasn't sure whether he either saw or heard her. He seemed to have retreated into another world.

Maybe I can make this work, she thought. If only she could get him to see it as some kind of thank-you for all his devoted service. But she knew in her heart that it was all wrong. His image of her as an aloof goddess had been destroyed, and all his respect for her had gone. Now his goddess had turned into a whore and he would never forgive her for it.

Neither would she ever forgive Nigel.

Chapter Seventeen

Ralph was trembling all over, his wretched organ hanging limp and useless between his weak thighs. The idea of his beloved mistress debasing herself in that fashion was filling him with loathing, but he was afraid that if he protested that monster Willoughby would make it worse for Cordelia, so he saw no other course than to endure their joint humiliation as best he could. Looking down, he saw her beautiful glossy dark hair and the splendour of her naked breasts and gave a little whimper of psychic pain.

A woman like her was never meant to kneel before another man. Rather, she should be worshipped, placed on a pedestal. Yet by now it was obvious that she'd been having a filthy kind of relationship with her bully of a boss. How he loathed Willoughby! That man was the real villain of the piece, not his beloved Cordelia. He had corrupted her, got her into his power by some unfair means. Ralph felt sickened. He should never have tried to turn that monster into his ally.

But the dreadful deed was about to be done and there was no escaping it. Cordelia was lowering her lovely head towards his pathetic apology for a cock, holding it gently between her silken lips and sending tremors of anticipation through him. He stood rigid, braced against the first onslaught of alien feeling, and was surprised to find his organ stirring a little, stiffening even. Was he to be betrayed by his own wretched tackle, too?

He glanced at the other two men. Nigel had a smug grin, his eyes gleaming with mischief as he watched his former secretary debase herself with her slave. Lucien's expression was more ambiguous. Ralph had the feeling he was biding his time, as if he knew that this charade must end and then he was confident that Cordelia would be his, and his alone. Did he regard all this as some act of closure, the last of the pantomime performances? A sick dread overcame him as he realized this was most likely to mean curtains for him and Cordelia.

But he couldn't deny the intense eroticism that was overwhelming him now as his mistress's skilled lips worked their way around his burgeoning erection. He took little pride in the way his cock was responding. It was making him feel all the more ignominious to have a penis that responded of its own accord, despite his best efforts to remain indifferent. His mind sought topics that might deflate his ardour: stepping in dogshit, being buried up to his neck in hot sand, having root canal work or an injection. But nothing did the trick. He could feel his dick hardening and tingling, the blood pumping him up towards the inevitable climax and the shame that he dreaded most of all.

Nigel came up and stood behind him, to whisper in his ear like a taunting demon. 'Enjoying it, aren't you? I bet you never thought you'd see the day when your mistress got on her knees before you and gave you a blow job!'

Ralph screwed his eyes tight shut, wishing he could do the same for his ears. He could feel the pressure building up in his cock and balls, preparing for the discharge. But what if she didn't pull back in time and he shot his load right into Cordelia's mouth? That was the worst outcome he could think of. He would never have wished to submit her to such an indignity. Tense and fearful, he braced himself to face the roller-coaster ride towards inevitable ejaculation. . . .

Despite her misgivings, Cordelia felt a certain pride at being able to revive Ralph's flagging erection and once she got into it her desire to give full satisfaction increased. She knew he was probably hating every minute of it emotionally, but on a sensual level his arousal was evident. Perhaps a part of him was enjoying this double-bind situation. Knowing that his sexuality was complex and involved, she wouldn't put it past him to be relishing the experience at a deeper level than he was even aware of.

Such speculation faded, however, as she felt herself becoming stirred. She had a sudden desire to feel Ralph's prick between her breasts, as she had done once before, to suck his glans while she rubbed his shaft with her fleshy mounds. The thought of it sent sexy prickles all through her. Maybe that compromise would ease Ralph's embarrassment. Besides, it felt nice.

She wiggled her torso around until she had him lodged in her cleavage, then bent her head to the task. Although her hands were still immobilized behind her back, Cordelia found that by flexing her chest muscles she could hold Ralph's cock firmly in her cleavage. She thought she could feel the tension in him easing a little as the balance of power was subtly shifted. Now he would be able to imagine her deriving more pleasure from the act than him. She squeezed his glans between her erect nipples and moaned softly as a hint to Ralph that she was getting off on it.

Her only fear was that Nigel would suss out the significance of her move and put a stop to it. The man was devious and bound to be curious about her relationship with Ralph, since it was the mirror-image of the one he had with her. Just what was he feeling now? Cordelia realized that he had always been an enigma to her and that was the main aspect of his attraction. But what if there had been less going on inside that handsome head than she had supposed? What if she had simply projected her own complicated feelings onto him? It was a weird thought.

At least Nigel didn't seem to realize what was going on between her and Ralph. On the contrary, he appeared to approve of the development. He stood behind her, watching the proceedings closely and from time to time giving her neck a brief caress.

'That's it!' he encouraged her. 'Rub him up the right way and he might just spurt all over your beautiful tits. You'd like that, wouldn't you – slut!'

Cordelia wished she had eyes in the back of her head so she could see how Lucien was taking all this. He was the only one she really cared about. Although she had some lingering affection for Ralph, Nigel had put himself well beyond the pale and she was relieved that soon he would be out of her life forever. But Lucien . . . nothing must put him off her. Somehow she must find a way to repair any damage to their tender new relationship that this episode might have caused.

Ralph's penis was dribbling now, a bead of pale juice appearing like the egg of some tiny creature in the eye of his organ. It wouldn't be much longer, she calculated, redoubling her efforts. The inner slopes of her breasts were growing slimy with his juices as the seepage continued and she could taste the bitter juice whenever she licked the glans with the tip of her tongue. Taking a deep breath she enclosed the whole glans with her lips and moved them slowly down the shaft until he was fully inside her mouth. Then she began to nod her head up and down as rapidly as she could.

All the time she could hear Ralph moaning quietly in distress and she wanted to stop, but she knew it was in both their interests to continue to the end. She knew he was trying to stop himself from coming, but that was only prolonging the agony. Her tongue flicked across the taut skin of his glans inside her mouth, then rolled around the stiff shaft while her lips sucked at him, teasing him mercilessly.

At last she could feel his ejaculation gathering force, like a volcanic explosion in his belly. She pulled back as his cock voided itself and his essence spilled over her breasts in a hot fountain, leaving a film of spunk that felt clammy as it cooled. Cordelia sat back on her heels, looking up at Ralph's mortified face. He opened his eyes, regarding her with fear and loathing. She smiled up at him, trying to indicate that it was all right. But it was impossible to know whether she'd succeeded in reassuring him.

Her ex-boss, on the other hand, seemed thoroughly satisfied with the way things had gone. He kissed the nape of her neck and then unlocked her handcuffs. She rubbed her sore wrists with relief, easing the chafed skin. Nigel looked around the room with a self-satisfied air, then said to Ralph, 'I think we've done enough to show these two how we feel about them. Shall we go?'

Ralph whimpered something incomprehensible. Cordelia said, 'Aren't you going to untie Lucien?'

Nigel grinned. 'Don't tempt me. You sort him out, if you like. He's all yours now.'

She hurried over to where Lucien was huddled up and struggled with his bonds. The dressing-gown cord had been knotted several times but it was silky-smooth and fairly easy to undo. When she released him he lay stretched out prone to ease the strain on his back and leg muscles. She gave him a rub.

'That's right, give the guy a massage,' Nigel sneered. She threw him a venomous look, then stroked her lover's dark hair, bending her mouth to his ear. 'Come on,' she murmured. 'Let's go. I don't want to stay here a minute longer than we have to. This place is too full of bad memories now.'

Slowly he rose to a sitting position, rubbing his shins and feet. Cordelia gave him a hand. The smooth warmth of his flesh was comforting beneath her fingers, inspiring her with hope that once they got away from that cursed cottage everything would be all right. She saw Ralph pocket the handcuffs with a sheepish air while Nigel was looking around the room curiously.

'Nice place you've got here,' he said to Lucien. 'Proper little love nest.'

'It's not mine. I'm just staying here.'

'Ah!'

Lucien got to his feet, pulling himself up to his full stature. 'But not for much longer. You've ruined our little weekend in the country, you'll be glad to know. We might as well get back to town now, although I don't suppose either of us is up to driving. Can I phone a taxi?'

Nigel nodded, losing interest. He went to make sure the door was closed after Lucien had gone downstairs, then turned back to Cordelia. She could tell from his stance that he was about to give her one of his pompous lectures. She deliberately turned her back on him and began to get into her clothes.

'Cordelia, when I found out about the double game you were playing I confess to being quite miffed,' Nigel said, regardless. 'And I believe the same is true of Ralph here. We both trusted you to remain true to us in spirit. It's not just a matter of physical fidelity, as I'm sure Ralph will agree, but it's more to do with keeping your sexual identity pure, unsullied. Now you can't tell me that you didn't relish the though of keeping me and Ralph dangling on strings while you played one of us off against the other.'

'But it's all a game, isn't it?' she reminded him, fastening her stockings. 'Only mine was a game of bluff and double-bluff. Are you trying to say I didn't give satisfaction – to you both?'

'No.' Nigel was giving her one of his long, intense stares that made her squirm. 'I'm saying you didn't give *you* satisfaction. Otherwise you'd never have taken up with your Froggie friend, would you?'

She pondered his words. He had caught her attention now. In the whirlwind of the past few weeks she'd had little time to sit and think about things. What was the truth? It was difficult to pinpoint.

Cordelia sighed. 'Maybe I just got bored with you both? It happens to the best of us.'

Nigel said nothing, but continued to stare at her balefully. She turned to Ralph, who still looked crestfallen. 'What do you think?' she asked, kindly.

He shrugged, acutely embarrassed. 'Things weren't the same after you met that Lucien.'

'I know, and I'm sorry. I've upset both of you, and that grieves me. But I think I . . . well, I know it sounds corny, but I think I've found true love at last.'

Nigel snorted. 'Well, that makes everything all right then, doesn't it?'

Cordelia felt as if she'd just thrown a bucket of cold water over herself. She'd never intended to say that. She'd just blurted out. But it was true. She had never felt more certain of anything in her life.

At that moment Lucien returned, looking more like his normal self. 'The taxi should be here in about ten minutes. Now, shall we all have some champagne? I put some in the fridge for later and it seems a shame to waste it.'

Cordelia stared at him in amazement. What a nerve the man had! Even Nigel was looking gobsmacked, but Ralph said, 'Yes, why not? I could do with a drink right now.'

'Good. I'll go and find some glasses.'

'Maybe you could whip up some canapés,' Nigel said to Ralph, scathingly. 'I've heard you're ace in the kitchen.'

'Leave him alone!' Cordelia snapped. It still felt strange talking back to her boss instead of kow-towing to him, but she was getting to like it.

When Lucien had disappeared for the second time Nigel said, 'You've got to hand it to him, that Frenchie certainly has more than his share of *savoir faire*.'

'Well, you didn't think I'd fall for a total nerd, did you?' Cordelia retorted. She felt on form again, as if she were among old friends – which, in a way, she was. But Ralph was still looking squashed, so she went up and placed her arm around his shoulders, then gave him a light kiss on the cheek. He seemed to cheer up.

'No hard feelings?' she asked him.

'I guess not.'

'Fun while it lasted, and all those old clichés.'

'Hm. It wasn't exactly as if I hadn't seen it coming.' His brow furrowed. 'But where will I live now? What on earth will I do?'

'Don't worry, I won't throw you out on the street. I'll make sure you're happily settled somewhere, introduce you to a few people. You have great talent as a chef, Ralph. Ever thought of running your own catering business?'

'But you've been my whole life!' he wailed as the enormity of his loss suddenly hit him.

Cordelia was giving him a hug as Lucien entered with the champagne and glasses on a tray. She invited Ralph to serve it and soon they were standing round in a circle with fizzing glasses. It felt strange, but somehow right too. Nigel, still the ostensibly dominant male in the room, raised his glass. 'I suppose we should all wish each other well. To Cordelia, Queen of Subdom, and may God bless all who become entangled in her web!'

As they were drinking there was the sound of a klaxon horn outside, followed by excited female voices and rapid footsteps ascending the stairs. Cordelia frowned. Had Lucien phoned the owner of the cottage? Was this some kind of a set-up? The door was flung open and two women entered with a flourish of bright scarves and flowing coats. It took Cordelia a few seconds to recognize them, but when she did she gasped in astonishment.

'Kristina! Tasmin! What are you doing here?'

She was even more astounded by what happened next. Before anyone else had a chance to realize what was happening, Lucien helped the girls to secure the wrists of the other two men with their scarves. Both Nigel and Ralph looked shocked: Nigel bordering on fury, Ralph near to tears.

'Lucien, what's going on?' Cordelia asked, sharply.

'I knew my friends were staying in Reading this weekend so I rang and asked them to come over by taxi. I think they'll have some fun with your two ex-lovers, darling.'

She didn't know quite what to think, or feel. 'I see. Revenge is sweet, is that it?'

'I think it will be particularly sweet for Ralph and Nigel. As you know, Kristina has little time for men while Tasmin has time for both men and women, so long as they are of a domineering disposition. I'm sure that some exciting little scenarios are going to take place in this room tonight. What a shame we can't stay to witness them.'

Cordelia stared at him in bewilderment. 'What? I don't understand . . .'

He reached out and took her hand. 'Come on, Cordelia, finish your champagne, then let's get going. Our taxi awaits us outside. Say goodbye to your gentlemen friends. Or should that be *au revoir*?'

Cordelia gave the others a puzzled shake of the head before she was whisked out of the room and down the stairs to the waiting taxi. Lucien bundled her into the back seat, gave the driver his address, then jumped into the back with her.

She was still dazed, events moving too fast for her to take in, but she was relieved to be leaving the cottage and glad that Lucien seemed not to bear her any grudge for what had happened.

On the contrary, he began kissing her instantly, hot passionate kisses that threatened to singe her lips and take the roof off her mouth. His hands were groping beneath her jacket too, finding the hard globes of her breasts and fingering the nipples through her clothes to make them just as hard. Cordelia felt embarrassed. She'd never behaved like this in the back of a taxi before and Lucien was giving the impression that it wasn't going to be just a kiss and a cuddle, either. She moaned and tried half-heartedly to push him away, hoping the driver wasn't watching in his mirror.

Lucien was fumbling with her buttons. 'It's a long way back to London,' he murmured. 'It's going to take us at least an hour.'

'But we can't . . .' she began, before his lips crushed her protest.

His hand came up beneath her skirt and found the hot, damp crotch of her panties. Without any hesitation he inserted his forefinger under the leg and wormed his way through to her vulva. She gasped as he probed within, finding her very wet indeed, while he continued to kiss her, exploring the inside of her mouth with his tongue. He tasted of champagne still, all yeasty and buttery, like rising bun-dough.

Cordelia couldn't resist putting her hand down to his fly and feeling the hard ridge of his cock inside. 'See how much I want you?' he grinned at her.

'How can you bear to wait?'

'I can't.'

'But what about the driver?'

His response was to pull her down so that she was lying on the thick leather seat with her knees up. Her sex was steaming now, unbearably hot for it, and far from worrying about being seen she started to worry about not being satisfied. Her clitoris was so swollen and sensitized that when she pulled her knickers further down she couldn't resist rubbing it a little with the cool tips of her fingers, bringing herself some temporary relief.

Then she saw him pass a roll of notes to the driver over his shoulder. 'Keep your eyes on the road, mate!' Lucien said, in an imitation cockney accent that had her helpless with laughter.

The man took the money nonchalantly. Cordelia had the impression that he often witnessed strange goings-on in the back of his taxi, so she stopped worrying. Lucien knelt down on the seat, his legs either side of hers, and unzipped his fly. She saw his cock jump up, pale and thick in the dim light, and her insides convulsed with longing. With one leg placed securely on the floor of the taxi, he braced himself against the side of the vehicle with one arm while he unclipped the straps of her suspenders and pulled her panties down to her knees. Her mons was exposed and she could feel the cool night air fanning it blissfully. She opened up to him a little more, feeling randy as hell.

She felt the domed head of his penis nudge at her entrance and soon he was plunging into her, a little cautiously at first since the taxi had not yet reached the motorway and was still twisting and turning round country lanes. Once they reached the A4, though, the speed they were going seemed to encourage him and he began to shaft her rapidly, skilfully taking her towards an orgasm. Cordelia could practically feel the road rushing away beneath her as he rammed into her over and over with exhilarating force, making her moan and sigh. She was quite oblivious of where she was, and heedless of the fact that a complete stranger was driving the car. All she wanted was to reach her fulfillment.

It came upon her suddenly, a rich vein of ecstasy that he hadn't mined before. It seemed to come flooding through her in a gush of love-juice that flowed out of her and into him, so that he groaned too and shot his seed with a hot urgency that only increased the pleasure she took in her orgasm. She clasped his shaft for as long as she could afterwards, reluctant to let him go, but at last he grew too soft and slipped out.

'God, I needed that!' he exclaimed, loud enough for the driver to hear. But he was the perfect gentleman and never turned round.

'So did I!' Cordelia murmured, with feeling. She was writhing on the seat in the heat of the afterglow, with her skirt up above her waist and her pussy still exposed to the elements. Lucien bent down, contorting himself, to kiss her open vulva and she moaned with the sheer excess of bliss as he bathed her overheated flesh with his cool saliva.

They settled side by side and lay embracing as best they could in the confines of the back seat. Cordelia could hear the wild thudding of his heart and feel the soft melting of his cock between her thighs, the gentle retreat of the flesh into repose. She kissed his cheek with utter tenderness and whispered, 'I think I love you, Lucien.'

'You only *think*? You don't *know*?'

He was playing at being affronted, and yet there was a tad too much conviction in his tone. Laughingly Cordelia said, 'Oh, all right, I *know* I do. I love you, Froggie!'

'Don't ever call me that!'

He sounded quite aggrieved and she half sat up in protest. 'Hey, it was just a joke!'

'And it was just a joke when that boss of yours called me that, too? Somehow, I don't think so! He's the sort of man who gives xenophobia a bad name, you know.'

Cordelia giggled. 'Oh Lucien, you can be so funny sometimes.'

'And serious too. I'm serious now. Will you marry me?'

'Oh God! No one's asked me that for . . . years! Do you mean it?'

'No, of course not!' Her face fell. He tweaked her nose playfully. 'What do you think, noddle head? Do you think I'm in the habit of going round asking women to marry me if I don't mean it? I mean, it's not trivial, is it? Not like, "Will you have my baby"?'

Cordelia punched him in the chest, softly. He caught her fist and raised it to his lips, kissing her knuckles one by one. There was a new lightness about the way they were that came from her having finally buried the past. Without needing to explain anything to him, because now he understood everything. And the best thing of all was that, if there was anything to forgive, he forgave everything too.

Kristina and Tasmin were having a ball. They had Nigel on his knees, blindfolded and chained to the bed, while they were dressing Ralph up in women's clothes. He was rather enjoying it, although he preferred not to speculate about what they had in store for him afterwards. He rather liked Kristina, even though she was supposed to be a man-hater. She had a wicked sense of humour.

The two women were obviously infatuated with each other, which fascinated him. He'd never had much to do with lesbians but the sight of them kissing and caressing each other turned him on. They'd brought a whole armoury of toys with them, too: whips and dildoes, French ticklers and novelty condoms. It looked as though they were in for a ball.

The only fly in the ointment was Nigel, who looked like thunder. They had taken off his trousers and pants and his big dick was lying across his thigh with a sullen air as if it was definitely refusing to play. Ralph was curious about how the girls were going to deal with him. In fact, he was curious about quite a lot of things. Now that his detective instincts had been roused they refused to settle down.

If anyone had told him, a month ago, that he would find being released from Cordelia's service a liberating experience he would have laughed in scorn. But right now that was exactly how he felt. As if things had run their course and he was ready for pastures new. It was possible to be stuck in a rut, after all. He remembered the strain of producing a new and exciting dish for his mistress every day. It had probably been equalled by the strain on her, constantly having to find new ways to discipline him and satisfy his needs. Perhaps they'd both needed a break but had been too locked into their cosy world to admit it.

Ralph thought he might take a holiday, since he had more than enough saved up. One of those singles tours to somewhere hot, where he could ogle girls' naked breasts behind his sunglasses and dream of starting over with someone new. Yes, that was a very good idea. He would peruse the travel agent's window tomorrow morning.

The big woman, Kristina, was oddly attractive to him with her huge mane of dark hair and ample bosom. She would make a wonderful new mistress, even though she disliked men. Maybe he could be hired to service her girlfriend, Tasmin, who apparently needed a man from time to time. In his imagination he soon had a nice little *ménage à trois* set up for himself.

Now Tasmin was showing him some attention. She was lifting up the skimpy little top she wore and showing him her lovely bare breasts. They were tanned and perfect, little round orbs that he could imagine fondling. Her blue eyes sparkled at him, knowing that she was making him randy, and she wiggled her little hips as she stepped out of her miniskirt showing her tiny flesh-coloured panties. They were made of soft chamois leather that was so harmonized with her skin colour that it was hard to see where the tan hide stopped and the tan skin began.

'He's a cutie!' she purred. Then she raised her voice, looking towards Nigel on the bed. 'I fancy you too, Nige! Can you hear me?'

'Yes, Tasmin, I hear you,' he responded, gloomily.

'I think your friend here would like to suck my tits and stick his cock in my pussy. Or maybe my arse!'

Tasmin giggled, and jumped onto the bed like a kitten. She crept up Nigel's bare, outstretched leg with her fingers until she reached his flaccid penis which she tugged softly.

'What's this, no excitement in the old loins? What's got into you, Nige?'

'I can't bloody *see*!' he muttered, brusquely. 'Perhaps it's escaped your notice.'

'Ah! You need to see to get horny, right?' She took his hand and placed it on her breast. 'It's not enough just to *feel*, is it? You must be the sort that has to make love with the lights on.'

'Oh, leave him alone!' Kristina called. 'Come here, I'm feeling left out.'

Tasmin waggled her bum backwards over the bed, hopped off and came skipping to her lesbian lover's side. Wide-eyed, Ralph watched Kristina stroke her small breasts, mumbling and mouthing at them in a frenzy of desire. She seemed rapacious, full of a macho energy that thrilled him as much as it intrigued him.

Suddenly she broke off and walked over to the case that held their equipment. She quickly removed her trousers and pants to reveal a flourishing dark bush. Then she strapped on a large black dildo and grabbed Tasmin's hand, pulling her into her arms with possessive urgency. 'What do you want us to do with these two?' he heard her mutter. 'What will turn you on so much that you'll let me fuck you till you come?'

Tasmin looked from one man to the other. When she saw the apprehension in Ralph's eyes she gave a slow, wicked smile. Pointing first at him, then at Nigel, she said, 'I want to see *this one* sucking *that one* off!'

8½-10

MARCH 2000